· Dogsbody ·

Also by Michael Molloy

Black Dwarf
Th Kid from Riga
Harlot of Jericho
The Gallery
Sweet Sixteen
Cat's Paw
Home Before Dark

MICHAEL MOLLOY

· Dogsbody ·

HEINEMANN : LONDON

First published in Great Britain 1995
by William Heinemann Ltd
an imprint of Reed Books Ltd
Michelin House, 81 Fulham Road, London, sw3 6rb
and Auckland, Melbourne, Singapore and Toronto

Copyright © Michael Molloy
The author has asserted his moral rights

A CIP catalogue record for this title
is available from the British Library
ISBN 0 434 00016 7

Typeset by Deltatype Ltd, Ellesmere Port, Wirral
Printed and bound by Clays Ltd, St Ives plc

· Prologue ·

It was a cold morning at the beginning of January and the dawn came with a surly reluctance. Finally the pale orb of the sun showed on the horizon through a thin veil of clouds, casting a shadowless light over an island on the upper reaches of the Thames. All was still, even where a man lay concealed among the reeds at the water's edge.

In the silence, he looked across the narrow channel to the near embankment and waited expectantly for a sign of movement. All he could see were the high walls of a great estate, fringed with leafless trees; and a small wooden jetty, the boards silvered with age, supported by rickety piles that merged into the mist shrouding the surface of the river. For a moment the watcher's attention was distracted by the flickering swoop of a passing bird and his eyes followed its passage. When he returned his gaze to the opposite embankment, a party of men had suddenly appeared before the wall, as if the earth itself had thrown them up.

Their mysterious appearance caused the watcher to feel a sudden lurch of superstitious fear that he quickly stifled. There must be a logical explanation, he told himself, and he raised a pair of binoculars to study the group that had now mounted the jetty.

There were five men in all, wearing country clothes cut in a similar sporting fashion, and there was a definite hierarchy to the group. The two leaders were much the same in appearance, although of greatly differing age. The older man was of average height, slim, but made to appear smaller by a slight stoop, although his step was sprightly enough. Long white hair framed his narrow features and the tip of his hooked nose dipped towards a prominently pointed chin.

Next to him stood a more youthful version of himself. The younger man's hair was still the colour of butter, and his complexion not yet mottled with broken blood vessels, but the cast was set as clearly as a potter's mould. Close behind them came a tall, middle-aged man whose well-cut clothes, sensuous, fleshy face and carefully brushed wings of yellowish-grey hair gave him a dandified air, although his shape was marred by a prominent belly.

Of the two others that followed, the first was a bow-legged, runtish figure, with a face as dark and furrowed as a walnut. He was one step ahead of a lumbering brute of a man; the great muscles under his tightly fitting coat gave him the appearance of an ox as he walked. His battered features were surmounted by a brush of hair cropped close to the skull. Both carried bundles of large white bathtowels.

When the party stopped at the end of the jetty they stripped off their clothes; then, with shouts of encouragement to each other, they hesitated above the mist on the icy water before plunging into the river. When they surfaced, the men continued to shout like noisy schoolboys as the lazy current began to carry them downstream.

The watcher had heard the same sounds the previous morning. They had aroused him from his sleep on the far side of the island, but when he had come to the water's edge there had been no sign of the bathers, just their clothes heaped on the jetty. Later, when he returned, the clothes had vanished. In his boat, the watcher had rowed across the channel to the far embankment and examined the undergrowth; but there had been no disturbance, and no sign of passage in either direction along the river's edge, except for the few feet of ground where the men had appeared before the wall. This mystery disturbed and angered him, and he decided that he must solve the puzzle before he left the island.

The voices of the bathers receded now, and he relaxed for a moment; despite the curious manner of their sudden appearance, he felt the sense of superiority and power that comes to the secret observer.

But then his attention was engaged by another sight. The shock of the new apparition was so terrible, he felt his body slacken with fear. Momentarily, he lay helpless on the muddy ground, the breath driven from him by the sudden horror.

Silently gliding towards him – disembodied by the clinging mist on the river – came the gigantic heads of two monstrous creatures. Reason told him they must be dogs, but he had never seen a breed like this before. Black as jet, their glistening fur was ridged over massive skulls that gave them more the appearance of prehistoric reptiles than of warm-blooded mammals. Even their eyes had a dead, alien quality that to the watcher made them as nightmarish as some mythical creatures guarding the gates of Hades. There was no doubt in his mind that they wished him harm.

As if in anticipation, their great mouths gaped open, revealing jagged teeth and jaws that he knew were powerful enough to strip the flesh from his body and crack his bones. He wanted to get up and run blindly into the thick wood that lay behind him, but – as if in a nightmare – his strength had drained away. All he was aware of was the terrifying sight before him and the pounding of his heart as he lay frozen with fear upon the cold ground.

They were now so close to his position among the reeds that he could see the circles of blood-filled flesh that rimmed their eyes. His breath began to come in tight little gasps; then there was a long, low whistle from somewhere downstream. At the summons, the dogs turned reluctantly and paddled away towards the sound.

The watcher felt a moment of elation at his deliverance, as if he had somehow conquered the monstrous opponents by his own endeavours, and a flood of self-esteem filled his breast so that he even managed a smile. He was about to rise when he felt himself suddenly seized by unseen hands. They gripped the back of his anorak, dragged him forward and pressed down, so that his head plunged through the mist and submerged in the icy river. At first the freezing water acted as a stimulant to his struggle so that he fought desperately, clawing in the stiff mud beneath his body; but he stood no chance. The last memory that came, as the life went out of him, was of the cloudy mist on the river before the water closed above his head.

· I ·

'Sit,' Sarah Keane said, in what she hoped was a commanding voice; but the young Labrador remained standing, tail wagging furiously, while he gazed with eyes of liquid devotion at her face. 'I know you love me,' she continued with a sigh. 'Why don't you do what I tell you?'

At that moment her father, Doctor Henry Linton, entered the kitchen and without pausing in his stride across the tiled floor, snapped his fingers and said 'Down' in a mild voice. Immediately the dog flopped to the floor and cocked his head to watch him as he reached into a cupboard and took down a packet of Alka-Seltzer.

'There's fresh coffee just made,' Sarah said and her father nodded, prodding the tablets as they dissolved in a glass of water. When he was satisfied with the state of his concoction he muttered, 'Physician, heal thyself', and drained the contents in one draught.

'Do you feel up to the drive?' Sarah asked.

Doctor Linton thought about the question before he answered. 'If the twins keep the dog quiet in the back and the sounds of Vivaldi don't leak from your daughter's Walkman I shall face the journey with my usual calm resolution.' He looked about him and said, 'Where's Colin?'

'A car came for him an hour ago. He should be on a train now.'

'What time did we get to bed?'

'Twoish.'

Doctor Linton nodded. 'I do enjoy those little talks where you can't recollect a bloody word you uttered the following day.'

'Colin said the same when he came to bed.'

'We woke you, did we?'

'I didn't mind – you like him, don't you?' Although Sarah and Greaves had known each other some time, her father, who lived in the country, had had little opportunity to get to know his prospective son-in-law.

'He'll do,' Doctor Linton replied, and Sarah knew that she would get no more than that from her father. But it was enough for her to know the depth of his approval. He had never really cared for Sarah's first husband; they had rubbed along well enough when they met, civil and distant with each other, with no warmth or intimacy: in-laws and total strangers. It had been hard for Sarah; she had adored Jack Keane.

Doctor Linton poured himself some coffee and looked from the window into the still gloomy garden. From above, the noise of bumps and crashes came to them, then the sound of Elgar's violin concerto.

Henry Linton shook his head. 'Why the devil doesn't she play pop records like any other sixteen-year-old?'

Sarah smiled. 'I didn't know you were so familiar with the behaviour of teenage girls, dad.'

'I'm not dead yet, you know – though I might be by the end of this bloody journey.'

'Are you sure you feel up to this?'

Linton waved a hand dismissively. 'Of course I am. It'll do them good to get some country air for a few days. The pollution in London is appalling. I don't know how you can stand it.'

Sarah resisted the temptation to point out that a quiet street in Hampstead, a few minutes from the Heath, was hardly living in the West End.

'It's a pity you can't come as well,' he continued. 'It wouldn't do you any harm.'

'I'd love to,' she answered, 'you know that. But I've really got to work.'

'Mmm,' he answered, some how managing to put all his disregard for her job as a reporter into the disapproving sound.

Half an hour later, Sarah's children were assembled outside the house with the dog on his lead and their luggage piled beside them. Martin and Paul were involved in some game that seemed to consist of kicking each other's ankles, Emily was detached from events, her Walkman clamped to her head. Doctor Linton fussily supervised the loading of the boot while Sarah moved her Renault so that he could back his BMW out of the drive, then stood in the road shivering in the raw morning air to wave them goodbye; she missed them already.

In the now silent house, Sarah sat at the kitchen table and drank half a cup of lukewarm coffee, glancing at the shabby walls about her. The skirting-boards were chipped and the white paint yellowed with age. There were fresh scratch marks on the door made by the Labrador and a crescent-shaped discoloration on the wall by the refrigerator caused by orange juice, splashed there during some piece of horseplay by the twins. She grimaced as she finished the last mouthful of coffee, then heard the front door open. It was Pat Lomax, her housekeeper. They had not seen each other since before the Christmas holiday, when Pat had gone to visit a sister near Hastings.

'Thank God I'm back at work,' she said fervently when she entered the kitchen.

'Was it that bad?' Sarah asked sympathetically.

Pat filled the kettle as she replied. 'I was rushed off my feet. There was our lot and Dave's brother's. Edie's got angina so she can't do much, so it was down to me and Iris. We didn't put our feet up until New Year's Day.'

'Couldn't the men help?'

'When there's snow in mid-July,' Pat sniffed. 'Women are just dogsbodies at this time of year.' She smiled. 'Still, they'll be coming round here this afternoon to make a start, so the boot will be on the other foot.'

The men in Pat's family were builders and decorators and Sarah had contracted with them to give the whole house a long-needed facelift. Secretly she had been astonished at their estimate for the work: it was far more than the deposit she and Jack had originally put down on the house. But then, she reminded herself, she could easily afford it.

Noticing the time was now nearly ten o'clock, Sarah refused Pat's offer of a cup of tea and, collecting her bag and coat, set off for the offices of the *Gazette*.

There was less traffic than usual on the journey and Sarah remembered that most children were still on holiday. Just a few more days' respite and the roads would be as clogged as always. Her own children attended a private day school close to their home which took a longer break at Christmas. Emily and the boys still had two weeks before commencement of term, and were going to spend them with their grandfather. Colin would be away for most of that time too, attending a conference. Still, it would make the disruptions the decorators were about to cause easier to handle.

She arrived earlier than she had anticipated, so there were still plenty of parking spaces in front of the *Gazette* building. Sarah left her car in the vanway and made her way to the newsroom on the third floor.

Christmas decorations festooned the various editorial departments but they were already looking tired. Paper chains had come adrift from their original moorings and the occasional balloon had given up the effort and half deflated. As she approached the news desk, she saw that Alan Stiles, the deputy news editor, was already on duty, but there was no sign of

George Conway, the head of the department, and the rest of the reporters' desks were still empty.

Stiles had seen her, but he kept his eyes on his terminal screen and made no attempt to greet her as she approached. Sarah called out a crisp, 'Happy New Year!' to include the two secretaries each side of Stiles and sat down at her own desk. She logged on to her terminal and then went to the coffee machine where she found a sub-editor from the sports department slapping the side forlornly. 'Bloody thing's eaten my pound coin.'

Sarah held on to her own change and headed for the canteen. The shabby maze of corridors off the newsroom always caused her to recollect her earlier days on the newspaper. The building had a curious quality now: parts had been modernised and redecorated, but others remained unchanged. Sometimes the effect was like looking through a family photograph album where old black-and-white prints brought vivid memories from the past.

When she had first joined the *Gazette*, nineteen years before, there had been a wholeness about the structure; all had aged to the same degree of shabbiness. The paper had been a broadsheet then. Once she married Jack Keane she'd left the paper to raise her family. Then the company had been taken over and many changes followed. New printing machines were bought and installed in Docklands, computers replaced the old-fashioned composing equipment and the newspaper was transformed into a tabloid. Thousands of print workers – compositors, engravers, machine-minders and warehouse staff – had lost their jobs; and what had once been a factory in the heart of the city was now simply an office building attached to a derelict print-works. Parts of it reminded Sarah of a haunted house.

In her youth, the building had been permeated with the smell of newsprint and ink; the sight of swaggering, confident artisans in overalls and aprons was commonplace. The vanway had been a sacred place, the heart of the paper's production and distribution, supervised by a yard marshal of absolute authority whose awesome duty was to ensure that the arteries of the newspaper were free to allow the flow of vital supplies into the building and the nightly outgoing convoy of vans heading for the main London railway stations.

Each night the great presses in the basement had begun the print run, and for a moment the structure of the building quivered from their impetus.

Now the vast press rooms were empty; as silent as Tara's halls. The canteen had also been a different place then. Tough cockney women, with rough bantering tongues, had produced mountains of fried food, an endless succession of toasted sandwiches, rock cakes, bread pudding and gallons of strong tea served in chipped china mugs. The air was always filled with cigarette smoke and evaporating fat. Now the room was half the size and leased to a catering company. Young men and women in smart uniforms offered selections from a salad bar, and the hot drinks were served in sterile polystyrene cups.

Sarah took her coffee and was about to return to the newsroom when she saw George Conway sitting at a table with Tony Prior and Pauline Kaznovitch, two of her fellow reporters. He waved for her to join them.

Pauline looked as fresh as ever, her mass of curling bright red hair and pale, freckled complexion unmarked by the rigours of the holiday season. But the faces of George Conway and Tony Prior told of sterner times endured. Conway's features looked as if they had been carved from a house brick: his nose, broken many times by vigorous sports in his youth, sat sideways in a face that gave evidence of hard living. His bright blue eyes were red-rimmed and the cropped hair on his bullet head grew in various directions, like corn blown by a storm. His powerful frame, blurred by fat, hunched over the Formica-topped table and he held a cup of coffee in both hands, as if about to pray.

Tony Prior, in contrast, was as pale as the new white shirt he wore. His mousy hair was limp and his narrow body appeared barely able to support a head that seemed large above the thinness of his neck.

'Don't they look awful,' Pauline said cheerfully.

'A trifle worn,' Sarah agreed.

'So would you if you'd been up all night with a new baby,' Prior said thickly.

Pauline raised her eyebrows to Sarah. 'So you were getting up to the baby were you?' she asked him.

Prior shook his head. 'I can't feed the bloody child, but every time Barbara moves she wakes me up. It's like doing watches in the Navy. I keep telling her: "I've got to work tomorrow", but I might as well be talking to the bedpost.'

'Barbara doesn't work during the day then?' Pauline continued.

Prior looked at her as if she was slow-witted. 'Of course not, the baby's only a few months old. We don't have a nanny.'

Pauline nodded her understanding. 'So she just lolls about at home during the daytime – feet up, sod-all to do?'

Prior saw the trap and tried to rally. 'Looking after babies is women's work, isn't it? I'm not responsible for the demands of nature.'

'Oh yes,' Pauline smiled. 'I forgot it was Mother Nature that made us slaves and lackeys.'

George Conway shifted slightly and his eyes flickered across to Tony Prior. 'You won't win this one,' he said. 'Take it from me.'

'You sound a little jaded,' Sarah said to him. 'Have you had a testing weekend?'

'On the contrary,' George answered. 'I have been keeping New Year with my customary devotion.'

'But it's the third of January today,' Sarah replied. 'New Year's Day was on Saturday.'

George massaged his nose as he said, 'You English don't understand how to do it properly. In certain parts of Scotland, Hogmanay has been known to go on for weeks.'

'I thought you were English,' Prior said.

'Only by an accident of geography. My great-grandmother was a Campbell.'

'How did your dear wife respond to this burst of nationalism?' Pauline asked.

'With frequent trips to the off-licence,' George answered in satisfaction.

Sarah looked at him reproachfully. 'You told me you were making a resolution to cut down this year.'

George glanced about the canteen at the scattering of people from other departments. To those who kept normal office hours it was the mid-morning break. 'That was before I met the new chairman,' he told her.

Sarah noticed the edge in his voice. The Christmas period had been a traumatic time for the *Gazette*. The previous owners had been ousted in a takeover bid and Charles Miller, a city financier, had gained control of LOC PLC, the company that owned the newspaper. Most of the staff had been delighted by the development, because a popular previous editor, Brian Meadows, had been brought back to run the paper once again. In fact, George and Meadows had always been fairly good friends so Sarah was slightly surprised by George's attitude to the new regime.

'What happened?' Sarah asked.

George didn't answer. He drank some of his coffee, and it was Prior who replied to her question. 'He had a heated discussion with the new chairman at the New Year's party.'

Sarah sighed. She was very fond of George; when she had needed to return to work after Jack's death, it had been Conway who had taken the chance of giving her freelance shifts even though she had been out of the business for years. He had always been a staunch, foul-weather friend, and noted for his loyalty to subordinates – but sometimes he had problems dealing with authority.

'How did all this come about?' Sarah asked. She had left the party early, but everything had been going smoothly, like a reunion of long-lost friends.

'I was standing with Meadows and Miller,' George began reluctantly, 'exchanging blandishments suitable to the occasion, when Fanny Hunter joined us.'

'Ah,' Sarah said softly. Fanny's name was enough to provide some pretty powerful guidelines to events. There was a malevolence in Fanny Hunter that caused her to spread poison wherever she went. It was not enough for Fanny to conquer all others; she had to see that her opponents were crushed and humiliated. Her attitude had always puzzled Sarah, whom Fanny saw as an enemy. Sarah could understand ambition – she had ambitions of her own – but in Fanny it was accompanied by a need to destroy all those whom she imagined were standing in her path.

'What happened next?' Sarah asked.

George held up the polystyrene cup in his hand as if he contemplated crushing it, then placed it gently on the table and gave Sarah a wintry smile. 'She told Miller that she'd enjoyed his interview on *The Money Programme*, then she turned to me and asked me what I thought of it.'

'Knowing you hadn't watched?'

He gave a short laugh. 'Well, it was a pretty good bet.'

Sarah understood. It was one of the paradoxes of newspapers that those who held high executive positions found it impossible to read all the vast quantities of information and catch up with the entertainment on which they were supposed to hold opinions. The best they could hope for was to catch a small percentage and be briefed by subordinates on the rest. Sometimes it led to extraordinary situations. Sarah had often heard angry debates in which none of the participants had actually seen or read the original broadcast or article in question.

'What did he say on the programme?' Sarah asked.

George took a moment to recall. 'Fanny explained to me that Miller had said that a good manager is similar to a forester. To make sure the wood stays healthy and productive, it is necessary to constantly clear the undergrowth, prune the dead wood and cut away the secondary trees that threaten the valuable timber.'

'What did you say?'

Again, Prior answered for him. 'He said, "The ability to make simplistic bollocks sound profound is the ultimate triumph of the politician."'

Sarah looked at George without comment.

'I meant it to be lighthearted,' he said sheepishly.

Prior paused, a match halfway to a cigarette. 'You should have tried something more subtle, boss. Like: fuck off, you prick.'

In the silence that followed, they were joined by Cat Abbot, another *Gazette* reporter. 'Bloody coffee machine's broken again,' he grumbled as he sat down.

'Did you have a good holiday?' George asked, attempting to change the subject. Abbot had been in Spain, visiting his daughter for the past few weeks. He slapped his waistline. 'Not bad, if you like paella for Christmas dinner.'

'How's the family?' Sarah asked.

Abbot tugged at his bow tie and sighed. 'I just don't understand girls these days. My daughter's got a new baby, no job, and she says she's going to go travelling around Europe for a couple of years. Thank Christ's she's married. At least her husband will be able to support her.'

'What does he do?' Pauline asked.

Abbot reached for Prior's cigarettes. 'He's got a degree in politics, economics and philosophy, so he can always get work as a barman.'

'Don't you think your daughter can survive without him?' Pauline continued.

Cat studied the stream of smoke he blew towards the ceiling. 'She's an attractive girl, she'll always find a bloke to look after her if he clears off.'

Pauline reacted to his provocation, just as Abbot knew she would. It was one of his diversions in life.

'Women can survive without men, you know. It's not like the old days any more.'

Abbot's smile goaded Pauline further. 'I was in the North before Christmas,' she said. 'It was the women who were working up there. The men were all on the dole. I think I could survive just as easily as a man.'

George began to show a flicker of interest. 'You're saying you could manage just as easily as a man if you didn't have a job today?'

'Yes,' Pauline said flatly.

'Well of course you could,' Abbot went on. 'You'd just pop over to Wapping and get your mates on the *Sunday Times* to fix you up with a few casual shifts.'

'I could survive without working as a reporter,' Pauline said.

'Yes, darling,' Abbot said, putting out his cigarette in the remains of his coffee.

George watched them, then said to Abbot, 'You don't think she could survive as well as you could?'

'No chance,' he replied breezily.

George sat back and drummed his fingers. 'Right,' he said. 'You can both prove it.'

'How do you mean?' Abbot said, his voice filled with alarm.

George stood up, and the conversational tone had gone from his voice. Once again he was head of the department. 'I want both of you to prove how you can survive on the streets without money. I don't care if you beg, borrow or work as skivvies. You can't use contacts or draw money from your bank, nor can you sleep at home.' He paused and studied Abbot. 'Don't worry, you'll probably win an award when you finish the series.'

'Series?' Abbot echoed.

George smiled. 'I can see it now: "Down and out in the Nineties. Two top *Gazette* writers report from the gutter." '

'You're not serious,' Abbot pleaded, but he knew that George was.

'See what you've got us into,' Abbot grumbled to Pauline as they made their way back to the newsroom. George, striding ahead, was suddenly in a better mood.

Pauline seemed not to mind the assignment but Cat grumbled about it for the rest of the day. Sarah was following up an agency story, trying to get quotes from people who lived in Derby. It meant long telephone calls and waiting to be connected with individuals mentioned in the copy. Each time she was on hold and her attention drifted back to the newsroom, she could hear Abbot telling someone else of his misfortune. Glad that she was not involved, Sarah continued with her own task until at 3.30 a news-desk secretary asked her to go to George's office.

His little room off the editorial floor was empty. A few Christmas cards had fallen from the top of a filing cabinet on to the floor and a piece of mistletoe hung from a light-cord. Sarah stooped down to pick up the cards and, as she reached for the last one, noticed a row of books on the bottom shelf of a half-open cupboard.

One caught her eye: a volume of Shakespeare's sonnets half out of the shelf. Sarah took out the slim book and it fell open where a small photograph had been used as a bookmark. With a sudden lurch, Sarah saw that it was a picture of her, taken many years ago when she had first joined the paper.

She read the first line of the sonnet, 'Shall I compare thee to a summer's day', then closed the book and replaced it.

Sarah knew that George had always carried a torch for her; it was almost a joke between them that had developed over the years. But this secret reminder of his real feelings brought a sudden ache to her throat. She knew what it was like to think of someone you couldn't have. When Jack had been killed she'd thought at one point that she might die of grief.

George entered the room and she smiled at him with sudden affection. He sat down, avoiding her eyes, and said, 'I'm not sure how to tell you this.'

'What?' Sarah asked, suddenly suspicious.

He leaned forward and rested his elbows among the scruffy piles of papers on the desk.

'The idea we had in the canteen this morning.'

'The idea *you* had.'

He sighed. 'Well, whoever . . . anyway, Brian Meadows loves it, he says it'll give the paper back its serious edge after all the trash Simon Marr published recently.'

Marr had been the editor replaced by Meadows's restoration.

'Well, that's good isn't it?' Sarah asked.

'Up to a point. The problem is, Pauline can't do the piece. We've got a sudden break on the insurance scam story. She's got to follow that up.'

Sarah knew what was coming. 'Oh, no,' she said. 'Oh, no. You're not going to put me on the streets, are you, George?'

He held his hands palms upward. 'Who else can do it like you can?'

Sarah groaned and sat down in the chair opposite him.

'Just this one for me,' he pleaded. 'I need a few Brownie points at Headquarters.'

She almost refused; then thought of her picture in the book of sonnets and sighed. 'OK,' she said. 'But I hope you know what you're getting me into.'

· 2 ·

The old woman knew what the others in the great house thought of her: that she was old and frail and witless. A senile, decaying cripple, living out the last of her life: to be fed slops and then forgotten. But she was sharper than they realised, and still able to move from the attic where they thought she was bedridden. And she knew the great house better than any of them: there were forgotten rooms that only she remembered. Lost passages and hidden places where she could listen, hear muttered conversations, and see things that others didn't want revealed to the light of day.

Last night she had woken to their drunken shouts and scuttled from her room, looked down on the stableyard. At first it had seemed like a game they played, but the man tormented by the others had squealed hopelessly with fear, like a pig going under the knife. Then the dogs had caught him and the sounds changed. The screams stopped after a few moments and there was just their grunting snarl and the terrible tearing sound their jaws made.

They were silent when they pulled the dogs from his body; but later she had found a place where she could hear their conversation. Long into the night they worked out the details of how they would cover up the crime. More secrets for her to hoard, to store away with all the other dark fragments of knowledge.

Sarah paused before the blackboard, chalk in hand, halfway through writing the word 'past', and suddenly wished she was a thousand miles away from the classroom where she now stood. Or she would have settled for her garden in Hampstead – breathing air fresher than the cloying mixture of dust and heat that rose from the ancient radiators lining the walls.

Muttering voices sounded behind her, and she did not have to turn round to know that it would be Garland and Hesketh-Pearson. Sarah finished the word, then turned to face the room.

'Can anyone tell me where the sentence I have just written comes from?' she asked. Ten callow faces, blank with boredom, gazed at the words and then back at her, mute with incomprehension.

She sighed, and once more had to remind herself that they were not children but youths on the edge of adulthood. But for the fact that their parents were all wealthy, they would have long ago been cast out of any normal educational establishment and would probably now be begging on the streets, without even the ability to find themselves a cardboard box for shelter.

The bodies of men and the minds of farmyard animals, she thought.

Garland and Hesketh-Pearson, who lounged together in the front row, did not even bother to conceal the magazine that was spread on the desk top before them. In fact they had turned it towards her and left it open at a sprawling centrefold so that her glance could not miss the naked body.

Sarah looked down at the model's pouting features and for a moment almost envied the girl in the picture. At least she knows how to hold the interest of an audience, she thought; and a fragment of poetry came to her from her childhood. Something about a clerk in a dusty office wishing he were swimming with polar bears.

'Put that away, Garland,' she said in a weary voice.

'We thought it might be you, Mrs Keane,' Hesketh-Pearson said in a lazy voice. 'I would say the hair and skin tones is identical.'

'Are identical,' Sarah corrected automatically. 'You wouldn't want people to say Hesketh-Pearson's brain and his vocabulary *is* very small, would you?'

The reply raised a feeble laugh from the rest of the class

because they recognised it as an insult, but Sarah regretted the remark. It was becoming easier each hour to share their Neanderthal sense of humour. I've got to get away from this dreadful place, she told herself, before my brain atrophies completely.

A bell sounded in the distance and the youths clattered to their feet.

'Read the first chapter of *The Great Gatsby* again tonight,' she called out above the noise, 'And note the narrator's remarks on the foul dust that Gatsby left behind him.'

Sarah turned to her desk and began to gather her books together. When she looked up she saw that the door was now closed, but Hesketh-Pearson was still in the room.

'Yes?' Sarah asked coldly, when she had crossed over to him.

The youth leaned smiling against a row of cupboards so that his body blocked the doorway. Slowly, but with casual deliberation, he began to push himself closer to her. 'I thought you might like to examine me when we were alone,' he said, his mouth now near enough for her to feel his damp breath on her face.

'Let me pass,' she said without any real anger in her voice.

'Come on, Mrs Keane,' Hesketh-Pearson continued. 'After all, you brought the subject up.'

'Get out of the way,' she said in a tighter voice. Instead of moving, he took a crumpled £50 note from his pocket and slowly tucked it down the front of her blouse.

Sarah removed the banknote and dropped it on the floor. 'It's a pity you can't buy yourself a new personality, boy,' she answered, and there was the warning of real anger in her tone now.

'You're the one who needs a lesson, Mrs Keane,' he continued. 'Didn't anyone ever tell you about servants knowing their place?'

She was tempted for a moment to hit him, but knew she had been wrong earlier to make a provocative remark. 'Let's just forget what you've said, shall we?' she said and attempted to pass again. Still he barred her way.

He reached out and took hold of her arm. To his surprise it was not soft and yielding as he had expected; and he was taken aback by the strength with which she now seized his shoulder with her free hand and swung him away from her.

He half-stumbled and scattered his books on the floor. Recovering, he was about to move towards her again when he became aware of the troubled stare of the headmaster, Adrian Hostler, who had pressed his face close to the reeded glass of the door and was watching suspiciously. Behind him, Sarah noticed another blurred figure.

Hesketh-Pearson scrabbled his books together as the door opened and quickly left the classroom with a curt 'Sir' to Hostler, who marked his passing with a brief nod. The headmaster turned to Sarah and pursed his lips in disapproval as he glanced down.

Among the books dropped by Hesketh-Pearson was the magazine, which had skidded across the floor and had come to rest at Sarah's feet. Hostler stooped down and held it up with prim distaste.

'I didn't expect to find anything like this in your classroom, Mrs Keane,' he said, as though accusing her of bringing the offending article on to the premises.

'Perhaps you would like to impound it, Mr Hostler,' she replied, 'in case the boy it belongs to wants it back.'

The headmaster walked across the room and dropped the magazine into a wastepaper basket with a theatrical flourish, then returned, his face grim with anger. In the few days she had worked in his establishment, Hostler had grown to dislike Sarah almost as much as he fawned upon the parents of the youths who attended his crammer. The school, located in a once elegant Georgian house off Ladbroke Grove, specialised in taking public-school failures who were boarded on the premises while they were coached for one more chance at university entrance.

Sarah was also staying in the house: she had a bedsitter high up in the attic rooms, where the central heating gave way to an occasional paraffin heater.

'Mrs Keane,' Hostler began, 'did I see you and that youth indulging in horseplay?' While he spoke, the emaciated little man blinked rapidly, as though his watery eyes were offended by her presence.

'No you did not, Mr Hostler,' she replied firmly. Then she noticed the other man, who was attempting to conceal the beginning of a smile. He seemed an unlikely figure to be seen about these premises. Tall, conventionally handsome, he was more Latin than Anglo-Saxon, but dressed as a prosperous member of the upper classes in a pinstriped suit, and dark blue overcoat. He carried a neatly furled umbrella and wore some sort of club tie she did not recognise. It occurred to her that he might be a parent.

Hostler took a firm grip on the edge of his gown with a claw-like hand, then continued, 'Well, it looked like it to me.' His rising voice reminded Sarah of chalk squeaking on a blackboard.

She stood as straight as she could and looked down on him. 'I think it was simply sexual harassment, not really horseplay,' she replied.

Hostler stiffened and transferred his grip to the lapel of his ancient tweed suit: 'It won't do, it just won't do,' he repeated. 'I always suspected that the presence of a . . . female, no matter how impressive her academic qualifications, would only bring disruption to an educational establishment such as this.'

Suddenly, Sarah knew she could not take any more. The effort to remain unaffected by the squalor of her surroundings, the brutish behaviour of the pupils and the constant attempts at bullying by the little man before her finally proved too much.

'Mr Hostler,' she began carefully, 'I don't have any academic qualifications – impressive or otherwise. Your deputy hired me because I could speak English. I saw the only other applicant outside his office. He would have had difficulty getting a job as a minicab driver.'

'What are you inferring . . .' Hostler spluttered, and Sarah could now see that the other man had given up his effort not to smile.

She continued in the same calm voice. 'I'm not *inferring* anything – I believe you mean "imply". I am stating bare facts. This is not an "educational establishment" by any stretch of the imagination. Real schools are still closed for the holidays – this is the headquarters of a confidence trickster, and you, Mr Hostler, are simply posing as a teacher.'

To give him his due, Hostler attempted to continue with his charade. Feigning outrage, he pointed an accusing finger at Sarah and said, 'I had the gravest reservations when Mr Milburne hired you. I am sad to say my misgivings have not proved groundless. I think it best if we terminate the arrangement forthwith.'

'Strange,' Sarah said, with an immense feeling of relief and in a suddenly cheerful voice, 'I would have sworn you were going to say "henceforth",' and with a brief smile she strolled past Adrian Hostler and his companion and out of the building.

By the time she reached Holland Park Avenue she had begun to regret her hasty departure: she was wearing only a light blazer over her silk shirt, and there was a cold wind blowing from the direction of Shepherd's Bush.

She stopped at a telephone booth and dialled George Conway's number.

'News desk,' answered the familiar voice.

'It's me, Sarah,' she said. 'Are you still keen on this nonsense?'

'As a newly honed razor.'

Sarah groaned in despair. 'I thought you might have passed on to another bright idea by now.'

'Sorry,' Conway replied briskly. 'What's the matter, losing your grip?'

'That'll be the day,' she answered and hung up.

When she came out of the phone booth she was surprised to find the man who had stood beside Hostler waiting for her.

'Forgive me,' he said quickly. 'I'm not usually in the habit of following ladies and accosting them in the street; but we did see each other with Mr Hostler – even though he didn't bother to introduce us.' He held out a hand. 'My name is Latimer, John Latimer.'

His voice was deep and expensively educated, and his handshake dry and firm. There was a small scar between his eyebrows she hadn't noticed earlier.

'Sarah Keane,' she replied.

'I wonder if we could talk; I gather you're unemployed.' He spoke now with an almost arrogant assurance that Sarah might have wished to undermine in normal circumstances; but now she had to remind herself that she was beholden to anyone who might offer work. She was about to answer when a pattern of raindrops appeared on the pavement about them. There was a sudden crack of thunder and after a momentary pause a torrential downpour began. Casually, Latimer unfurled his umbrella and covered Sarah with a proprietorial flourish. It seemed like a moment of intimacy. The dull roar of the traffic changed pitch as cars and buses swished past on the rain-slicked road.

'What do you have in mind?' Sarah asked.

Latimer glanced around him and then at his watch. 'I have to be back in town,' he said. 'Perhaps you could come with me. We can discuss it then.'

'What part of town?'

'Lincoln's Inn.'

He had turned away from her now and was gazing imperiously into the traffic. He raised his hand a couple of times, but the cabs he signalled sailed on.

'You won't get a taxi in this,' Sarah said. 'It would be easier to take the underground.'

'Would it?' he answered. 'Where from?'

'The Central Line, just along here at Holland Park. That will take us all the way to Chancery Lane.'

Latimer smiled. 'You see, you're just the type of resourceful young lady I'm looking for.' Again the manner was that of effortless superiority. Sarah felt like a native guide showing the great white hunter where game was to be found. 'Don't you ever use the underground?' she asked.

'I did twice, when I was a boy,' he answered without much interest, and she knew he was telling the truth.

The rain was easing a little when they reached Holland Park station. Sarah could see that Latimer did not know what to do but he gave no indication of dismay. Instead he waited while she stepped forward and bought them both tickets to Chancery Lane.

The storm had brought more people than usual on to the train and it was impossible for them to talk in the crowded carriage. Latimer seemed intrigued by the bustle and slightly aloof from the crowd; it made Sarah feel responsible for him – until they emerged once again on the surface.

'Well, that was entertaining,' Latimer said. 'I had no idea it was like that down there.' He gestured with his umbrella, having regained his bearings. 'This way.'

About halfway down Chancery Lane, which curved south from High Holborn towards Fleet Street, they turned into an ancient gateway that led into the rear entrance of Lincoln's Inn and made their way along a stone-flagged passage that eventually opened out on to handsome brick cloisters. Even though it was still raining slightly there were plenty of pedestrians in the narrow lanes threading between the Dickensian buildings. Brisk serious women carrying briefcases and papers jostled with hurrying clerks. Occasional barristers, wigless but wearing the rest of the costume necessary to perform their duties at the nearby Law Courts, strolled among them, protecting their black-gowned figures with large umbrellas. Latimer nodded to people a few times. Clearly he was on familiar territory.

Sarah was beginning to feel decidedly damp and a little scruffy in her trainers, blazer and jeans. Passing out of the imposing gates at the entrance of the Inn, they entered Lincoln's Inn Fields, a wide square of trees, lawns and tennis courts overlooked by imposing buildings. Skirting the square they arrived at the north side, and a large block of Edwardian mansion flats.

The name CORTON COURT was set in a bronze plate above the main entrance. Latimer strode on, up a short flight of stone steps and passed through heavy, brass-bound oak doors into the building. Inside, was a bleak echoing hallway with a floor patterned in a mosaic of black and white marble. Ignoring the open-caged lift he began to climb the wide staircase, Sarah following a few steps behind.

He stopped on the fifth landing; Sarah looked from a large window as he searched for a key. The wind blew steadily from the west and she could see more stormclouds darkening the sky over Harrow in the distance.

Turning from the view, she followed Latimer into a large hallway that was piled with an odd assortment of items that looked as if they had been culled from the attic of an old family house. There were leather suitcases patched with exotic labels, tea chests full of children's books and battered toys, hat boxes and sporting gear. She examined the clutter for a few moments before Latimer led her along a wide gloomy passageway lit with a single bare light bulb. Sarah noticed patches of paler wallpaper where pictures had recently hung.

Suddenly she began to enjoy this new development. Although her usual demeanour gave the impression that she was reserved, she possessed an acute sense of the ridiculous that sometimes caused her to behave recklessly when confronted by situations that appealed to her liking for surrealism. There was something deeply intriguing about this new direction.

Latimer stopped at a doorway and shook his head. 'Forgive me, I'm forgetting my manners. Would you care for some tea? My sister should be here but she appears to have gone out.'

Sarah nodded and he led her into a largish living room which was in better order than the rest of the flat. A fire was burning and the room contained some good pieces of furniture. Bookshelves flanked the fireplace, faced by two deep, comfortable-looking armchairs and a large chesterfield in faded brown leather. Oriental rugs lay on the polished wooden floor and a dining table against one wall held silver objects. A grand piano with a collection of framed photographs stood by the windows. The pictures on the walls, surprisingly, were abstracts in primary colours, and, Sarah guessed, rather valuable.

Latimer gestured to the armchairs and they sat down. 'Now, about this job,' he began easily. 'What I'm really looking for is a resourceful and presentable young woman who can act as – ' he paused to find the suitable phrase – 'a guardian angel, might be the correct term.'

'What makes you think I could do this work?'

He smiled. 'The person I need must have spirit and intelligence. I could see you possessed those qualities from your dealings with the wretched Mr Hostler.'

'How did you happen to be there?'

Latimer waved a hand. 'I'm a solicitor – I was telling him of some business connected with his family.'

'And you were able to form an opinion of me from that one brief encounter?'

'I think so,' he answered after giving her question a moment's thought. 'I'm used to making immediate judgements in my work. I find that I'm seldom wrong.'

'Whom do you wish me to protect?'

Latimer paused while he looked her over again. 'One of my clients, who has . . . certain problems,' he answered slowly.

The fire gave a sudden crack of exploding gases and a red-hot cinder the size of a walnut was thrown on to the rug at his feet. Without hesitation, Latimer reached down, picked it up and flung it back into the grate. Sarah watched with interest and saw that he looked slightly sheepish. 'I didn't mean to show off. It doesn't burn if you do it quickly enough,' he said. 'The trick is not to hold on too long.'

'I shall remember that,' Sarah answered. Her damp blazer continued to feel uncomfortable.

There was the sound of a door banging open and Latimer looked up. 'That will be my sister.'

Before he could speak again, the door opened and a woman entered, awkwardly carrying two plastic bags. She stumbled momentarily as she caught a shoe heel on the edge of a rug.

After a flash of bright colours, the first thing Sarah noticed was how thin and dishevelled she was. It wasn't that the clothes she wore were of poor quality; in fact Sarah could tell that they were, if anything, rather expensive. It was more a lack of judgement about their suitability for such a gaunt frame. Even her stockings bagged at the ankles and the violent clashes of colours of her skirt, blouse and loosely draped shawl gave her the appearance of a child who has spent a rainy day dressing up from her mother's wardrobe.

From beneath a mop of dark, frizzy hair, a narrow-featured face, with the same dark complexion as Latimer's, peered myopically towards them. 'Have you seen my spectacles?' she asked, placing the bags on the floor. Latimer reached to the table next to him and picked up a pair of wire-framed glasses. 'They're here,' he answered gently and held them out. When she had put them on she noticed Sarah.

'Oh, hello,' she said. 'I'm Polly Latimer.'

'Sarah Keane. How do you do.'

'Did you remember the milk?' Latimer asked.

Bird-like, the woman put her head to one side and suddenly Sarah realised how appropriate her name was. In her bright plumage she looked rather like a parrot. And there was the same ageless quality, although, Sarah thought, she was probably older than her brother.

'Do you know, John,' Polly Latimer replied in a puzzled voice, 'I wrote down a list of things to do and when I got to the shops in Holborn I realised I'd forgotten my spectacles so I couldn't read it. I think I got most of the items but I'm afraid I shall have to go again.'

Latimer inclined his head. 'As you wish.' He turned to Sarah again and sat with his hands making a steeple. 'Polly shares this flat with me,' he explained, then continued, 'Now tell me, what made you decide to come?'

'I would have thought that was quite obvious,' Sarah replied. 'I need a job.'

Polly peered from one to the other then said to Sarah, 'I hope you'll be happy with us.' She turned to Latimer: 'I take it you are going to offer the position to her?'

Latimer turned his head to his sister. 'Possibly,' he said, then, to Sarah, 'Tell me, do you have any questions you want to ask me?'

She looked from one to the other. Somehow the situation had changed. Now it was as if Sarah was the supplicant. She should have reminded Latimer that it was he who persuaded her to accompany him, but she was still intrigued; and she did want to know the answers to some questions. 'Why didn't you advertise the position?' she asked.

'Because we would have got too many replies,' Latimer answered briskly. 'We don't have time to interview a long list of people, and we need a smart woman immediately.'

'Couldn't you have asked for just that?'

Latimer sighed and shook his head. 'Not so simple in this politically correct world, I'm afraid.' He shifted in the chair. 'I want a woman who is bright; but if you specify that you want someone of a particular sex these days, you open the doors to all sorts of wearisome people who delight in challenging "sexual stereotypes". I can assure you I know what I'm talking about.'

'Is it really that bad?'

'Just the other day one of my clients wanted to hire a new housekeeper. He was hoping for a middle-aged woman – a widow with a young child would have been ideal. Some of the young men who applied became quite abusive when he rejected them. I didn't want the same problem if I advertised for a smart, presentable woman with a good speaking voice.'

A good speaking voice, Sarah thought. The second time I've been hired for my pronunciation. So much for the classless society.

'So I pass your initial tests,' she said. 'But aren't you interested in seeing any references?'

'I don't think so,' Latimer answered in almost a cold tone. 'As I said before, I pride myself that I'm a pretty fair judge of character – but there is one caveat.'

'What would that be?'

'I want to offer accommodation here as part of the salary.'

'Why?'

Latimer made a steeple of his fingers again as he replied. 'I have a busy practice to serve. It would make life easier if I could discuss the work I want you to perform in the mornings and evenings. Do you have any objections?'

'None at all,' Sarah said. 'I needed somewhere to stay.'

Latimer smiled again. 'Well, that's settled then. Now let's have some tea.'

'Oh, dear,' Polly said apologetically. 'The milk.'

'Never mind,' Latimer answered. 'I'll go this time, it may be quicker.' He turned to Polly. 'Why don't you show Mrs Keane the rest of the place while I'm out?'

Latimer departed and Polly led Sarah around the other rooms of the flat. It was even bigger than she had expected. There was a large bathroom, furnished in marble, mahogany and brass, part of the original apartment.

'This is John's room,' Polly said, indicating the open door to a room that was crowded with dark, heavy Edwardian furniture. Next door was a large office that looked as if it had been furnished at the turn of the century. The telephone was made of black Bakelite mounted on a mahogany stand. Sarah lifted the receiver experimentally and found it heavy enough to club somebody insensible. Polly looked about her at the wooden filing cabinets, brass-handled partner's desk and leather swivel chairs. 'I love this room,' she said. 'I'm trying to persuade John not to change it. What do you think?'

Sarah noticed the very English enthusiasm in her voice, a sort of girls' boarding-school heartiness. 'I take it you haven't been here long,' she said.

Polly shook her head. 'Just a few weeks in the flat. John has an office in Lincoln's Inn, just across the way. He used to live in our father's house in Kensington until recently.'

'And you?'

'I lived with an aunt in the country, but she died.'

'Why did John move here?'

'Oh, the house in Kensington was very big and John says it's hard to get servants these days. We used to have five when I was a little girl.' She held out her hands. 'Well, do you like the flat?'

'A vast improvement on what I've been used to recently,'

Sarah replied truthfully. There was a ring on the doorbell. 'I'll get that,' she said.

The young police constable strolling across the concourse of King's Cross station thought there was something familiar about Colin Greaves's companion. Greaves could tell from the momentary double-take he gave Detective-Sergeant Nick Holland; but he didn't really notice Greaves at all.

He did not mind the lack of recognition; in fact he preferred anonymity. His picture was published in police magazines, and even in the national press from time to time, but he had the ability to appear unremarkable: a slim, grave-looking man of average height, conservatively dressed, although the discerning observer would notice that his clothes were more expensive than those of most police superintendents.

Nick Holland was the striking figure: tall, powerfully built, he had open, handsome features and the walk of an athelete. In the recent past he had been a star performer with the Metropolitan Police rugby team until a knee injury had ended his days as a player.

Greaves and Holland stopped for a moment to exchange farewells. 'I thought for a moment that Constable was going to ask for your autograph,' Greaves said.

'Not this season,' Holland replied. '*Sic transit gloria.*'

Greaves smiled. 'Is that a pun, or are you being philosophical?' he asked. The constable had been in the transport police.

'More philosophical,' Holland answered. 'I'm the one who has to go back to work.'

'Rank has its privileges.'

It was Holland's turn to smile. In his experience, Greaves had never abused his position of power. When asked why he stayed in the job of the superintendent's assistant, which many in the force considered a cul-de-sac for a man of Holland's talents, Holland simply answered that he enjoyed the work. It wasn't in his nature to tell people of the deep regard he had for Greaves. To others, their relationship seemed distant – even formal – but the two men knew how they counted on each other; and that was enough.

'I'll be in touch,' Greaves said, and nodded his goodbye.

While Nick Holland walked to the entrance of the underground, Greaves found a telephone booth on the edge of the concourse and made a couple of calls. The first was to his home number. He was answered by a recording from Sarah advising him to ring George Conway, who knew of her whereabouts. The news desk of the *Gazette* informed him that Conway was in the Red Lion public house. Greaves was about to call there when he realised that he would quite like a drink; the pub was only a few minutes away along the Gray's Inn Road.

Usually he would have walked the short distance, but his suitcase was heavy enough to justify a taxi. The snarled traffic slowed his journey through the wet, shabby maze of streets dictated by the one-way system leading south from King's Cross, and he began to compare his present surroundings with the elegant country house where he and Holland had spent the last few days. He wondered why he'd decided to live in London: he had enough money to go anywhere else they chose.

Sometimes he imagined moving with Sarah and her children to a house in the shires and leading the life of a country gentleman. But it was only a daydream. In his heart he knew that they both needed to work. Leisure could never be a way of life for them; only a reward for doing something they considered worth while.

The taxi halted outside the Red Lion and Greaves entered the crowded saloon bar and he spotted George Conway, standing in a group with a cluster of reporters. Greaves knew them all slightly. Mick Gates, Tony Prior and David Rose were all in their twenties; only Cat Abbot was of a similar age to Conway and himself.

Abbot was reminiscing when he joined them. 'You don't get sieges like you used to,' he said wistfully. 'I had a page lead every day when that lot were banged up in the Guildford Bank snatch.'

'You were giving one to the wife of the security guard who was inside as well, weren't you?' Conway added.

'I don't remember you complaining about the copy I got out of it,' Abbot protested.

Conway ignored the remark and turned to Greaves. 'What will you have, Colin?'

Greaves asked for a whisky and Conway raised his eyebrows. 'Hello, you must be on duty.'

Taking the drink, Greaves shook his head. 'Actually I'm on leave. Have you seen Sarah?'

'She's on a job,' Conway replied. 'She told me you were away until the end of the week.'

'I was, but the conference broke up early. There was a salmonella scare at the hotel. The brass decided to make a strategic withdrawal.'

'And that broke up the meeting?'

Greaves nodded and reached out for the soda siphon on the bar. Conway's idea of a whisky was 50 per cent too strong.

'Salmonella, eh,' George mused, making a mental note to follow up the possibility of a story later in the afternoon. 'We need a dose of that over there.' He indicated the drab grey stone building that housed the offices of the *Gazette*.

'How's the new regime doing?' Greaves asked.

'*Plus ça change*,' George said. 'It doesn't matter who's in charge, the poor bloody infantry still gets to do all the fighting.'

'I thought you liked Brian Meadows.'

George drank some of his own whisky. 'Oh, Brian's all right. A thousand times better than that last clown. But I still have my reservations about Charles Miller.'

'Miller's not bad,' Greaves said. 'He just likes making money. He was even like that at school.'

'You knew him at school?'

Greaves looked into his glass. 'Different houses – but yes, slightly.'

'What was he like then?'

Greaves searched his memory. 'Average sort, quite a good runner. Sharp enough.'

'Anything else?' George pressed. He was a firm believer in the child being father to the man. Any clues to the character of his new employer might be valuable in the future.

Greaves was aware of the purpose of the questions but he liked Conway and was prepared to co-operate. 'He ran an insurance scheme against punishments with a very sophisticated sliding scale of premiums depending on the risk factor.'

George pondered that piece of information as Greaves bought a round of drinks.

'Where is Sarah exactly?' asked Greaves.

'She's out and about on a story. She'll be away from home for a few days. Didn't she phone you?'

'I was out of touch.'

George looked at him shrewdly. 'You were at the anti-terrorist conference, weren't you?'

Greaves glanced at the other reporters, but they were engrossed in their own conversation. 'How do you know about that?'

Conway smiled, his battered features assuming an air of innocence. 'Just a whisper I heard.'

'Not from Sarah,' Greaves replied. 'She didn't know anything about it. Now where is she, George?'

Conway shrugged. 'I'm not really sure. She calls in once a day, normally at about six o'clock. She's working on a piece about what it's like to get work in London without any qualifications.'

Greaves frowned. 'That sounds the sort of job that could take her anywhere.'

'At the moment she's working at some school in Notting Hill. I don't know the address.'

Cat Abbot had been listening to the last part of their conversation. 'I hope she's having better luck than I had,' he said. 'I bloody nearly starved.'

'What were you doing?' Greaves asked.

Abbot waved a hand in a semicircle. 'I started out applying for a job as a stockbroker and ended up washing windscreens on Westway.' He shuddered. 'The days weren't the worst part; it was those nights in the dossers that finished me off.'

'Nights?' Greaves repeated.

Abbot glanced to Conway before he answered. 'The idea is you're not allowed to sleep at home. It's no use checking into the Strand Palace and putting it on your credit card.' He smiled. 'Still, look on the bright side, she'll have saved a few bob on the current account by the time she's back home.'

Greaves finished his drink, picked up his case and said to George, 'Ask her to give me a ring at home when she calls in, will you?'

'Sure,' he replied. 'Won't you have the other half? After all, there's no one to nag you when you get home.'

Greaves shook his head and held up a hand in a salute of farewell. I hope you know what you're doing, Sarah, he thought to himself as he looked for another taxi in the Gray's Inn Road. The streets of London can be a nasty place when you're alone.

· 3 ·

When Sarah opened the door she saw that it was John Latimer, returning from his errand. 'Magritte,' she said as he stood framed in the doorway.

'What do you mean?' he replied, entering as she stood aside.

'The surrealist,' Sarah said. 'You look like one of his paintings.'

Latimer examined himself in the long mirror in the hallway. 'It's just the hat,' he said, taking off a rather elegant curly-brimmed bowler.

Sarah disagreed. 'It's the bowler *and* the bottle of milk. Put them together and you have surrealism.'

'The only thing surreal is forgetting my key,' he said, taking off his long blue overcoat and placing his umbrella in the coat-stand in the hall.

'I'm glad you didn't have to go far,' Sarah said.

'And how do you deduce that?' he asked as she followed him into the sitting room.

Sarah pointed towards the windows: 'It's only just stopped raining, but your umbrella is quite dry and so is your coat and hat.'

'I might have gone by taxi.'

'Your shoes are splashed with rainwater, so you walked somewhere.'

'Quite right,' Latimer replied. 'My office is nearby, I got a bottle from my secretary.'

Sarah studied him as he stood warming himself before the fire; it was clear he had something on his mind.

'Well,' she asked finally. 'Have you decided to tell me what you want me to do?'

He stretched his hands towards the fire again and smiled. 'I want you to keep somebody under observation for me.'

There was still a certain reluctance in Latimer's manner. For a moment, Sarah was reminded of one of her children, when they wanted permission for some undertaking to which they knew she would object. 'Has this person committed some offence?' she asked.

'Good Lord, no,' Latimer said quickly. 'He's an old and valued client of mine. I'm simply concerned for his safety.'

Sarah remained standing and folded her arms, suddenly more aware of her shabby appearance.

'Why exactly do you want a woman to do the job? Most people would prefer a man.'

Latimer now took the chair opposite her and crossed one leg over the other, carefully arranging the crease in his trousers. 'My client is something of an eccentric,' he said. 'Already he has bodyguards who accompany him everywhere, but the men are almost simpletons. I want a person who can observe what is going on and make intelligent deductions, and, if necessary, quickly get in touch with me.'

'You still haven't said why you want a woman for the job.'

Latimer smiled again as he replied. 'Now, this part is rather delicate, so I must ask you to bear with me while I explain.' He raised his hands and made his fingers into the familiar steeple before continuing in a slow and measured voice. 'Sir Silas Nightingale is a baronet. The family has always been astonishingly wealthy. But because Sir Silas's ancestors chose to marry into the same small group of acceptable families – ' he paused and raised his eyebrows – 'the Nightingale genetic pool has become . . . shall we say . . . overtaxed.'

'You mean he's inbred – barking mad?' Sarah suggested.

'I *was* going to say eccentric,' Latimer answered. He held up a warning hand. 'And I would prefer the term "colourful" in any future conversations.' He paused to collect his thoughts, then went on: 'Sir Silas lives most of the time on his estate in Oxfordshire, but twice a year he comes up to town to stay at the place he has made his London headquarters.'

'He has a town house?'

'He does, but he prefers to use another place where he feels more at home.' He paused, but Sarah said nothing so Latimer continued.

'The place he chooses to stay is an exclusive and discreet establishment in Jermyn Street, called the Corinthian Club. Whenever he stays there he is accompanied by his entourage, which consists of his nephew and heir, Tobias Nightingale, a young man whom he has raised since childhood. Then there's an ex-boxer called Trooper Stone, a great thug of a man; and his horse trainer and valet, a former jockey called Nathaniel Scroat.'

'He pays for all these people?' Sarah asked.

'Oh, yes. And there's one more . . .' Again Latimer paused, as if the name he was about to utter was distasteful to him. 'His personal physician, a Doctor Pendlebury.' Latimer looked down when he had finished and arranged the crease in his trousers again.

'You don't sound too keen on Doctor Pendlebury,' Sarah said.

Latimer pursed his lips. 'Frankly, the man is a charlatan. I think old Silas just keeps him around for the pills that boost his . . . energy.'

'And what does Sir Silas get up to on these trips?'

Latimer looked at her sharply. 'He carouses, Miss Keane – in the manner of an eighteenth-century gentleman.'

'By that you mean you mean whoring and gambling.'

'Exactly,' Latimer replied with a relaxed smile, pleased by Sarah's perception. 'That is the whole purpose of the Corinthian Club. The clientele pay a great deal of money to a discreet management so they can indulge in their pleasures without fear of untoward publicity.'

'So where do I come in?' Sarah said.

Latimer raised his eyes and studied the moulding on the ceiling. He continued: 'Although he is very old, Sir Silas has the constitution of an ox. He is nearly eighty but he still rides to hounds and when he is at home he swims every morning in the River Thames, no matter what the weather.'

'So what's caused your concern?'

Latimer frowned. 'In the past few days Sir Silas has suffered a bout of severe food poisoning.'

'Why is that suspicious?'

Latimer sat up in his chair and leaned forward. 'Nightingale always eats the same food and drinks the same wine as his entourage, yet none of the others suffered a moment's discomfort.'

'That's not uncommon, you know,' said Sarah dismissively.

Latimer looked at her with an almost faraway expression. 'I'm aware of that,' he said. 'But the morning before last he fell the entire length of the grand staircase at Gaudy, his country home, and he was stone-cold sober at the time. He insisted the ghost had pushed him.'

'Ghost?' Sarah said with raised eyebrows.

Latimer smiled thinly. 'Tell me, Mrs Keane, have you ever heard of an old house that didn't have a ghost?'

'But Nightingale believes in it?'

Latimer held up a hand. 'I told you he was eccentric. The Nightingales are known for their wealth, not their . . . intellect.'

Sarah thought for a moment. 'So you think there could be something in it?'

'I don't think the family ghost is causing harm . . . but – '

'But you're suspicious of something,' Sarah asked. 'Do you think the nephew is hurrying along his inheritance?'

Latimer shook his head. 'I don't think that at all. The two have been inseparable since Toby was orphaned as a small child. I've no doubt of the affection they have for one another. Sir Silas wouldn't even let him go away to school, he had him tutored at home. There's a great physical resemblance too.'

'They sound like two peas in a pod.'

'They could be – but with one difference. While Sir Silas would like to have lived in the eighteenth century, Toby actually thinks it *is* the eighteenth century.'

'You mean he's as colourful as his uncle.'

Latimer sighed. 'No, Miss Keane, Toby Nightingale *is* barking mad.'

'That bad?' Sarah said.

Latimer did not smile this time. 'Oh yes. If it weren't for the cloistered life he leads at Gaudy, I'm sure Toby would be in a nursing home.'

'So what exactly do you want me to do?'

'I want you to get a job at the Corinthian Club for the duration of Sir Silas's stay. Watch him and report to me if you see anything odd.'

'How can you be sure they'll hire me? Jobs are hard to come by these days.'

Latimer laughed. 'Believe me, you have the necessary qualifications. There is always a demand for beautiful women at the club.'

Sarah was flattered, but still not convinced. 'I'm a bit past the ideal age for a bunny girl,' she said.

Latimer wagged a finger. 'You're quite wrong,' he contradicted. 'A lot of men prefer maturer women; they find them less threatening. And I have a certain influence there. I shall tell them I'm your solicitor and you want to research a book. There's no need for them to know you're really watching Sir Silas. All you will have to do is present my card. I need hardly add, I will charge Nightingale a substantial sum for your services and you will receive 23 per cent of that fee – on top of your salary.'

'Really,' Sarah said. 'How substantial is my salary to be?'

'Shall we say, one hundred guineas a day?'

'I appreciate the guineas,' Sarah answered, keeping a deadpan expression as she spoke.

'Call it an anachronism of the legal profession,' Latimer said drily. 'You see I also have my eccentricities.'

He stood up and spoke in a sudden brisk voice. 'So, are you prepared to go ahead with the arrangement?'

Sarah did not have to think about her decision. She rose and held out her hand: suddenly the story was getting better and better.

· 4 ·

When the taxi dropped Colin Greaves in Hampstead, at the house he shared with Sarah and her children, he found a van blocking the driveway to the garage. He had forgotten that Sarah had arranged for the ground floor to be redecorated during his absence. He paused for a moment at the gate to look over the house, as if seeking reassurance that all was the same. In the months that he had lived there, Greaves had discovered an affection for this suburban property that he had never expected to develop.

It was strange now to remember that he had even wanted Sarah to move, so that they could begin their life together in surroundings that were new to them both. Sarah had refused even to contemplate his proposal. She had lived in the house throughout her marriage to Jack Keane; and she loved the old rambling redbrick villa with a fierce devotion. While Jack had roamed the world over the years, she had remade the garden, knocked down walls, created rooms, bought pictures and gradually found the furniture she wanted.

Now it was too much part of the fabric of her life for her to be parted from it. Greaves had come to understand that. He no longer saw it as the place where she had lived with Jack Keane, a journalist she had met on the *Gazette* when they were both young. She had given up reporting to raise their children and make this home. When Jack, who had moved to television reporting, had been killed in the Middle East she had returned to the *Gazette*.

She'd met Greaves on a story and they had been instantly attracted to one another. He had been married before but when his children were killed in an accident his marriage had not survived. Now Greaves knew that the house in Hampstead had a hold on him too.

It was easy to understand why: he had never lived anywhere he had actually considered home before. In his early childhood in Hong Kong his father had been a member of the ruling elite: Greaves, of the House of Greaves, head of one of the dynastic families whose trading empires had ruled the colony for over a hundred years. Their 'residence' had been more an opulent hotel than a home. Scores of servants saw to its smooth running while his parents, gracious and magnificent, loved him from afar. School in England had followed, then university and a time in the army, after which he had been expected to join the family business empire. But Colin Greaves had had other ideas. He chose to be a policeman, a decision that had astonished his family and appalled his new wife.

Looking back now, he recalled many places; but this was his first true home; and it was something he wanted to share with Sarah for the rest of his life.

Opening the front door, he picked his way through the clutter of paint cans, shrouded furniture and builders' ladders to the kitchen, where Mrs Lomax, their housekeeper, was making a pot of tea. Four men in overalls sat at the table, eating bacon sandwiches of heroic proportions.

Pat was flustered by his sudden appearance. 'I've been out shopping all day,' she explained. 'I wasn't expecting you back until the weekend. There's not much food in the house.'

Greaves looked at the workmen's sandwiches and felt a sudden stab of envy. Like many who have attended the grander public schools, food of a certain sort was his primary obsession.

Pat Lomax, still surprised to see him, recovered enough to introduce the men, who were all related to her. They were friendly enough, but somehow Greaves felt like an intruder.

'Can I get you anything?' Pat asked.

'A sandwich just like one of those would be perfect,' he replied. 'I'll be in my room, I've got some work to do.'

Greaves went to the bedroom at the top of the house. It was big enough to also serve as a study, and he had brought a few pieces of his own furniture when he had moved in with Sarah some months before. Through the open door paint fumes had filled the room. Greaves opened a window that overlooked the back garden and saw that two of Pat's relatives had now left the kitchen and were stacking equipment on the stone-flagged patio beneath him.

Their voices were quite distinct. 'He's a bit posh for a copper, isn't he?' asked the younger one, whom Greaves recognised from the recent introduction as Terry.

Bob, the elder, grunted. 'He's loaded, doesn't have to work at all, Christ knows why he bothers. If I had his money I'd be off to Spain and spend the rest of my life on holiday.'

'She's got money as well, hasn't she?'

'Nah, she didn't have two ha'pennies to rub together. That husband of hers left her flat broke when he died.'

'I thought he'd been on telly. He must've been worth a bob or two.'

Bob disagreed. 'She was going to have to take the kids away from the school. According to Pat, that's why she got her old job back as a reporter.'

'But she doesn't have to work now?'

'No, they both do it because they like it.'

'They must be bloody mad.'

'Well don't let Pat hear you say that. She thinks the world of them.'

'Oh, they seem all right – still bloody mad, if you ask me.'

45

Greaves drew away from the window and crossed the room to sit on the sofa. He thought for a while and then realised he had nothing to do. It was an unusual condition. Even when he had been married, he had driven himself. That had been in Hong Kong, where he had lived with his family.

His wife, Marion, had really hated him being a policeman. She'd found it incongruous and occasionally embarrassing that he should have been devoted to a job that she considered to be beneath her social station. When their son and daughter had been drowned in a boating accident she had blamed Greaves, accusing him of caring more for his work than his children.

The accusation had eaten into him, as she had intended. Still he wondered if he could have prevented the accident, had he gone with them to the club that Sunday morning instead of to the scene of a murder in the old city quarter.

A deep numbing melancholy was beginning to enfold him when Pat Lomax knocked and entered with his food. She left the tray and he looked at the sandwich now without appetite. Then the telephone rang: it was Emily, Sarah's teenage daughter.

'Colin?' she said with surprise. 'I thought you were away until the weekend.'

'There was a drama,' Greaves explained. 'One of the chief constables thought he was poisoned.'

'Really?'

'Cross my heart.'

'Did you tell mum? Is she writing a story about it?'

'I've temporarily lost contact with your mother.'

'Why – is she all right?'

'She's doing some job. I hope she'll ring me later. How are you all?'

'Fine. I'm a little bit bored, it's raining and freezing.'

'What about Martin and Paul?'

'They're all right, they're out fishing with grandad. Is Pat there? I want to know if there's a letter from Ric.'

'Hold on,' he said. 'I'll transfer you.'

Greaves buzzed the extension and handed the call on. Talking to Emily had lightened his mood. He bit into the sandwich, and while he was eating remembered that he wanted to do some work on his old Riley that was parked in the garage. Half an hour later he was happy, hands covered in oil, mind occupied with the arcane intricacies of the Riley's fuel pump.

Her conversation with Latimer over, Sarah accompanied him to the kitchen where they found Polly making tea. 'Toast, I smell toast,' he said with boyish enthusiasm.

'Go and sit next door, it's nearly ready,' Polly instructed.

A few minutes later she brought a silver tray into the living room, where Latimer was attending to the fire once again.

When they had finished tea, Sarah looked down at her crumpled clothes. She now really wanted to change. The rest of her wardrobe was still at Hostler's crammer and she was due to call George Conway. 'Well, if I'm going to move in, I'd better get myself organised,' she said, standing up. 'I'll be back in a couple of hours.'

'Would you like me to give you a lift?' Latimer offered.

Sarah declined the invitation, but did realise she was broke. After a moment of hesitation, she asked Latimer for an advance on her salary. He was happy to comply. Pocketing the money she said she would see them later, and left the flat. In Chancery Lane she stopped at a bar and called the news desk.

'You're still employed, I take it?' George said when he answered the phone.

'How's Cat Abbot doing?' she asked.

'Back in the office,' George chuckled. 'He tried begging for a time, but he says that's a young man's game. He gave himself up in the front entrance hall after seventy-two hours.'

'Well I'm going the whole distance,' Sarah said. 'This is beginning to make good copy.'

'By the way,' George said as she was about to ring off, 'call Colin, he's at home. The conference ended early.'

Sarah redialled. A few moments later she had Greaves on the line. 'Where are you?' he asked.

'El Vino's wine bar in Fleet Street.'

'When are you coming home?'

'I can't for a few days.'

'Can I come and see you?'

Sarah thought. 'I don't see why not, providing you don't give me any money.'

'That shouldn't be too difficult. I'll be there in about half an hour.'

Greaves smiled wryly when he joined Sarah at a small table in a corner of the bar.

'Don't say anything,' she said, aware that he had noticed her dishevelled appearance.

'Can I get you another drink?'

'I suppose so,' she replied. 'I can always pretend you're picking me up.'

When they were settled, Greaves asked her how she had managed for the last few days. She told of the tedium at Hostler's Academy, then of the intriguing developments of the last few hours, but didn't mention the part of the job relating to the Corinthian Club.

'So you're going to carry on,' he said finally.

Sarah looked up at him. 'I think so, at least for a few more days. Will you come with me to Notting Hill and collect my clothes?'

'As long as you give me the money for the petrol.'

In the Riley, Sarah said, 'Can we go via Jermyn Street? I want to look at a club there.'

'Club?'

'A place called the Corinthian.'

Greaves glanced at her as they passed along the Strand. 'Why do you want to look over the Corinthian Club?' he asked.

So Sarah explained the next part of her duties.

'Are you sure?' Greaves said in an ominous voice. 'I don't think you'll be happy there, it's no better than a knocking shop. Did you know it's called the Bawdy House?'

'No,' she admitted, 'but I do know what goes on there. It's all right, I can manage it.'

'I'm really not very happy about this,' Greaves said in a worried voice. 'I know some of the people who belong to that place.'

'There's no need to be concerned,' Sarah said. 'I really will be quite safe.'

In Jermyn Street, Greaves slowed down as they passed the premises.

'It looked innocuous enough,' Sarah said, when they reached Hyde Park Corner.

'So does quicksand – until you step in it,' Greaves replied.

They drove along the Bayswater Road which was crowded with traffic and slick from the rain that had begun to fall again. She waved to the right: 'Turn down Ladbroke Grove and I'll direct you from there.'

Hostler's Academy looked more forlorn than ominous to Sarah now. As they passed by, she could see the flaking paintwork and seamed cracks in the plaster by the light of one low-powered bulb burning in the porch. They found a parking space quite close to the house and hurried back through the rain that was now falling more heavily. Passing an uncurtained window they saw Adrian Hostler seated at the head of a refectory table where the staff were dining. There were a few students at other tables in the gloomy room, but Sarah knew that most were rich enough to eat at the many restaurants in the vicinity. Pleased that she would not have to meet any of the residents, she led Greaves into the dingy entrance hall. 'This way,' she said and led him up the stairs to the attic floor. He noted the peeling wallpaper and a smell of paraffin.

'This is my room,' Sarah said, pausing in the corridor. 'Wait here, it won't take me a moment to get my stuff.'

Quickly she packed her clothes in a canvas bag and with one last brief glance at the dismal room smiled with relief and said, 'Come on, let's get out of here.'

She was as good as her word about the money. She bought Greaves dinner in a Chinese restaurant in Gerrard Street. As always, she was fascinated when he engaged the waiter in conversation. It was odd to know someone so intimately yet hear him speak a language that sounded alien to her own ears.

'What did he say?' she asked when the waiter had departed.

'He wanted to know if English women liked sex,' Greaves replied with a straight face.

'Well, if you'd care to make a diversion by way of Hampstead, you can always find out.'

'Do you have to go back to that place tonight?'

'Afraid so, those are the rules of the job.'

'I'm glad I only ordered two courses then,' Greaves said, then he saw that Sarah was making a sign with both thumbs up to the waiter who had just re-emerged from the kitchen. The white-coated figure doubled up with laughter and pointed to Greaves with glee.

When Sarah returned to Corton Court later that night she found Latimer and Polly reminiscing about their family. They sat at the table in the living room which was softly lit by candles and the glow from the fire. She accepted a glass of brandy and joined them.

'Do you remember Uncle David's stories at Christmas?' Latimer asked Polly.

'Only the one about the lion attacking the kitchen boy when he was on safari,' she replied.

'Uncle David spent all his time in Africa at a club in Durban.'

'You mean he never went on safari?'

'Only to the bathroom after the eighth or ninth drink.'

'What about that leopardskin and the buffalo's head he had in his cottage?'

Latimer poured them another brandy. 'He bought them from a man he met in a railway carriage when he was on his way to Hastings for Aunt Maude's funeral.'

'Who told you that?'

'Dad.'

Polly looked dejected by the news. 'Oh,' she said sadly. 'It must be true, then. He never lied.'

'And little good it did him,' Latimer said with a sudden note of bitterness.

'It made him happy,' Polly answered.

Latimer nodded. 'I suppose so, but it was a big price to pay.'

Sarah, feeling that the conversation was straying on to personal matters that were none of her concern, decided to steer the talk in another direction. 'Did you have a big family?' she asked.

'Yes,' Polly replied, 'scattered about, but we kept pretty close. What about you?'

'Hardly any on my father's side,' said Sarah. 'I don't really know my mother's family.'

'Don't you like them?' Polly asked.

'Oh yes, but they objected to my father because he wasn't a Catholic. It split us up, I'm afraid.'

Latimer cast a warning glance at Polly, who was going to ask another question. Sarah saw his expression and smiled. She had often noticed that some Protestants found the fact that she was a Catholic a slight embarrassment, and that any discussion of religion was considered almost in bad taste. Noticing the awkward pause, Latimer offered to do the washing up. It was something of a grand gesture, like an officer serving other ranks on Christmas Day.

Afterwards they played Scrabble until after one o'clock. It was a pleasant enough ending to the evening.

When she and Polly went to the room they were to share, Sarah tried a few casual questions about Latimer's personal life.

'He nearly got married a few years ago,' Polly told her, 'but she went off with another chap who had money.' She waved towards the bed in which Sarah was to sleep. 'Take that one, it's the more comfortable. I want to buy another one for myself as soon as I can.'

'How sad for John, the woman leaving him like that,' Sarah said, steering the conversation back to Latimer. 'Was he very upset?'

'I think he was a bit cut up for a while,' Polly answered as she applied face cream. 'But the family was rather pleased. None of us could stand her. She was a dreadful snob.'

They got into bed and Sarah arranged her duvet, then said, 'But he got over it?'

Polly replied through a yawn: 'I don't think it bothered him much. Actually, I think he was rather relieved in the end. He saw her recently and apparently she's got enormously fat. Goodnight.'

Polly seemed to fall asleep in an instant, but Sarah lay awake, listening to the rain. It was strange sharing a room with another woman, almost like being back at boarding school. As she went to sleep she thought of Colin, and how reassuring his concern had been about her working at the Bawdy House.

The following morning it was still raining, but there was a hint of better weather to come, Sarah thought, as she looked out of the bedroom window and noted patches of blue between the stormclouds. Latimer had already gone to his office but he had left a note with the number for her to call and arrange the interview at the Corinthian Club.

As he had predicted, there was no difficulty after she had mentioned his name. She and Polly spent some time making preparations for the appointment, which was due to take place at eleven o'clock, then examined the results in a full-length mirror in the bedroom.

Bird-like, Polly cocked her head to one side and said, 'You look a bit . . .' Her voice trailed off.

'Tarty?' Sarah said, smoothing down the red dress she had brought from Hampstead. 'Surely that's how I'm supposed to look.'

'It wouldn't seem the same on me,' Polly added. 'Being tight makes a difference.'

'Where did you get these high-heels?' Polly asked.

'Camden Town market,' Sarah said, telling a white lie. In fact they were a pair she had impounded from her daughter – along with the red dress. 'I don't know why I bought them, I just wobble about when I put them on.' She stood back and gave another critical stare.

'Well I think you look spendid,' Polly said after a moment. 'Do you want me to drive you there?'

'I'd better take a taxi.'

Polly nodded. 'Yes, there is something glamorous about arriving anywhere in a cab – a black taxi, that is. Minicabs don't seem to have quite the same style.'

· 5 ·

Sarah walked, rather uncomfortably, on Emily's high heels towards the Strand and stopped to make a quick call to George Conway from a telephone box outside the Law Courts.

'I may not get a chance to ring you this evening,' she explained, then she told him a little of the recent developments. He sounded pleased, but distracted.

When she had rung off, George gathered a notebook and the day's news schedule from his desk and walked with the other department heads towards the editor's office.

The door was open and they filed into Brian Meadows's room to take their customary seats. Conway noticed that Fanny Hunter, the *Gazette*'s best-known columnist was already there, in the chair closest to the editor's desk, a position usually occupied by the deputy editor. A faint sensation of unease came to him. George possessed acute antennae for detecting shifts of power in the complicated relationships of a newspaper office. Fanny Hunter's presence heralded trouble.

Gordon Brooks, the deputy editor, entered the room and hesitated when he saw Fanny in his seat. She noticed him hovering and smiled, but made no effort to give up her place.

Gordon sat down on the sofa next to George and muttered, 'I had hoped we'd seen the last of Fanny.'

George replied in the same undertone. 'Restorations aren't all rosy. The bad often comes back with the good.'

'The same thing happens when you throw up,' Gordon said

bitterly. Fanny was not liked in the office; even the previous editor had attempted to force her resignation; but since Brian Meadows had returned, it seemed to be a case of: my enemy's enemy is my enemy.

Meadows, seeing that all the executives were present, nodded for George to read through the news schedule. After him came pictures, foreign desk, politics, features and finally sport. Each executive read from a prepared list, interrupted occasionally by Meadows when he wanted clarification on a point, or to make a personal comment on how a piece should be approached.

The ritual finished, Meadows thanked them all and told the leader writer that he would discuss the editorial column later in the day. They rose to leave but Meadows held up his hand. 'George, I want you and Fanny to stay – and you, Gordon.'

The others left the room exchanging glances of interest. When the door closed, Meadows buzzed his secretary. 'Tell the chairman's office conference is over,' he instructed. He looked about him at the expectant faces.

'I know you've all met Charles Miller, but that was socially. He's coming down to talk about work this morning.'

'Oh God,' Gordon Brooks muttered in the same soft voice. 'He's going to be a hands-on proprietor.'

'That's right, Gordon,' Meadows said.

Fanny Hunter shifted in her chair and crossed her legs in a manner copied from Sharon Stone in *Basic Instinct*. 'What would you prefer, Gordon,' she said. 'To be pissed on from a great height, or face to face?'

Gordon looked at her with unconcealed distaste: despite her obvious attractions there was a deep streak of vulgarity in Fanny which some men found erotic – and others repellent.

'Personally, Fanny, I don't like being pissed on from any angle – but I'm unaware of your sexual peccadilloes.'

A brief knock on the door prevented Fanny's reply. Charles Miller entered the room, accompanied by a younger man.

George was struck by their similar appearance. Both were of average height, thickset and with athletic frames. Both were in shirt-sleeves, and had expensive silk ties. The young man carried some large sheets of card but they could not see what legends they conveyed.

'This is Roger Mantle, our new marketing director,' Miller said briskly. He made the introductions and then gestured for Mantle to take a seat while he remained standing.

'Let's get down to business,' he began. 'The *Gazette* is in trouble.'

'Thank God he didn't say deep shit,' Gordon whispered to Conway.

Miller took one of the sheets of board which had been placed on Meadows's desk and held it up. The figure 1,513,000 was printed on it in large letters.

'That's the current circulation,' he said flatly. He held up another board: it showed a thick declining line on a graph.

'This is the trend of our sales over the last nine months.' Miller pointed to a point further along the graph. 'If this trend continues at the present rate, the circulation in the next year will fall well below one and a half million. And if that happens –' he paused and glanced towards Gordon – 'we *will* be in deep shit. We'll have to lower our advertising rates – and less in the honeypot means less to go round. We're a publicly quoted company; and shareholders expect us to perform – or suffer the consequences. I didn't take over this newspaper to get myself a peerage. I did it because, potentially, we can make a fortune. But it's a "winner takes all" sport; losers have to get out of the game. Do I make myself clear?'

'Loud and clear,' Fanny said enthusiastically.

Miller walked over and stood beside Meadows. 'Now I don't claim to know anything about editorial matters, but I do know about selling,' he said, then gestured towards Mantle who wore a grim expression. 'And so does Roger here. The opposition are expecting us to take our time. They think it will be months before we can formulate a plan of attack, so they're unprepared. In fact Brian and I have spent the last months of his exile planning for this day.'

He looked towards Meadows with a smile. 'I want to say now I have every confidence in him – after all, we're practically related.'

There was a ripple of knowing laughter at the last remark. They all knew that Brian Meadows was going to marry Miller's estranged wife once their divorce was final. 'Roger, tell them what we're going to do,' Miller ordered.

Mantle stood up and seemed to lean forward towards the audience, like a boxer going on the attack. When he spoke it was with a broad cockney accent.

'There's no use poncing about,' he said flatly. 'You know this and I know this. Three things sell newspapers – the right product, at the right price, with the right advertising.' He paused and reached for a board which he held up. The legend £20,000,000 was printed on it. 'That's the amount we're putting into the pot,' he said. 'As from next Monday, we're cutting the price of the *Gazette* by 10p for a year. That's about seven and a half million quid straight down the Swanee.'

When he paused all they could hear in the room was the sound of distant traffic in the Gray's Inn Road. Mantle saw he had their attention. He clicked his fingers and spoke again. 'You journos get another million to spend on editorial.'

Meadows interrupted. 'That's just if there's any big properties worth buying,' he said quickly. 'I've agreed with Charles not to hire any more staff.'

'What about foreign?' Gordon Brooks asked. It was one of his particular complaints that the *Gazette* had closed all its offices abroad under the old regime.

Charles Miller held up a hand. 'I'll answer, Brian, if you don't mind?'

Meadows nodded his assent.

Miller looked directly at Brooks. 'It was costing the *Gazette* more than a million pounds a year to run the New York office alone before it was closed down in 1986. Paris and Rome were nearly as much. If we get the circulation up and the profits follow, I'll be the first one to encourage expansion. But until that day we stay lean.'

'Thank God for CNN news,' Brooks said softly.

'Right,' Miller said, and he turned back to Mantle, who began again. 'The rest of the 20 million goes on television advertising. That takes care of the right price and the right advertising.'

Miller interjected again. 'And the right product is up to you people. Brian,' he continued, 'would you like to explain what's wanted from your side?'

Meadows nodded. 'Our Treasure Island promotion goes on, but we're upping the first prize by 10,000 a week. I'm shifting Fanny to be overall in charge of features again. She will have assistant editor rank, alongside George. Now, as Roger has told you, we're going on television all next week with sixty-second spots – so I want something red hot to put into those adverts. Fanny, I want you to come up with a features series that's a real grabber.' He turned to Conway. 'George, we need a big news story – something that will run all week and knock them out of their socks. I know you can do it – all of you. So go to it, and good hunting.'

A beam of sunlight had streamed through the window as Brian Meadows spoke, but it brought no comfort to George Conway.

The same sunshine pierced the clouds and bathed Saint Clement Danes in golden light when Sarah came out of the telephone booth beside the Law Courts. She took it as a good omen. The stormy weather had passed at last, but it was colder than she had anticipated. She didn't have a suitable coat to go with Emily's red dress so by the time she arrived at Jermyn Street her body was so chilled it caused her nipples to show through the thin material with a boldness she found slightly disconcerting.

I look as if I've got acorns stuffed down there, she thought; but she got a wolf whistle from a window-cleaner when she turned from paying the taxi. Smiling her appreciation, she entered the pillared doorway of the Corinthian Club and found herself in a gloomy hallway that was more like the lobby of a grand country house than an hotel.

Suits of armour flanked a staircase, a grandfather clock ticked in a stately fashion and a variety of stags' and foxes' heads glared sightlessly from the walls.

Sarah stood in the centre of the black and white chequered floor and looked around her. An emaciated figure with a face shaped like a weasel's emerged from the depths of a porter's chair and shuffled towards her. Sarah studied the top hat, bottle-green coat, tight fawn trousers and riding boots he wore, while he eyed her up and down in turn.

'I'm Wedge. Come to see Mr and Mrs Purse, have you?' he said, his tone an equal mixture of familiarity and contempt.

'How did you know, Mr Wedge?' she replied.

'Just Wedge,' he said in a dusty voice. 'The Thin End, the members always say. I could tell right away you weren't a new member.'

'How perceptive of you,' Sarah answered. 'And how do I find Mr and Mrs Purse?'

'I announces you, that's how – follow me,' he commanded and led her along a short corridor under the curving staircase to a door marked PRIVATE. Here he knocked and waited for a summons, which came after a few moments.

'Woman to see you by the name of . . .' he turned. 'What's your name, girl?'

'Keane,' she replied, holding on to her temper. 'Sarah Keane.'

'She *says* Sarah Keane,' he repeated, his voice edged with disbelief.

'Show her in,' said a rather harsh voice and Wedge stepped aside.

Mr and Mrs Purse were sitting side by side on an ornate little Regency sofa when she entered. They had very pink complexions and their bloated little figures were garbed extravagantly. Mrs Purse wore an Empire dress in lavender silk that revealed a great deal of her ample bosom while her husband favoured a blue chalk-striped suit with a handkerchief that matched his wife's dress. Sarah was reminded of two piglets in an illustration for a nursery story. She saw that both were drinking champagne and eating from a tray of hand-made chocolates. The room, which was crowded with fake Georgian furniture, smelt as perfumed as a hothouse filled with orchids.

'Have a glass of bubbly, dear,' the harsh voice said; Sarah was surprised to see that it came from Mrs Purse. Mr Purse reached out to the ice-bucket, looked up at Wedge with glittering little eyes and then spoke in a higher voice. 'Don't just stand there like a spare part. Go and get a glass for the lady – then wait outside.'

Wedge shuffled over to a sideboard and returned with a champagne flute. Mr Purse filled her glass and gestured for Sarah to sit in a chair opposite them. 'Nice figure, Mrs Purse,' he began enthusiastically and Sarah felt his eyes roaming over her body.

'Nice legs, too,' she added. 'Have you done this sort of work before, dear?'

'Mostly abroad,' Sarah replied evasively, not quite sure what kind of work the woman was referring to. She took a sip from her glass and noticed that the champagne was very sweet.

'You did get a call from Mr Latimer, I take it?' she asked.

Mr Purse nodded. 'He was in a bit of a rush though, so he didn't have time to tell us much about you,' he explained.

Sarah took a deep breath before she answered. 'Did he tell you about the book I'm writing?'

Mr Purse looked at his wife. 'He did say something about a book – but no real details.'

'It's a work of fiction,' Sarah said quickly. 'No real names and the location will be heavily disguised. Mr Latimer said he would fix it so that I would be able to gather background material here.'

'Yes,' Mr Purse said. 'He did mention that. But you'll be prepared to pull your weight while you're here?' he asked.

'Of course.'

Mr Purse looked thoughtful. 'You do realise, my dear, some of the girls have – what shall we say? – a *special* relationship with the customers?'

'Oh yes,' Sarah answered. 'That's just the sort of material I'm looking for.'

'So you won't be shocked if some of the goings on seem a bit . . . well, frisky?'

Sarah shook her head firmly. 'Believe me, I'm very broad-minded.'

'Broad-minded, eh,' Mr Purse repeated. 'I like that, Mrs Purse.' He turned to Sarah again. 'So you're ready to go to work.'

Sarah looked into her glass. 'As a waitress, certainly.'

'And this book, would we be in it?' Mrs Purse asked. Sarah smiled with relief. She knew she had their interest: vanity was a curious business. Most people seemed happy to be included in a book, but were hesitant if there was a possibility that they might appear in a newspaper.

'I'm always looking for good strong characters,' Sarah continued. 'Of course I wouldn't want any of the members to know I was writing a novel. Some people find it hard to be their natural selves when they know they're being watched, but I can tell you two wouldn't be bothered by that.'

'Grand,' Mr Purse said, rubbing his hands again. 'We'll tell the members you're shy, make them think you're a nice ordinary sort of girl. We can bill you as the shy one for the time you're here.'

'But you'll have to wear the costume,' Mrs Purse said.

'Costume?' Sarah asked.

Mr Purse took another chocolate and talked on: 'It's the club gimmick, dear. You know like the Playboy has its bunny girls. Our members tend to be a little old-fashioned in their preferences. Nothing wrong with that. We're here to give them what they want.'

'It's more comfortable than a bunny outfit,' Mrs Purse added quickly.

'What does it consist of?'

'Milkmaid stuff, you know: like Bo-Peep.'

'And a wig. Our wenches must look the part.' Mr Purse insisted. 'Unless you want to play the part of a serving boy and wear footman's clothes?'

'I think I'll wear a wig, thanks,' Sarah said quickly.

'Probably just as well,' Mr Purse said. 'Some of the members wouldn't leave you alone if you was dressed as a boy. Still, each to his own, as Mrs Purse and I always say. Now, the pay's a hundred a week, but that's just for the taxman. Our customers are big tippers, particularly at the gaming tables, we don't call it a casino here. Of course, if you were turning tricks, the sky's the limit, but me and Mrs Purse take 33 per cent of everything you get.'

'That seems fair,' Sarah said.

'What a nice sensible, mature girl,' Mr Purse said, beaming. 'I knew it the moment I clapped eyes on her.' He poured more champagne and called for Wedge in a loud voice. The top-hatted figure reappeared in the doorway and Mr Purse said, 'Get Mollie down here.'

'More champagne?' he asked Sarah.

She shook her head with a smile. 'I mustn't drink if I'm going to work. I haven't got a very strong head.'

'Quite right, dear,' Mrs Purse said approvingly. After a few minutes, a tall, attractive woman came into the room. Sarah guessed she was about the same age as herself. She was dressed as an eighteenth-century milkmaid, with a mob cap on her mass of flame-red hair and most of her snowy breasts bulging from a low-cut blouse and laced waistcoat. She eyed Sarah professionally and said, 'Pity we've got to cover those legs with a long dress.'

'Good figure, though,' Mrs Purse added. The woman agreed. 'When can you start?' she asked.

Sarah looked towards the couple on the sofa. 'As soon as you like.'

'She's only hired as a waitress, Mollie,' Mrs Purse told her. 'No extras. Let her work with you for a few days.'

Mollie looked at Sarah shrewdly for a moment, then smiled. 'Come on, love, I'll show you the ropes.' And she led Sarah from the Purses' private quarters.

From the features of the building, it was clear to Sarah that the Corinthian Club had once been a private town house. 'The Purses live on the premises,' Mollie said. 'But you never see her about the club, just Purse.'

'It all looks very grand,' Sarah said.

'There's even a Turkish bath in the basement,' Mollie added as they walked up the wide curving staircase. 'The kitchens are on the ground floor, the restaurant and gaming room on the first, next to the bar and library. The top two floors are all bedrooms and suites. We live in the attic.'

It sounds a bit like Hostler's Academy, Sarah thought as she looked about her. 'How many guests are there usually?' she asked.

'There's only twenty rooms,' Mollie replied. 'But a lot of members come in during the day. The action starts at lunchtime. They're usually sleeping off the night before until then, so if you've got anything personal to do, save it for the mornings. We work a six-day week, with a rotating day off, but you can usually swap with one of the other girls if you want a particular day free; just make sure you fill in the score sheet.'

'How do Mr and Mrs Purse calculate their percentage?' Sarah asked.

'Club money,' Mollie replied. 'When the members come in they cash cheques with Mr Purse for a bag of guineas. It's not real, just imitation, but it looks like gold. Any tips or payments we get are paid in the stuff, so the Purses make their deduction when we cash in what we've taken.'

'That's smart.'

Mollie laughed. 'Don't let their looks fool you. They're both as sharp as broken glass. They thought of the idea for the whole place. It's turned out to be a gold mine for them.'

'What are the members like?'

'I don't know what they're like in real life – but in here you've got to remember they're living out a fantasy of how they would like women to behave. So remember to take out your brain when you put on your costume. They just want chattels here.'

Something Pat Lomax had said came back to Sarah. 'Dogsbodies,' she said softly. Mollie caught the word. 'You've got it,' she said cheerfully.

At the top of the house Mollie walked her along a narrow corridor lined with doors, until they reached a largish room filled with cigarette smoke and women in various states of undress. The room was furnished with black imitation leather armchairs and two cheap whitewood writing tables against the windows were scattered with dogeared magazines and paperbacks. A large television set was switched on to a morning chat show; no one was watching. Nothing about the scene would stir the erotic imagination. Most of the women wore comfortable dressing gowns; some of their faces were still puffy with sleep and shining with face cream.

'Morning ladies,' Mollie called out briskly. 'This is a new recruit. What's your name, my love?'

'Sarah,' she replied. The girls nodded or smiled at the introduction.

'Get a move on,' Mollie said to the room. 'First shift is due on duty in forty minutes.'

She led Sarah into a further room that was filled with costumes hanging on coat rails. 'Wigs in the boxes over there,' she said. Looking down at Sarah's high heels she said: 'I should wear some comfortable shoes if I were you. The dresses come down to the floor so the punters won't notice. They're mostly retarded schoolboys anyway, so most of them are only interested in your tits. Get yourself changed and come downstairs to the bar and I'll tell you what to do.'

'Do we have to live on the premises?' Sarah asked.

'Not if you don't want to, but it suits most of the girls. The hours are long and the streets are pretty rough at night these days. Some of them go off partying after hours but I'm usually ready for bed. I gave up doing turns a long time ago.'

'So you don't have to turn tricks if you don't want to?'

Mollie smiled, 'I'll let you into a little secret, love: most of the hellrakes downstairs can't get it up anyway, they're either too old or too pissed. Half the time the girls go to bed with them and then say "you were wonderful" in the morning, and the punters think they're bloody Casanovas. They like to feel you up now and then, but that's just part of the job. There *are* one or two rams about the place, but you'll soon learn to spot them.'

Mollie departed and Sarah set about selecting a costume. Half an hour later she descended the staircase, wearing milkmaid clothes and an extravagant blonde wig. She found Mollie at the bar.

'Oh, very good,' Mollie said with approval. 'No make-up is a nice touch, you look fresh as a new-laid egg.'

'It feels as though I'm still carrying the chicken on my head,' Sarah replied and she gave the wig another tug.

'You'll soon get used to it,' Mollie answered. 'I feel naked without mine these days.' She looked sharply at another girl who had just entered the bar. 'Jean,' she called out. 'How many times do I have to tell you? No smoking in the club rooms. They didn't make Silk Cut in Regency days.'

'Sorry, Mollie,' the girl replied.

'Next time you get fined.' She turned back to Sarah. 'I'm going to start you on serving drinks,' she said and she pointed to the bar. 'I work here and you go to the tables. There's no tick, so the punters pay for everything in club money, and we limit the range we serve. Nothing fancy. If they want to pretend it's 1805, they can put up with the same drink they served then. Champagne is only sold by the bottle and it's twenty-five guineas a throw. The same with burgundy or claret but the price is fifteen guineas a bottle. They can have a pint of porter at five guineas a tankard and a club brandy is seven guineas a glass. Got that?'

'I think so.'

'Remember to keep chiding them about how much they drink, it makes them feel wicked.' Just as she finished speaking two middle-aged men entered the bar. They were well dressed, overweight, and laughing loudly as they approached.

'Morning, Mollie,' one of them called out. 'A large heart-starter for Mr Brian, and a bottle of bubbly for me.'

Mollie wagged her head in mock disapproval as she poured the brandy. Sarah did not wait to be asked: she found a large refrigerator behind the counter and started to open a bottle of champagne. Mollie smiled at her and looked up at the members.

'Brandy at this time of the morning, Mr Geoffrey? I don't

know what the world's coming to, truly I don't. You mark my words, there'll be tears before bedtime.'

'Then I shall kiss them away, my dear,' he replied with heavy gallantry.

Mollie whooped with laughter. 'Your tears, Mr Geoffrey, not mine.'

Sarah was amused to hear that Mollie had assumed a country accent for her banter. She placed the bottle of champagne on the counter and the man said, 'In my silver tankard, if you will, my dear: the one hanging third from the end.'

Sarah poured the champagne to the brim and served it with a smile.

'Hello,' he said. 'You're new, aren't you?'

Sarah bobbed a small curtsy. 'If you please, sir,' she replied shyly.

'Well, we do *squeeze*, don't we, Brian?' he said to his companion.

'Now, gentlemen, none of your roguish chatter,' Mollie said severely. 'This is my cousin, just up from the country, she's not used to your London ways.'

Mr Brian looked at her dreamily. 'Do you know, Mollie, you often remind me of my nanny. Have I ever told you that?'

'Often, Mr Brian, usually late at night when you want me to tuck you up.'

'*Fuck* you up, Mollie?' the man said with a wink to his companion, and he slid a pile of gold-coloured coins across the counter. 'Surely not?'

Mollie whooped with laughter again as she scooped them up. Sarah noted that she worked hard for her guineas.

'Heavy duty last night, Mollie?' Mr Geoffrey asked.

'Always heavy when Sir Silas and his lads are here, sir,' she replied. 'That man breeds mischief, like a gamekeeper does pheasants. The girls are worn down like butchers' knives. And did you hear about Lord Bletchley?'

The men shook their heads.

Mollie leaned across the bar. 'He lost 30,000 at the tables on one hand of bezique against Sir Silas. And he's not well – his doctor told him he mustn't have any excitement.'

Sarah's admiration for Mollie grew. Her earlier remark about taking out her brain was not really correct: the role was as demanding as that of any actress in a West End play. She had clearly missed her real vocation in life: every sentence she uttered would have been prized by a romantic novelist.

More members began to trickle into the bar until just after one o'clock, when there was a sudden rush of arrivals and the room was filled. Sarah and the three other girls on duty were now moving behind the bar and about the room without pause; but despite the crowd, the noise wasn't loud and the feeling of the room not that different to a popular public house at any lunchtime.

Then, quite suddenly, the atmosphere changed. Sarah saw the crowd part as a group of men entered the room and made their way to the bar. The leader was a gaunt, white-haired figure, and beside him walked a young man of such remarkably similar appearance that they almost seemed an old and young version of the same person, brought together by some accident of time.

The pair sauntered through the crowd, like royalty passing among a mob of commoners. Both held themselves erect, heads and shoulders well back, and in time-honoured fashion gazed down their noses, as if at their inferiors. They were dressed as dandies, their clothes cut and flared to emphasise their slim figures. They should have appeared ridiculous; but there was such an air of certainty in their self-confidence that no one in the room dared challenge their disdainful gaze.

Three others followed: a giant bruiser, a shifty, bow-legged little man and a tall heavily set figure. They obviously played a more subservient role.

When they reached the bar, the old man stood for a moment, swept his gaze about the room to take in all the assembled members, then banged down a bulging leather purse on the mahogany counter. 'No man pays for drinks until my winnings from Bletchley are spent,' he shouted, and the other members at the bar let out a roar of approval.

Now Sarah observed how the mood of the Corinthians changed. It was as if some collective will had taken control of the men in the bar and determined that they should compete in rowdiness as champagne and brandy began to flow in even greater quantities.

'Oh Christ,' Mollie muttered to Sarah as they hurried to serve the demanding crowd. 'Watch out if they start throwing glasses. Old Sir Silas is bad enough, but that Toby Nightingale is certifiable.'

Sarah turned to follow Mollie's gaze as the old man called out. 'Hold me up, Trooper,' to the bruiser beside him. The bodyguard encircled the old man's waist with two massive hands and lifted him effortlessly above the heads of the crowd. Then Sir Silas shouted: 'Corinthians! A thousand guineas to any man who can beat my nephew Toby at storking!'

A hush of anticipation fell on the bar as the yellow-haired youth jumped on to the counter and was handed a full bottle of champagne by the bow-legged little man. Standing on one leg, he raised it to his lips and the crowd began to count. When they reached twenty-seven he threw the empty bottle aside.

'Three seconds outside the club record!' Sir Silas shouted. 'I'll pay to see if any man here can match that.'

Several tried – and failed. Some, after their efforts, slumped at tables unable even to raise their heads. To Sarah it was an extraordinary sight. She had seen heavy drinking before, and had always thought that reporters in the right mood could hold their own against most revellers, but this was a new dimension.

The bar was awash with spilt champagne and reeling figures; rolling bottles littered the floor.

Finally, Mr Purse appeared at the doorway beating a gong. When the noise had subsided he squeaked: 'Lamb chops, roast beef, venison pie and baked ham are now being served for luncheon, gentlemen. Take your places, and a good appetite to you all.'

The room emptied of those that could still walk, leaving the rest to be tended by Wedge and the bar staff. Sarah joined in as they slowly helped those who were unable to walk unaided to the rooms above. When they were back in the bar, Sarah looked at Mollie across the debris of empty bottles, broken glasses and smouldering ashtrays.

'You did well,' Mollie said; and Sarah felt a strange pleasure in her praise, like a raw recruit glad to receive an accolade from a veteran soldier after his first battle. 'Let's see how much we made before we clean up,' Mollie added in a businesslike voice. She counted the heavy little discs of imitation gold in what to Sarah seemed an astonishingly short space of time. Finally she slid half of the stacks across the bar. 'Your cut's £327 in real money,' she said.

Sarah was astounded. 'That much?'

'It won't always be like that,' Mollie said. 'The Nightingales get them all going. When they're not in town usually it averages about fifty quid at lunchtime.'

'What happens in the afternoons?' Sarah asked.

Mollie scooped the neat piles of club money into the pocket of her little apron before she answered. 'Usually most of them sleep it off; but there's always the odd few who go on boozing, so one girl stays on to take care of the stragglers. Mind you, it's different now the Nightingales are here. I'll be staying on this afternoon, and I'd like you to as well. The other girls can get a few hours to themselves. The evening rush starts again about six o'clock, and then goes on till God knows when.'

Sarah watched her walk from the room with the loaded tray and then set about clearing the devastated bar. Shouting voices and roars of muffled laughter came from the dining room.

· 6 ·

Mollie was correct in her assumption: after lunch a small crowd did follow the Nightingale entourage back to the bar, and they called for more champagne. Sarah recognised a few of the men: there was an actor whom she had seen in television commercials, a well-known sports commentator, and a politician who had once been in the cabinet before he had been hustled out of office over some indiscretion involving an exotic dancer.

'Ah, the new girl from the country,' Sir Silas called out as Sarah approached his table with the first order of champagne. When she had placed the bottles before them, he pulled her down on to his lap and said in a stage whisper, 'Purse tells me you don't roll in the hay.'

Remembering Mollie's earlier instructions, Sarah made an effort to enter into her role. 'That's right, sir. I'm a good girl,' she simpered as she squeezed her elbows to her sides to stop the old man's exploring hands reaching her breasts. Nightingale gave a giggling wheeze and jiggled his knees so that she bounced up and down. Despite his age, there was still strength in the man.

'So who would you like to be the first through the gate?' he asked. 'How about Natty Scroat?' he asked. The pinch-faced little man lounging opposite smiled and brought his hand up to cover the yellowing stumps of teeth as he chuckled at the suggestion. 'Or Trooper Stone?' Nightingale continued, swinging her round to face the huge figure. The man returned her gaze impassively; there was no detectable expression on the brute-like features. It was like exchanging glances with a beast of burden. 'How about Doctor Pendlebury?' he continued. 'Mind you, he don't count. You wouldn't have to open your legs for what he likes to do with women.' Nightingale leaned forward and punched the doctor on the arm. 'Eh, Pendlebury,' he leered. 'We could probably train a monkey to satisfy your wants.'

Pendlebury smiled, or at least his moist lips twitched for a moment. There was no movement in the other muscles of his face. Nightingale hadn't finished. He now turned Sarah towards his nephew, who seemed completely uninterested in the events around him.

Sarah glanced at the pale, narrow face, which was now scowling with an expression of anger as he examined a beautiful gold pocket watch attached to the chain on his waistcoat. 'How about young Toby here?' the old man whispered loudly. 'He's got a cock on him that would touch the bottom of a wishing well. He gets that from my side of the family.'

Sarah had to exercise a great deal of self-control in order not to make some demonstration of her true feelings. Before she could answer the old man, Toby Nightingale laid the watch on the table, slowly picked up one of the empty champagne bottles and began to beat the watch to pieces. The gold case flattened and delicate little cogs and wheels spilt across the table.

'Why did you do that, Toby?' Sir Silas asked with interest.

'It stopped,' he answered in a petulant voice. 'I noticed this morning. Damn thing's worn out.'

'Why didn't you wind it?' the politician asked from his seat on the fringe of the crowd.

'Wind it?' Toby repeated, puzzled. 'How do you do that?'

'I've always done that for him,' Scroat interjected. 'I forgot this morning.'

There was silence as the assembled crowd contemplated the curious quality of Toby Nightingale's ignorance, then an explosion of wheezing laughter from Sir Silas. 'How do you do that,' he repeated. 'My God, didn't I bring him up to be a gentleman?' He leaned forward and slapped the young man's arm. 'Quite right, my boy. Who needs a watch anyway – only tradesmen.'

He looked about him. 'I want everybody who considers himself a friend of mine to follow Toby's example,' he ordered.

To Sarah's astonishment, the men began to take off their watches and place them on the table, with the exception of the politician, who, she noticed, slipped a Rolex from his wrist and into his jacket pocket.

'In the middle,' Sir Silas demanded.

A pile was made and the old man nodded to his bodyguard. Trooper Stone picked up an empty champagne bottle and was about to bring it down on the timepieces when Sarah felt one of Sir Silas's hands scrabbling at her leg. Frustrated in his attempts to grope her breasts, he was attempting to reach beneath her dress. She slipped forward on the old man's lap, so that her feet touched the floor again; and when Sir Silas's hand reached the inside of her thigh, she gave a loud giggling shout of 'Mercy, Sir Silas, you undo me', and leaped to her feet. At the same time she thrust back an elbow with all the force she could muster and felt the satisfaction of hearing it come into contact with the point of his nose.

Sir Silas roared with pain and clapped his hands to the tender spot as blood flowed between his fingers. Mollie, who had been watching, hurried to the table with a towel. The old man took it from her and then, seeing her snowy breasts close to his face, reached out and smeared a bloody hand between them.

At the sight of the gore on Mollie, Toby Nightingale's clouded mind started on another train of thought. He began to shout: 'Scarlet showing – Corinthian fox-hunt! Corinthian fox-hunt!'

It seemed to be the signal for some kind of ritual to begin. The men around the table rose to their feet and Sarah nervously stood back against a wall, next to Mollie, who was wiping her breast clean with the towel.

'What's happening now?' Sarah whispered as the men formed a circle.

Mollie tossed the towel on to the table. 'They always do this when the blood of a member is spilt,' she said wearily. 'Just stand back and keep out of the way.'

'I'm the fox,' Toby Nightingale shouted, but before he could move the door of the bar opened and Mr Purse stood in the doorway.

'Gentlemen,' he appealed, 'I must ask you to limit the hunt to the bar and the dining room. Lord Bletchley has suffered a stroke and the doctor is with him even now.'

'Bar and dining room it is, Purse,' Sir Silas replied. Then he shouted: 'Set the fox running.'

Immediately, Toby Nightingale dived over a table and, whooping gleefully, the other members followed one by one. He crawled rapidly on his stomach across the floor to the bar. Hauling himself up, he ran along the counter-top before leaping to a wide windowsill that overlooked Jermyn Street, the other members in pursuit. Sarah noticed that Nightingale's entourage took no part.

She was used to the bad behaviour of small boys and knew that their games frequently ended in tears. There was a recklessness in the male that, encouraged by the pack, could quickly spiral out of control and lead to disaster. She had never felt this need in herself to follow blindly in the pursuit of danger, nor seen it in her daughter; but her sons were capable of similar folly. That's what they are, she told herself. Naughty boys, with no one to smack them or curb their excesses. As she continued to watch the game Toby Nightingale swung on a curtain and just made it to the seat of a sofa against the wall. The rest of the crowd did their best to imitate his every action, as he led the procession across obstacles about the rooms.

'How long does this go on?' Sarah asked.

'Until another member's blood is spilt,' Mollie replied in a jaded voice.

'What if it's one of us?'

She shook her head: 'We don't count.'

Toby was on the bar again. This time he made an even greater leap for the splendid chandelier that hung from the centre of the ceiling. Catching the edge, his hanging body made a graceful arch. Just then another serving girl entered the bar, unaware of the game in progress, and Nightingale's swinging body collided with her. She was knocked to the ground and the chandelier tore loose, crashing down on both of them in a cascade of glittering crystal. Sarah thought they might be injured, but after a moment the girl struggled free and said, 'Are you all right, sir?' to the youth, who lay momentarily dazed.

Shaking his head, Toby rose slowly to his feet and Sarah could now see that he appeared to be in a state of shock. His entire body trembled and his arms made jerking convulsive movements, as if beating off invisible tormentors. Then, to Sarah's horror, he began to make a sound that chilled her body and stilled the babble of voices in the room. It was a rising howl that was more like the baying of an animal than a human being.

The girl stood next to him, eyes now filled with fear as he reached out and long fingers curled around her throat to pull her closer. His other hand drew back as if he were about to punch her in the face. A harsh voice rang out in the silence: 'Toby – enough,' it commanded. Then Sir Silas hurried forward and the youth released the girl.

'Only a game,' the old man said quickly, and he thrust a handful of the coins into the girl's hands. 'Hunt over,' he called out and slapped Toby on the shoulder. The youth now leaned against Trooper Stone panting like a dog. Sarah exchanged glances with Mollie, who shrugged dismissively.

A murmur of conversation started among the members who

had witnessed the scene; then Purse entered the room once again. He gazed about him at the wreckage without emotion and said, 'The bar is temporarily closed for repairs, gentlemen.' Gazing with an unperturbed smile at the chaos, he announced. 'Drinks will be served in the dining room for the next few hours.'

'I think I'll take a nap now,' said Sir Silas, like a suddenly weary child. 'You too, Toby.' He pointed towards Sarah. 'Bring me a pot of coffee and a bottle of brandy at six o'clock.'

When Nightingale and his men left the room, the other members drifted away, and soon the dining room was empty. Sarah and Mollie sat down at one of the tables that was now set for dinner, then Mollie looked at the front of her blouse: 'Damn,' she said, 'I'd better change, I've still got some of Nightingale's blood on me. See you in a little while.'

Sarah sat alone for a time, thinking about the extraordinary events of the afternoon and how she would write her story. It would make good copy. Then she saw Wedge shuffling towards her. 'There's someone to see you,' he said. 'Waiting in the hallway.'

'Who is it?' Sarah asked.

Wedge thought for a moment. 'Can't remember,' he answered eventually. 'But I can tell he's a gent.'

Sarah followed him downstairs and found Colin Greaves standing before the grandfather clock.

'I thought you might like to come out for some tea,' he said, eyeing her wig with a flicker of amusement.

'I can't really go out dressed like this,' Sarah said, sweeping a hand over her milkmaid's costume.

'I suppose not,' he replied, then turned to Wedge, who was watching from the depths of the porter's chair. 'Is there anywhere we can be private for a few minutes?' he asked. Wedge shook his head. 'Not if you ain't a member, sir,' he replied.

Greaves took a £20 note from his pocket and held it out. 'Why

77

don't you go into the dining room,' Wedge suggested. 'The girl will show you the way.'

Sarah led him up the staircase and past the wreckage in the bar. 'You missed the lunchtime fun,' she said lightly.

Greaves did not reply until he was seated at one of the tables in the deserted dining room: 'I came to give you some information about this man Nightingale you're supposed to be watching.'

'Go on,' she answered; but before he could speak again, a workman in blue overalls entered, whistling.

'Sorry, guv,' he said when he saw them. 'I thought we had the place to ourselves. I'm just replacing the chandelier. Hope we won't be disturbing you.'

'No, carry on,' Greaves replied.

'We're going to have to turn the lights off,' the workman said.

'We can manage in the dark,' Sarah answered.

'I bet you can,' she heard the man mutter, deliberately clear enough for her to hear. Then he called out in a louder voice: 'I'll shut the doors, guv, so as our noise won't disturb you.'

And as he spoke, the room was plunged into total darkness. There was sudden intimacy about sitting together now. Colin's voice was softer when he spoke.

'How are you coping?' he asked.

'Fine,' Sarah answered. 'But I wouldn't want to do it for a living, despite the money.'

'The money's good?'

'I made three hundred pounds at lunchtime.'

'Good God, what did you have to do for it?'

'Serve champagne to a lot of retarded schoolboys.'

'I think even I could manage that.'

'No you couldn't,' Sarah answered after a pause. 'They wouldn't have the same sort of fun if you were doing it.'

'I don't understand.'

Sarah continued. 'A lot of their enjoyment comes from

treating the women as lackeys. I never realised that could be a pleasure in itself before. This has been an eye-opener.' She paused. 'I've worked for people who have no manners, or any consideration that you might be a human being with feelings and sensibilities.' She hesitated again and then continued. 'But I've never actually been treated as a sex object before. It's almost interesting – in a horrible sort of way.'

'What about the boys at Hostler's Academy?'

'That was different,' she answered, 'although I suppose their attitude was about the same – I'm sure they'll all end up as members here one day – but I could fight back against silly boys. These people know you want the job and are prepared to be humiliated to keep it. The money is generous, but you pay a high price to get it.'

'Why don't you leave?' he said. 'Just walk out of the place with me now.'

Sarah reached out and found his hand. It was hard and dry but she could feel the warmth when he held hers. 'Thank you, but I can manage, I just keep telling myself it isn't real life.'

'As you wish,' he said after a pause, then his voice became brisker. 'Actually you won't be here for long; I've been finding out a few things about this man Nightingale. He'll be going back to his estates quite soon.'

'What else do you know?'

'Apparently the family is mad.'

Sarah laughed. 'I've already discovered that for myself.'

'Do you know about the Gaudy revels?'

'Go on.'

'Nightingale has a vast estate in Oxfordshire,' Greaves began. 'It's called Gaudy. It was actually named by the Prince Regent, after an exhausting weekend he spent there with one of Nightingale's ancestors. The land runs along the edge of the Thames. Apparently Nightingale is very rich, mining in Australia, farms in Africa and South America and investments going back for ever. Their affairs have always been managed by the Latimer family; they've been solicitors to the family for generations.'

'What are the Gaudy revels?' Sarah asked.

Greaves continued. 'Every year, the Nightingales celebrate the Prince Regent weekend by re-enacting exactly the same festivities. A lot of Nightingale's friends take part, fellow members here, I would imagine.'

Sarah was interested. 'What happens exactly?'

'They start the fun off with a steeplechase around the grounds on the Saturday afternoon. Then, in the evening there's a grand ball, followed by a bare-knuckle prize fight. The next day there's a shoot in the grounds. They round each day off with an orgy.'

Sarah nodded in the darkness. 'It sounds tailor made for the Corinthian Club. How did you find out all this?'

'I talked to some people I know.'

'And when does all this actually take place?'

'This coming weekend.'

Sarah sighed. It was as if a life sentence stretched before her.

'What happens to you now?' he asked as he stood up.

Sarah tugged at her wig as she answered. 'The evening rush starts at about six o'clock. I have to take a bottle of brandy to Nightingale's rooms then.'

'I'll come back later,' Greaves said. 'As my mother always used to say: try to be good.'

Sarah walked with him to the entrance hall and when she had said goodbye saw Mollie descending the staircase.

'Who was that?' she asked. 'He looked a bit of all right.'

'An old friend who dropped in,' Sarah answered. 'He's been telling me about the Gaudy revels.'

'Are you going?' Mollie asked.

'Do we get invited?' Sarah asked, as they walked back to the bar together.

'Not me,' Mollie answered. 'I'm past it, but some of the

members take our girls – if Sir Silas approves of the selection, one or two take their wives. Mind you, there's not a lot of difference, except some of the wives get a kick out of swapping partners whereas it's just another working weekend for our lot.'

The two workmen were still in the bar, packing away their tools. 'All done, George?' Mollie asked.

'Until the next call,' he answered. 'Thank God for these prats smashing the place up all the time, this is the best contract I've got on my books. I hope to hell there's never a revolution in this country.'

Mollie laughed: it was genuine this time, not the version she saved for the members. 'Then it'll be your turn to swing on the chandeliers, George,' she said.

'Not me,' he answered. 'I'm a bloody capitalist, just ask any of my men. Screw the workers, that's what I say.' He sauntered away with his companion and Mollie turned again to Sarah. 'There's a bit of time until six,' she said. 'Why don't you go and put your feet up? It's bound to be a heavy night, you'll be glad of it later. I'll give you a call.'

Sarah did feel a little weary. She thanked Mollie and went to the top of the house, where one of the girls told her she could use a room off the corridor. It was furnished like an inexpensive motel room. She was glad to escape. After removing her costume she lay down on the single bed, and after a few minutes drifted into a deep sleep.

She awoke to find Mollie shaking her gently. 'Time to get up, you're due downstairs in ten minutes. I let you sleep on because you don't have to bother with make-up.' Sarah looked around the little room for a few more seconds then slowly began to prepare for her return to the eighteenth century.

George Conway had retreated to the little office off the editorial floor which he used as a refuge from the news desk. Through the open door, he could see the momentum of the paper picking up as they approached closed copy time for the first edition. There was a certain intensity in the air and the telephones rang with greater frequency; but somehow it lacked the clamour and excitement he had known in his youth. His thoughts went back to the days before the new technology had transformed everything so completely. The newsroom had been another place then: scruffier, noisier, but pulsing with vitality. There was a different feeling to the atmosphere too. In the old days it had all seemed more exuberant, but although the tension was still there it was no longer channelled into face-to-face confrontations. People simply sat in front of their screens, charged with the adrenalin pumping around their bodies.

Sometimes he was sorry that he was living at a time of such change. His grandfather had been in the army most of his life, in a cavalry regiment that had gone over to tanks in the Twenties. When he was a boy, George had listened to him talking about the days of his youth, when he had roamed across Salisbury Plain mounted as cavalrymen had been since the Middle Ages. That's how George felt now, he told himself. A fragment of the past, a hot-metal man trapped in a time of electronic news-gathering. They called it cold set now, he reminded himself. Cold set. The words themselves chilled him.

'You look disenchanted,' Gordon Brooks said as he appeared in the doorway.

'Not me, Gordon,' he replied. 'I'm full of beans and ready to go over the top.'

From his vantage point at the doorway, Brooks could see Fanny Hunter standing at the door of her own office. She was shouting at her secretary, who was starting to wilt under the verbal beating. 'Fanny seems to be having a happy time,' he said drily. 'A man would be put under arrest by the politically correct police if he behaved like she does.'

'She must have had some good ideas,' he said gloomily. 'How about you?'

George shrugged. 'Like Mother Hubbard, my cupboard is bare.'

'Come and have a drink,' Brooks said. 'You might as well be miserable in the pub as in here.'

George stood up and tucked his flapping shirt back into the waistband on his trousers: he had one of those heavy bodies that seemed to fight his clothes. Opposite the news desk he made a drinking gesture to the night news editor, who waved his understanding. Halfway down the newsroom they encountered Harry Porter, the *Gazette*'s chief photographer, who was clearly heading in the same direction. He fell into step with them and, like three ageing Musketeers, they made for the Red Lion.

As they entered the bar, a group of reporters who had been laughing in a carefree manner fell silent when they came under the baleful gaze of George. 'What's up with that lot? They seem chastened by something,' Brooks said as he took his drink from Harry Porter.

'They're brooding about the little talking-to I gave them this afternoon, I hope,' George answered as he splashed a small amount of soda into his whisky.

'A bit much of Brian to expect you to come up with a big news story on demand, I thought,' Brooks said sympathetically. 'He knows better than anyone that you can't manufacture news like you can features. What have you set in motion?'

George put down his drink and counted off on his fingers. 'Prior is working with Sinclair on the rumour that one of the cabinet wants to have a sex-change operation, Pauline Kaznovitch is trying to pin down the insurance scam, the others are supposed to be out in the field, looking for leads.'

He raised his voice at the end of the sentence and Brooks saw three of the crowd put down their drinks and leave the pub. Harry Porter raised his glasses to his forehead and massaged his beefy features. 'Maybe Sarah will come up with something,' he said in a sepulchral voice.

· 7 ·

When Sarah reached the bar there were already a few members drinking at the counter; but unlike the lunchtime crowd, their mood seemed somewhat sombre. She also noticed that they were all wearing a wide black sash from left shoulder to right hip and secured with a rosette. Once again the bar gradually filled, but the same gloomy mood prevailed. 'What's the matter?' Sarah eventually asked Mollie.

'Lord Bletchley died when you were asleep,' she answered. 'The members are in mourning until dinner-time.'

'Nice of them to take so long,' Sarah answered. Mollie handed her a tray containing the pot of coffee and bottle of brandy Sir Silas had ordered.

'On your way, collect some sashes from Wedge for Nightingale's party to wear when they come down to dinner,' she instructed her.

Sarah did as she was told, and a few minutes later knocked on the door of Sir Silas's suite. Natty Scroat opened the door. He was in shirt-sleeves, smoking a clay pipe and holding a hand of cards. When Sarah entered the room she saw that Sir Silas lay fast asleep in a four-poster bed, wearing a white linen nightgown. In the vast room, the rest of the group were gambling noisily at a card table.

'Shall I wake Sir Silas?' Sarah asked.

'If you can, after one of the doctor's sleeping draughts,' Toby

Nightingale answered with a snorting laugh, but he didn't take his eyes from the game.

Sarah leaned over and reached out gently to shake the old man's shoulder. He did not stir. Sarah tried again without success: she could detect no sign of breathing and his body felt cold through the heavy nightgown. She turned to the men in the corner again. 'Gentlemen, I can't seem to wake Sir Silas,' she called out.

'Give it another try, girl,' Toby Nightingale replied, still not looking up. Sarah turned back to the old man and found him now lying with the covers back and his nightgown pulled up to reveal an enormous erection, which was made to appear even grosser by the shrunken body from which it protruded. She looked down for a moment and pretended to shy away as if shocked by the sight; at the same time she made sure the pot of coffee was spilt towards Sir Silas's naked parts.

With a screech of fear, Sir Silas just managed to avoid the scalding liquid. 'God's beard and trousers!' he shouted as he stood quivering beside the bed. 'This girl's more dangerous than a cocked revolver.' He picked up the bottle of brandy and nervously took a swig. Sarah, as if recovered from her surprise, moved towards him with arms outstretched as if in supplication. 'Sir Silas, forgive me,' she cried out.

The old man dodged away from her like a startled rabbit. 'Keep away from me girl,' he answered. 'You're as unlucky as a new moon through glass.'

He picked up the sashes that Sarah had now discarded on the bed and asked, 'What's this? Has a Corinthian died?'

'Lord Bletchley, sir,' Sarah answered.

'Poor old Bletchley, I shall miss his game. Come on, lads,' he called out, 'I mustn't miss making the mourning toast. Scroat, where's my damned shirt?'

Sarah withdrew and returned to the bar.

'Where's Sir Silas?' Mollie asked. 'The other members are ready to make the toast.'

'He's just coming,' Sarah answered. All the girls on duty were lined across the room with downcast eyes and hands folded in front of them. 'What's going to happen now?' she asked in a whisper.

Before Mollie could answer there was a sudden murmur from the assembled crowd. They turned to see Nightingale and company enter, accompanied by Mr Purse.

Purse took a place at the bar and beat a gong. 'Corinthians,' he called out. 'Sir Silas Nightingale, as senior member, will propose the mourning toast. Be pleased to charge your glasses.'

Sir Silas lined up with the other members, raised a glass of champagne and shouted: 'Gentlemen, to the memory of a great Corinthian.'

The men swallowed the drink in one gulp and the next moment there was the crashing splinter of fine crystal as they hurled their fluted glasses into the ornate marble fireplace.

'Is that all?' Sarah whispered. It didn't seem much of a ceremony to her.

Mollie replied in muted tones. 'The glasses they just smashed were supposed to be made for the coronation of Napoleon. Each was worth seven hundred pounds.'

'I don't believe it,' Sarah replied, shocked by such vandalism.

'Neither do I,' Mollie muttered. 'Purse buys them for a fiver each in Bermondsey antique market, but he tells them they're the real thing and they're happy to pay.'

The ceremony of wastage seemed to stimulate the Corinthian appetites. A lot of heavy drinking was done until an exodus from the bar began when Purse banged the gong and announced the serving of dinner.

'Come and get something to eat,' Mollie said to Sarah when the room was cleared. Sarah realised that she was quite hungry.

With the other girls she followed Mollie into the kitchen area below, where there was a large table set aside for the staff.

The food was excellent. Sarah had pea and ham soup and a delicious steak and kidney pie, but couldn't manage the trifle offered to her by one of the cooks who manned the grills and ranges alongside the table where they sat. The girls who were on duty returned frequently for baskets of the delicious little rolls that were being baked in one of the massive ovens.

'They eat a lot of bread,' Sarah remarked.

Mollie laughed, 'That's what they throw at each other during dinner,' she explained. 'Corinthians don't eat much, the drink kills their appetites.'

'What a terrible waste.'

Mollie shook her head. 'None of it gets wasted. The Purses have a farm. Everything that doesn't get eaten here goes into their pigs.'

The girls chatted and smoked for a few more minutes, then Mollie stood up and called out, 'OK. Everyone back to work.' She touched Sarah's shoulder. 'You're on duty in the gambling room now.'

'What does that involve?'

'Encouraging them to drink and play.'

'How do I do that?'

'The drink part is easy, you just keep bringing it to them. A Corinthian feels that an empty glass is a challenge to his manhood.'

'What about the gambling?'

'Just go on applauding their daring and keep saying, "My life, Mr Aubrey, I've never seen such courage!" That sort of thing. And now and again laugh in admiration, and warn them they're playing like madmen – they all like that.'

'Do you think there are women who behave like they do?' Sarah asked as they trooped back to the upper floor.

'I've known women who get the gambling bug, usually with

their husbands' money, but no, I've never known any women who wanted to get together and drink until they throw up. Mind you, I've known some women drinkers – but they usually do it alone.'

'What about the sex?'

'They're not here for the sex either. They could get the same thing cheaper and quicker at any of the Mayfair hotels. It's something to do with not growing up. Did you know there's a club outing whenever there's a production of *Peter Pan*?'

'No, I didn't.'

Mollie nodded to her as they entered the gaming room. 'And nearly every member attends. That should tell you a lot about the Corinthians.'

A large florid-faced member came up to them with his lower lip jutting. 'Mollie, you promised to ride me in the Club Derby tonight. I hold you to it.'

'Of course, my lord,' she answered with a brief bob, linking her arm through his. 'Who are the other runners?'

'That scoundrel Wickham, Toddy Newheart and the Nightingale set.'

'What time is the off?'

'Parade at 10.15, race-time, 10.30. Wickham is expecting a division in the House.'

'Are you sure you want an old jockey like me, my lord? I go ten stone these days. That's a lot of weight to carry.'

'Pah, that's nothing for an old warhorse like me. Mind you, I've given up National Hunt racing since I took that fall in the billiard room last season.'

'I shall see you in the paddock at ten o'clock then, my lord. Now excuse me, I must attend to the dice game.'

Mollie waved towards a large, green baize-covered table near the french windows, where Nightingale's group were playing cards. 'Go and deal for them,' she ordered. 'The girl doing it now can get the drinks.'

'Damn your eyes,' Sarah heard Sir Silas say as she approached the table and saw him throw down his hand. 'I'm tired of your dealing. That's the tenth hand in a row I've bottomed on.'

Sarah joined them and Sir Silas looked up at her. 'Do you know this game, girl?'

Sarah could see it was blackjack. 'I've played it in France, sir,' she answered.

He turned to the girl who had been dealing. 'Bring more champagne,' he demanded then, to Sarah, 'You girl, deal the cards and make sure you don't poke out anyone's eyes when you shuffle.' He addressed the table. 'Watch out if she comes near you. This one is sprung like a gin trap: brush up against her and she strikes.'

Sarah dealt out the cards and Sir Silas turned over his down card in triumph. 'Twenty!' he exclaimed, pushing the two queens across the table. Nightingale won the next five hands, each time raking the piles of club money towards him with whoops of pleasure.

'By the mark, you've brought me luck girl. Now I know what you're good for,' Sir Silas said. 'I want you for my jockey in the Derby, later. What weight do you go?'

'One hundred and seventeen pounds, sir,' Sarah answered.

'That's in the buff, I'll be bound. Them clothes must weigh another five pounds at least.'

'Four pounds, I'd say,' Toby interjected with a yawn.

'Nearer eight in my book,' added another member.

'I'd go for seven,' said Natty Scroat.

Sir Silas banged his fist on the table. 'Wager book!' he shouted, and Purse came waddling over with a leather-bound volume.

'Nightingale bets one hundred guineas that the clothes of the wench weigh five pounds.'

The other players called out their estimations and Mr Purse wrote them down.

'That's settled then,' said Nightingale. 'Take your clothes off, girl.'

'Not until there's snow in August,' Sarah answered firmly. Her play-acting had gone far enough, she decided. Nightingale leaned across the table with fists clenched, and his eyes bulged as he shouted, 'Dammit, girl, will you do as you're told. Take off your clothes. I'm not after your body, you know.'

'And I said no! you scrawny old river rat!' Sarah shouted back.

They were now leaning so close their foreheads almost touched. Nightingale stood quivering with rage for a moment, then burst into laughter.

'Old river rat,' he repeated with a snorting laugh. 'That's what I am, right enough. As you wish – the bet's off.' He slapped his hand on the table. 'Will you do me the honour of riding me in the Derby, young lady?'

Sarah was about to refuse when she remembered her undertaking to Latimer. She was supposed to be protecting the old man – after a manner. 'If I can do it with my clothes on,' she answered.

'I like your spirit, girl,' he said. 'By God, I truly do. You may ride me in a suit of armour, if you wish.'

They continued with the cards while Purse, assisted by Wedge, marked out the racecourse with tapes. At ten o'clock all other gambling was suspended while everyone crowded into the library, which served as the paddock. Each member who had decided to enter was led around the room by his tie by the girl who had been selected as jockey. Purse, acting as bookmaker, called out the odds, which were chalked upon a blackboard by Wedge.

Toby Nightingale was clear favourite: partly because he was to be ridden by a girl called Sharon who couldn't have been more than five feet tall, although, Purse was quick to point out, she did have extraordinarily large breasts.

When the last bets were struck, the riders and runners were allowed to walk over the course.

'Twice around the gaming room,' Nightingale explained to Sarah. 'Once around the dining room, then down the staircase to the entrance hall and back again. The head of the stairs on the return trip is generally considered by connoisseurs to be the Tattenham Corner of this course. If we don't have a good position by then, we're finished.'

They returned to the starting tape, and each girl mounted the back of her Corinthian. Tension heightened and the assembled members crowded the edges of the course, calling encouragement to their selections. Finally, Purse dropped a red silk handkerchief and the race was on. To Sarah's surprise, Sir Silas moved faster than she would have imagined and immediately took them into the lead. Jogging forward, he maintained their position until they were coming out of the dining room and heading for the staircase, then Sarah saw that Toby, carrying Sharon, had drawn level.

Undaunted, Sir Silas edged over and managed to trip his nephew, who stumbled and collided with Mollie and her mount so that they all tumbled in an ungainly heap at the foot of the staircase. Sir Silas had a clear lead once again and he entered the final straight without opposition. Purse dropped the handkerchief at the winning post and the members crowded around to congratulate them.

Sir Silas was glowing with pleasure. He tossed the bag of club money to Sarah and said, 'It's yours.'

But Toby Nightingale was not satisfied with the result, 'I demand a stewards' inquiry,' he shouted. 'I was interfered with on the staircase.'

'We was nobbled,' agreed the little wench, Sharon, who was now holding a piece of ice to a bump on her forehead.

While the stewards' inquiry was going on, Nightingale held court at the bar, insisting that Sarah stay beside him to share in the triumph. Colin Greaves found them there when he entered a little later. Sarah extricated herself from Nightingale's company, and they managed a few words of muttered conversation.

'I'm staying here the night,' he said in a low voice.

'I thought you had to be a member,' she replied.

'Money can alter a lot of rules,' he said softly and gave an almost imperceptible nod in the direction of Purse. 'It seems a room has suddenly become vacant.'

Sarah nodded. 'Lord Bletchley died. It must be his.'

'Just remember,' Greaves continued, 'if there's any trouble I'm right here; room 18.'

'I shan't forget.'

'Where's my lucky wench?' Sir Silas shouted out. 'Come back here, girl. I don't want you running off with my good fortune.'

Sarah raised her eyebrows at Greaves. 'I *am* supposed to be keeping my eye on him.'

Purse banged his gong again: 'Gentlemen, the findings of the stewards' inquiry are ready to be announced. The chief steward, Mr Wedge, will now read the result.'

Wedge shuffled forward holding a piece of paper. 'In my capacity of chief steward of the Corinthian Club,' he intoned, 'I find the accusation of boring by Sir Silas Nightingale, on the grand staircase, to be unsubstantiated; and the result will therefore stand.'

Nightingale slapped his knee with pleasure. 'I feel like a short nap,' he announced. 'I need a wench to lie with me.' He reached out for Sarah's hand and then, remembering her attitude, said, 'Ah, perhaps not.' Instead he seized another, more compliant girl around the waist. 'All of you, up to my rooms,' he called out.

Sarah remained standing at the bar, but he shouted out, 'Come on, Lady Luck, I want you to serve the drinks – and that's all.'

Sarah was coming from the bar, her arms filled with more bottles of champagne, a few minutes later when she saw John Latimer in the entrance hall, handing his coat to Wedge.

'How are you coping?' he asked.

'I didn't realise having fun was so exhausting,' she replied drily.

'I take it you're speaking ironically?'

'You could say that.'

'Where's Sir Silas?' he asked and he tapped a little leather document case he carried, 'I have a few papers for him to sign.'

'I'm on the way to his rooms with this,' Sarah replied.

'May I help you?' Latimer offered.

She shook her head. 'I'd lose my status as a wench if I let a Corinthian lift a finger for me,' she answered.

'Oh, dear,' Latimer replied. 'Do I detect a note of feminism creeping into your demeanour?'

'It could be,' she said. 'And only this morning I would have laughed at the charge.'

'How is the old man?' Latimer asked as they neared Nightingale's rooms.

Sarah glanced sideways at him. 'I can't say that I noticed any danger that hasn't been self-induced. At the rate he lives, death must be very near without the need of outside assistance.'

'Burning the candle, is he?'

'The middle and both ends, I'd say,' Sarah answered. 'But you can judge for yourself,' and she indicated the door of Nightingale's rooms.

A half mile or so away, on the edge of Shaftesbury Avenue, George Conway was in his own club, an establishment that was very different to the Bawdy House. The little basement room was clouded with cigarette smoke and noise from the shouted conversations that echoed around the roughcast walls and tiled floor. George sat at the crowded bar with Cat Abbot. To one side of them, three young actors argued with simulated rage and passion about who had seen the greatest Hamlet; to the other a Scottish film director, fuelled by a long day's drinking, was leading a group of enthusiastic but profoundly flat singers in a run-through of *Guys and Dolls*.

Abbot leaned close to George and shouted: 'I said: Pauline Kaznovitch is wasting her time. My contact tells me there's not going to be any arrests in the insurance fraud for at least three months; but when there are it will be the case of the decade.'

'What do you mean, your contact?' George shouted back. 'You've only been talking to the press office at the Yard.'

Cat looked hurt. 'Be fair,' he protested. 'I've known Reg Williams since he was a DC at Savile Row. We've been mates for fifteen years.'

'I know,' George bellowed. 'I've got your expenses to prove it.'

There was a tap on George's shoulder and he half turned towards the singers.

'Can't you two belt up?' the director asked indignantly. 'You're ruining a great song.'

'Sorry, Joe,' Conway replied.

'On the count of three, let's take it from the top again,' he instructed. He pointed to Cat and George. 'And you two take the harmony.'

He held up his hand. 'One, two, three.'

'Luck be a lady to night, luck be a lady tonight,' they all sang, George's voice made even more plaintive by the depressing news that Cat had just given him. Get lucky, Sarah, George thought as he sang on.

· 8 ·

Latimer opened the door to Nightingale's rooms and a heavy cloud of cigar smoke billowed into the corridor, engulfing them both. When they entered, the bedlam of noise almost numbed their senses. Through the smoke, Sarah now saw a scene like the re-enactment of a Hogarth print.

The large, candlelit room was filled with shirt-sleeved Corinthians who had formed a semicircle to watch Trooper Stone and Toby Nightingale put on an exhibition bout of bare-knuckle boxing. Both men, stripped to the waist, hammered relentlessly at each other to shouts of encouragement. Toby Nightingale's body looked as if it had been slapped all over with a piece of raw meat from the blows landed by Stone. The small bloody marks on Stone's face and upper arms came, Sarah could see, from the torn knuckles of Toby Nightingale rather than from any wounds inflicted upon the bruiser.

The open end of the semicircle was to allow Sir Silas to lie upon his four-poster bed and fondle the girl he had selected while he watched the sport before him.

Latimer, who walked over to the bed, was clearly not impressed by the scene.

'Sir Silas,' he said with enough force to be heard over the shouting voices, 'for God's sake stop this, the boy will be killed.'

Nightingale cocked an eye at him. To Sarah, he now looked like an old farmyard cockerel. 'Latimer, you're behaving like an old woman,' he replied. 'They're not hurting each other.

Trooper could punch a hole in his skull if he wanted to – this is just horseplay.'

Sarah saw that Doctor Pendlebury was straining to eavesdrop on Latimer's conversation. Latimer now beckoned him angrily to Nightingale's bedside. As Sarah continued to watch, Pendlebury left his position and came towards them, wearing an expression of sullen reluctance. She was reminded of an old dog, caught by its master wallowing in some unsavoury mire and returning, tail between its legs, in expectation of the chastisement to come.

'Yes,' Doctor Pendlebury said sulkily, when he stood beside John Latimer.

'Do you think all this is good for your patient?' Latimer asked.

Pendlebury drew himself up and ran his fingers through the long lock of hair that dangled over his forehead. 'Sir Silas is in remarkable health for a man of his age,' he replied, in a voice as soothing as honey. 'And I must point out to you, I am here purely as a friend. If he were to become unwell the position would be altered, but at present I am merely a companion and fellow member of the Corinthian Club.'

'He's got you there, Latimer,' Sir Silas chortled as his hands roamed about the body of the woman who lay beside him.

'For God's sake, man,' Latimer persisted. 'You must see that living like this is suicide. I enjoy a good time as much as anyone, but a normal person would need a gas mask just to breathe the air in here.'

Sir Silas threw the counterpane over his head and they could see the two forms wriggling beneath it. 'I'm breathing filtered air now,' he called out in a muffled voice.

Latimer leaned towards the heaped bedclothes and shouted: 'I have some papers that you must sign.'

'Later,' came the reply. 'This girl has needs that must be attended to first.'

Latimer gazed down in frustration for a few moments, then

indicated for Sarah to join him in the corner of the room furthest from the milling crowd around the boxers.

'How much has he had to drink today?' he asked.

Sarah attempted to calculate, but gave up: 'I can't be sure, but enough to pole-axe a normal human being, I would say.'

'That bloody Pendlebury,' Latimer said tightly. 'He should be reported to the BMA.'

Sir Silas emerged from beneath the bedclothes and beckoned Natty Scroat. The little man scuttled towards him and stood by the bedside.

'I want to review the women for the Gaudy revels,' Sir Silas instructed. 'Get them in here now.'

'Is it just to look or are we going to test 'em out, guvnor?' Scroat asked, his body as rigid for action as a bird-dog's.

Nightingale looked about the room. 'I think this lot can manage more than a look, don't you?'

Scroat smiled. 'Full-scale rehearsal, eh, guvnor?'

'Just so, just so.'

Latimer caught Sarah's attention after she had finished distributing the champagne. 'I don't think you'd better stay here,' he muttered. 'Scroat is about to organise an orgy.'

'I think you're right,' Sarah replied hurriedly.

Latimer turned to Sir Silas again. 'Will you sign these papers before the other women arrive?' he asked.

'Wait downstairs,' the old man instructed. 'I'll ring for you when I'm ready.' He shouted to Natty Scroat again: 'Come on, Natty, round 'em up, round 'em up.'

Latimer and Sarah descended to the bar once again, where they found Colin Greaves drinking a tankard of beer. Sarah steered Latimer to him. 'Do you know Superintendent Colin Greaves of Scotland Yard?' she asked.

'I don't think I've had the pleasure,' Latimer answered as they shook hands.

'This stuff is really quite good,' Greaves said, holding up his tankard. 'Would you care for one?'

'Perhaps a brandy,' Latimer answered. It was clear he was a little surprised to find that Sarah had such an acquaintance. 'I didn't know we had any policemen as members.'

'Just visiting,' Greaves replied easily. 'We try to keep in touch with all aspects of life, even when we're off duty.'

Latimer was used to policemen; and their position in the social scale. This one interested him. 'How do you know Sarah?' he asked.

'She tutored a nephew of mine for the common entrance examination last year, and we became friends,' Greaves replied glibly. 'I must say I was a little surprised to hear she was working in a place like this.' He raised his eyebrows to her.

Latimer suddenly made a connection. 'You're the policeman whose family controls the House of Greaves, aren't you?'

'That's right.'

Latimer's attitude changed: now he could accept Colin as an equal. He lowered his voice. 'You know she's doing a little background work for me?'

Greaves laughed briefly. 'Sarah didn't tell me that – she's always discreet.' Latimer looked at her with approval.

'What's going on up there now?' Greaves asked when he had ordered the drink.

'Rehearsals for the Gaudy revels,' Latimer replied. 'We decided that it would be taking Mrs Keane's duties too far to expect her to stay for that.'

'What time do you go off duty?' Greaves asked Sarah.

'When Mollie, my supervisor, says the day is done,' she replied.

'It might be a long night,' Latimer said.

Greaves nodded. 'I'll stick around, in case any of that lot upstairs forget their manners and try to include you in their games.'

Latimer sipped some of his brandy then said to Greaves, 'Look, old boy, there's really no need for you to stay. I've got to wait for Sir Silas to sign some papers, so I can keep an eye on Sarah if you want to toddle on home.'

'There's no problem,' Greaves replied. 'In fact, I'm staying here tonight.'

Latimer looked at Sarah. 'Then you won't lack company,' he said.

Sarah smiled. 'You forget I am supposed to be the one watching Sir Silas; and I am quite capable of looking after myself, gentlemen,' she interjected with a little more emphasis than she intended. 'As far as I'm concerned you can both go to bed.'

Latimer touched his document case which rested beside him on the bar. 'Well I've still got to wait up so that the old monster can sign these papers.'

'You see,' Sarah said to Greaves. 'I won't be alone, Colin, although it's sweet of you to be so concerned.'

'Are you sure?'

'Quite sure,' Sarah said firmly.

'Then I think I will turn in,' he said. 'That is, if Lord Bletchley's body has been removed.'

'I assure you the bed has been changed, sir,' Purse said. He had been hovering at the edge of their conversation.

Greaves drank the last of his beer, looked about the deserted bar, then made his farewells, leaving Sarah and Latimer alone.

'Do you play chess?' Latimer asked after a few minutes of silence.

'I know the moves.'

'Let's get a pot of coffee and retire to the games room.'

'I'll get the coffee,' Sarah suggested.

Latimer smiled. 'No need to act like a waitress when you're entertaining me. We'll ring for Wedge.'

'I don't think he'll like that.'

'I'm sure he won't,' Latimer replied drily. 'But I never could stand the man, so it will be my pleasure to remind him of his place in the order of things.'

Latimer won the first two games easily, but Sarah began to remember her father's lessons and forced a draw on the third. The night dragged on and both of them felt their bodies grow chilled and weary as it came to the small hours. Occasionally they could hear distant thumps and shouting laughter; and from time to time Mr Purse or Wedge returned to the bar in the next room for further supplies of drink.

Latimer yawned as Sarah set out the pieces once again, and felt the cold coffeepot on the table beside them. He was about to ring for Wedge again when the old man shuffled into the room.

'Sir Silas says you're to go up now,' he announced. 'And you,' he said addressing Sarah, when he saw that she had remained seated.

'Are the festivities over?' Latimer asked.

'They're paying the bills now,' Wedge said.

Latimer found his document case and they made their way to Nightingale's room. This time when they entered Sarah was reminded of a battlefield. Most of the earlier smoke had cleared, and the last of the candles guttered in the breeze from the open windows. Long lace curtains curled into the room like fluttering banners and empty champagne bottles littered the floor like discarded weapons.

Corinthians and wenches, casualties in various states of undress, lay everywhere. The only people standing were Mollie, who passed among the bodies collecting the club money, and Doctor Pendlebury who stood in the centre of the room, naked except for a pair of silk shorts, his great hard belly streaked with the champagne that dribbled from the bottle he held to his mouth.

'Come on, Latimer,' Sir Silas called out from the four-poster, where two of the girls sprawled beside him and Natty Scroat lay curled up like a dog at his feet. 'I'll sign those damned papers now.'

Latimer and Sarah picked their way through the carnage.

'Aren't you sorry you missed all this? Don't you feel your blood stir, girl?' Sir Silas said to Sarah.

She looked about her and could think of nothing to say that would express her true feelings, but she was willing to try: 'I had my blood stirred like this once before,' she answered.

'When was that?' the old man asked.

'Passing a traffic pile-up in the fog on the M1,' she replied. 'They looked as if they'd had the same amount of fun.'

Sir Silas didn't appreciate the comparison: 'Go and tell Wedge I want the Turkish bath prepared,' he ordered. 'And tell him we're going to drink bumpers down there.'

'Are you quite mad?' Latimer protested. 'You must get some rest, man.' He turned to Pendlebury, who was pulling on a pair of trousers that didn't seem to belong to him, judging from the tightness of the fit and the shortness in the leg. 'Can't you tell him, Pendlebury?'

The doctor walked over and lifted Sir Silas's wrist. 'The pulse of a boy,' he declared smoothly, 'I wish it were mine.'

'There you are,' Sir Silas chuckled gleefully, and he started to kick Natty Scroat awake. 'Come on, Natty,' he ordered. 'Get them all down to the Turkish bath. A good broiling will wake them up again.'

Scroat went about his master's bidding and the huddled bodies on the floor began to groan into life once more.

'What about these papers?' Latimer asked.

'Changed my mind,' the old man said petulantly. 'You'll have to wait until after the bath.'

Latimer turned to Sarah with a helpless shrug. 'We'd better stay with him,' he said apologetically.

Sarah was beginning to feel she was earning her fees.

It was the first time she had visited the basement and Sarah was struck by the splendour of the Turkish baths. The first room they entered was decorated with Grecian pillars supporting an ornately carved ceiling. Richly decorated tiles were laid beneath scrubbed wooden duckboards; and in the centre a cold pool, lit from beneath, glowed like a great sapphire. Sir Silas had led the crowd into the steam room, and through the misted windows Sarah could see the naked figures crawling over each other, like a vast basket of pink and white newly-born puppies. Sarah refused to join them; instead she sat at the edge of the pool and bathed her aching feet in the almost freezing water.

Mollie and Wedge arrived with trays of tankards and more supplies of champagne and brandy. The door of the steam room swung open and Sir Silas called out: 'Mix the bumpers, Wedge and make sure they're ice cold or you go in the pool with the rest of us.'

'Just as you like 'em, sir,' Wedge answered and he had to stand aside quickly as two of the naked girls burst out of the steam room, pursued by waddling Corinthians. They plunged into the cold pool: Sarah and Latimer had to step back to avoid being splashed. Moments later the rest of the group emerged, followed by Sir Silas who reached out for one of the tankards prepared by Wedge. He was about to raise it to his lips when Latimer stepped forward and grasped hold of the silver mug.

'Remove your hand,' Nightingale growled.

'Sir Silas,' Latimer pleaded in a low but urgent voice. 'For God's sake, man, enough is enough.'

'Nothing is enough for the Nightingales, sir,' the old man roared and he shook Latimer's hand free and raised the tankard to his mouth once again. As he drank, the mob in the pool stopped splashing and began to chant: 'Down in one, down in one.'

Standing with his back to the edge of the pool, Sir Silas finished the drink and, holding his arms wide in triumph, turned and looked contemptuously at Latimer. But then, Sarah saw, his expression began to change to one of sudden, growing fear. Eyes now widened in horror, he flung aside the tankard and clutched at his throat with a scrabbling motion. His body straightened convulsively and with a tiny, choking gasp, he crashed backwards into the pool.

There was a moment of silence then all of the women apart from Sarah began to scream. She moved forward quickly, but John Latimer was even faster. Reaching from the edge of the pool, he managed to pull Nightingale out of the water and with frantic speed thumped him violently on the chest. Pausing momentarily to listen to the old man's heart, he then began to try and breathe life into him – but it was obvious to Sarah that it was too late.

Sir Silas lay on the duckboards like a dead fish, sprawled under the body of John Latimer, who still fought to revive him.

Eventually, Pendlebury gently pulled him away and examined the still form. 'He's quite dead,' he announced after his examination.

There was silence until Toby Nightingale walked forward. Taking up another of the bumpers, he raised the tankard and said, in a quiet voice, 'To the death of a Nightingale.' Tears were streaming down the youth's face.

The Roman quality of the salute was slightly spoiled by the fact that a number of Corinthians were now furtively slipping away from the scene.

Pendlebury now took charge. He sent Wedge to rouse Purse and instructed a few of the more sober members to remain; others were ordered to their beds or told to leave the premises discreetly by the back exit. The tipsy and near-hysterical girls were sent to their quarters, with the exception of Sarah, who was clearly sober. Satisfied that all was ready, he instructed Purse to witness the scene as it now was, and then have the body carried to Nightingale's bed. 'I shall make out the death certificate,' Pendlebury said. 'Cause: heart failure.'

Taking advantage of the confusion, Sarah slipped upstairs, found the correct room and woke Greaves. Quickly she told him what had happened. He thought for a time. 'Did anything seem strange about it to you?' he asked.

Sarah didn't have to think. 'Nothing I could see,' she answered. 'Pendlebury signed the death certificate. But if it came to an inquest I would say it was virtual suicide.'

He reached out and put his arm around her. 'Well at least you can quit the job now and come home.'

Sarah leaned her head on his shoulder for a moment and then said: 'No, I'm going to see this through. I think I'll wait until Latimer is done with me.'

'Haven't you got enough to write about?' Greaves said softly.

Sarah paused. 'I don't know – I've just got a feeling there's more to come on this one.'

Greaves hugged her for a moment, then said, 'Well I'm going to stick around as well – it's starting to interest me now.'

Sarah changed, and rejoined Latimer. As they left the building it was raining again. Sarah waited in the hallway while Latimer brought the car to the door, then Purse emerged from his office and handed her a wad of money. She looked at him questioningly and he said: 'Your tips for today, I've taken our percentage,' then he paused. 'See you tomorrow?' he asked.

'I don't think so,' Sarah answered. 'It's been a busy day.'

'Got enough material, eh?'

'More than enough, Mr Purse. Goodbye.'

It was almost light by the time they reached Corton Court. When Latimer stopped to let her out of his car, she looked towards the still darkened trees shrouding the centre of the square. 'I didn't do a very good job, did I?' she said flatly.

'Nonsense,' he replied firmly. 'You did everything asked of

you. Nightingale's death was tantamount to suicide. Besides, I was there. If anyone failed, it was me.'

'Nonetheless, he's dead.'

'If anyone is to blame it's that charlatan, Pendlebury,' he said grimly.

'Well, I won't be making any charges for the day,' Sarah added.

'On the contrary,' Latimer said. 'I insist that you are paid for everything.' He glanced at his watch. 'And double time, too. Now let's go and get some sleep.'

Sarah got out of the car and watched Latimer drive away to park in a nearby garage. It was cold in the rain and a faint bluish light showed in the eastern sky. She shivered in the red dress and entered the block of flats.

'You're up early,' Sarah said, when Polly opened the door before she could put the key in the lock.

'I'm used to getting up. How did it go?' Polly asked.

'Not a good day,' Sarah replied. 'I'm afraid we lost our client.'

'Dead?' Polly asked incredulously.

Sarah nodded.

'Tell me about it over a cup of coffee.'

A few minutes later Latimer joined them. Sarah sat at the table in the kitchen and described the events at the club to Polly.

'You never told me about this place, John,' Polly said when she had finished. 'I didn't even know you were a member.'

'Ex-member,' Latimer said. 'I think I shall resign after this business.' He got up to go and take a shower and Polly leaned across the table. 'Tell me more about the girls who work there,' she said wistfully. 'Are they very beautiful?'

Sarah reached for her handbag to take out a paper tissue and the thick wad of money spilled on to the table top. Polly stared, wide-eyed. 'How on earth did you earn all this?' she asked breathlessly.

'By behaving myself,' Sarah answered with a tired smile.

Polly picked up the notes and flicked through them. 'Just imagine what the badly behaved girls must earn,' she said in wonder; and she held one of the £50 notes up to the pale light from the window.

· 9 ·

When Sarah got up after a few hours' sleep, Latimer had already gone to his office. It was just before midday. Polly was out so she took the opportunity to telephone George Conway: his voice sounded hoarse.

'Have you been shouting at people?' she asked.

'Singing, actually,' he answered.

'Amateur dramatics?'

'Some of the ensemble were professionals, if you must know. Are you getting any good copy?'

'I worked at the Bawdy Club yesterday. Two of the members died.'

'What of?'

'Natural causes.'

'That doesn't sound particularly exciting. Are you going to file?'

'Not yet – it might turn out to be good stuff, though.' She heard the front door open. 'Got to go, call you later.'

When Polly entered the room, Sarah was calling Latimer at his office. 'I wondered if you still wanted to go on with the arrangement,' she said when she was put through. 'I perfectly understand if you have no further need of me.'

'I want you to stay,' Latimer answered quickly. 'I'm a bit tied up at the moment but we'll talk later. There's nothing to be done today.'

Sarah hung up and sat thinking. She felt a stirring of guilt about the deception she was perpetrating on Latimer and his sister. If it had been a simple office job the task would have been easier; but he had invited her into his home. Now she was beginning to feel there was an element of betrayal in her actions. She would not have been so bothered, but Nightingale's death had altered everything; there was a black edge to the business now – and deeper, more profound feelings. Sarah knew that she would have no need to write anything that would reflect badly upon the Latimers – but there was still a nagging doubt that caused her discomfort.

She was staring moodily from the window when Polly came into the room and suggested they should buy a bed.

Polly insisted they go to the market in the Portobello Road where she knew a shop that sold brass bedsteads. She led them towards the Strand, a strange figure in flowing clothes that attracted the attention of passers-by.

'We can go by the underground from Holborn,' Sarah said.

'Oh, I don't think so,' Polly said. 'John doesn't approve of the underground. I think we should go by taxi.'

Polly did the bargaining with surprising firmness. While the transaction took place Sarah stood on the pavement looking at a display of framed prints in the shop next door. She was studying one when Polly joined her.

'That's that done,' Polly said briskly, 'and they say they'll deliver it before five o'clock.' She followed Sarah's gaze and saw that she was examining an old travel poster of a snow-capped mountain glowing in moonlight.

'That seems familiar,' Polly said. 'What is it?'

'The Matterhorn.'

'I like the bend on the top,' Polly said, and then, in a moment of intuition, 'You've been there, haven't you?'

Sarah nodded. 'With my husband.'

Polly looked at the picture again. 'When did you get a divorce?'

'I didn't, he was killed,' Sarah answered, still looking at the poster. 'We went skiing near there – the year before it happened.'

Polly looked at the picture again: 'It's a nice-looking poster – why don't you buy it?'

Sarah considered Polly's question. She had been about to say no, but now she changed her mind. 'Do you know, I think I will,' she replied.

'Let me do the bargaining,' Polly said; and Sarah watched as she beat down the shopkeeper from £20 to £15.

'Where did you learn to do that?' Sarah asked as they carried the picture towards Westbourne Grove. 'I wouldn't have the nerve.'

'From an uncle,' Polly answered. 'You should see the way farmers haggle on market day.' She pointed to the antique shops about them. 'They make this lot look like charity workers.'

'What was it like to grow up on a farm?' Sarah asked. 'I only used to read about it in children's books.'

'Lovely when I was a small child; hell when I left boarding school and had to live there all the time.'

'I thought it was supposed to be lovely all the time.'

'Did you never live in the country?'

'Half and half. My father is a doctor: we lived in a little market town but most of his practice was in the country. Not the same as a farm.'

'That's true,' Polly said with feeling.

Sarah hailed a taxi before she could ask her any more questions.

The traffic was heavy all the way to Lincoln's Inn Fields but Sarah didn't mind the slowness of the journey. There was something pleasant about riding around London without the pressure of work to distract her. It was almost like a holiday.

In Corton Court, Sarah remembered there were some tools in the box room. She found a hammer and nail and hung her picture in the bedroom. While she was making the final adjustment, she heard the telephone ring and Polly answer.

After a final admiring glance at the snowcapped peak, she went into the office where Polly now sat with her feet on the desk, flicking elastic bands at a calendar that stood on one of the wooden filing cabinets. She said, 'That was John's secretary, he wants you to ring him back.'

'Why didn't you call me?' Sarah asked.

Polly closed one eye and aimed a rubber band at an old account book, then turned to Sarah. 'It was his secretary, I can't stand her. She makes everything she says sound like she's a magistrate sentencing you to transportation.'

Reaching across Polly's legs, Sarah dialled the number. The phone was answered by an imperious voice. Sarah raised her eyebrows and Polly smiled knowingly.

'Mr Latimer wishes you to attend his offices this evening at six o'clock,' the voice informed Sarah, then the line went dead. A few moments later the telephone rang again. Polly raised her eyebrows and gestured for Sarah to answer. It was Latimer. 'I just caught the tail-end of your instructions from Miss Burton,' he said apologetically. 'She tends to be a little curt.'

Sarah laughed: 'What do you want to see me about?'

'Would you mind if I told you later? I think Miss Burton may be listening on the extension.'

'In that case, I'll see you at six,' she said, and hung up again.

Polly watched her with interest. 'Well, well, so John is protecting you from the dragon,' she said. 'It's more than he ever does for me,' and she fired an elastic band with enough force to knock over the calendar.

'Is that act of violence intended as a comment?'

'No, just killing time,' Polly answered.

At five minutes to six Sarah left the flat and, following Polly's instructions, walked the short distance to Latimer's chambers in Lincoln's Inn. Passing through the tall brick gates, she followed the pathway to a wistaria-clad Georgian building that overlooked lawns edged with flowerbeds. It was more like a private house than a set of offices. She had expected something equally elegant inside, but the outer office, occupied by a disdainful grey-haired woman who introduced herself as Miss Burton, was furnished with characterless, modern, grey-painted furniture and Latimer's own room was no more than a dusty hovel.

He sat Sarah in a crumbling leather chair and she glanced from his splintery wooden desk, which was heaped with papers, to the threadbare carpet.

'Sordid, isn't it,' he said when she had completed her examination.

'More homely than I expected.'

Latimer laughed. 'Full marks for tact,' he replied. 'But it is deliberate. Most of my clients are extremely wealthy and, in my experience, the rich hate spending money on anything but themselves. If they see me housed in poverty, they assume their money isn't being wasted on frivolities.'

'Well, you've created that impression perfectly,' Sarah said.

Latimer glanced at his watch. 'I hope you don't mind waiting a bit longer,' he said with a slight sigh. 'Sir Toby Nightingale is joining us and I would prefer to explain only once.'

Sarah, intrigued, said she could be patient.

He offered her tea, which she accepted, and by the time it was finished she could hear the sound of raised voices in the outer office. It was clearly Toby Nightingale demanding to see Latimer. Before Miss Burton could announce him he strode into the room, accompanied by Natty Scroat and Trooper Stone.

A grim-faced Miss Burton entered behind them and said, 'I'm sorry, Mr Latimer, these persons just barged in.'

'This is Sir Toby Nightingale, Miss Burton,' Latimer said quickly.

'I see,' Miss Burton replied. She stood very straight and looked over her half-moon spectacles at the young baronet, who now lounged in the chair next to Sarah's. 'I thought it might have been one of the criminals who call.'

Sarah smiled at the woman's comment and thought: she may be an old bat, but she's certainly got backbone.

'Thank you, that will be all,' Latimer said. He glanced at Sir Toby but he was oblivious to the other people in the room and had not even noticed Miss Burton's words. 'Got anything to drink, Latimer?' he asked, like a child demanding a treat.

'I think there may be some sherry.' Latimer opened a cupboard that was piled with dusty files. 'By the way,' he added, 'you've met Sarah Keane.'

Nightingale glanced at her without interest; Sarah looked quite different without the extravagant blonde wig. 'Never seen her before,' Nightingale said, then he nodded: 'Your servant, ma'am.'

Latimer decided not to remind him of the Bawdy House. Instead he handed him a glass of sherry and said, 'What arrangements have you made about Sir Silas?'

'He's already at Gaudy, in the family vault.'

'No funeral?' Sarah asked. She had intended to remain silent, but his remark interested her.

Nightingale looked at her lazily. 'The Nightingales don't believe in all that nonsense,' he said.

Latimer coughed to regain his attention. 'I have something confidential I wish to discuss. Perhaps it would be better if Mr Scroat and Stone would care to wait outside.'

'What about her?' Nightingale asked with a cursory glance towards Sarah. He downed the glass of sherry in one gulp and reached for the bottle Latimer had placed on his desk.

'Mrs Keane is a colleague. I think it is necessary for her to know what I am about to tell you.'

'Natty, Trooper – outside,' Nightingale said shortly; and they moved like trained animals at his command.

Latimer waited until the door had closed behind them and then he looked down at some papers on his desk. When he raised his eyes again, his manner was businesslike.

'Sir Toby,' he began, 'it is my duty to inform you of certain secret matters that involve your late uncle.' Sarah watched Toby carefully. He now sat with the sherry bottle in one hand and one leg looped over the arm of his chair. 'Go on,' he replied without much interest.

Latimer consulted his documents again, then cleared his throat: 'It seems you are not the only heir to your late uncle's estate.'

Now he had Nightingale's full attention. The young man let the bottle rest on the floor. 'Nonsense,' he said ominously. 'I am the last of the Nightingales, Uncle Silas often told me that.'

'You are the last of the Nightingales in name, undoubtedly – but you are not actually Sir Silas's nearest living relative.'

'This is damned lies,' Toby said with increasing force. 'How can there possibly be anyone else?'

Latimer paused and then said, 'Please let me explain. In his youth, your uncle had many liaisons with a variety of women. It fell upon this firm to make the arrangements when he wished to end any involvement with which he had become disenchanted.'

'So?'

'Some were more complicated than others?'

'Bastards, you're talking about?'

Sarah watched him with interest. There was no sign of instability: if anything, Nightingale seemed hard-headed and shrewd.

Latimer nodded. 'Just so.'

'How many?'

'Two that he wanted to make provisions for.'

'So what's the bill?' Nightingale said without much concern. 'Pay it and send them on their way.'

Latimer shook his head slowly. 'I'm afraid it's more complicated than that. The first natural child of your late uncle is now quite an eminent gentleman in his field. Professor Edwin Perceval of Oxford University, a specialist in medieval history.'

'And who is the other?'

'That's more difficult,' Latimer said with a half-smile in Sarah's direction. 'Apparently, Sir Silas had a son by a young lady with whom he later developed quite a bitter relationship. Eventually she moved to some remote region of the United States of America, where a child, Sir Silas's natural son, was born.'

'So where is the boy now?'

'Harold Crow is dead.'

'Crow?' Sir Toby repeated irritably. 'What kind of a name is Crow?'

Latimer clasped his hands together and spoke apologetically: 'Harold Crow, the gentleman in question, was appalled by the treatment of his mother by Sir Silas. He stated that if that was how Nightingales behaved in England, he'd rather be a Crow in the United States.'

'So if he's dead, why should that bother me?'

'He had a daughter.'

'Ah,' Sir Toby said thoughtfully. 'So what does that mean?'

'It means she inherits,' Latimer looked up. 'You don't seem particularly surprised by all this, Sir Toby.'

Nightingale shrugged. 'I might have heard something about all this, things I was told as a child by an old woman. I can't really remember . . . Go on.'

Latimer looked down at the papers again. 'Your late uncle's instructions were quite specific. The Sunday after his death, his heirs – that is yourself, Professor Perceval and Jane Crow – are to be present when the will is read at Gaudy.'

'This weekend,' Sir Toby said angrily. 'Impossible. The Gaudy revels are due to take place. It will have to be some other time.'

'I'm afraid that cannot be so, Sir Toby. The instructions are quite plain. Invalidate them and you may cause unnecessary difficulties. Remember this Miss Crow is American, and Americans are notorious for litigation. A lawsuit could cause all sorts of problems with your claim to the estate. You would win, but it might take years.'

Nightingale stood up, his usually pale features now beginning to colour. His head began to twitch uncontrollably and he scrabbled at the edge of Latimer's desk, scattering papers on to the threadbare carpet. 'No, no, no!' he shouted in a voice that broke into a screaming note.

'I'm afraid it is so,' Latimer said quietly.

Toby reached for the empty sherry bottle and threw it at Latimer's head. His aim was wild and the bottle shattered against the wall, smashing into shards of broken glass. Leaning forward, he screamed: 'Damn you, sir, and damn Uncle Silas. Gaudy is *mine*, I'll fight for every inch of it if necessary. Let these people come. I'll give them a welcome they won't forget.' He stood up and shouted, 'Trooper! Natty!' The door swung open instantly and Nightingale stormed from the room.

After a few moments, Latimer walked over and closed the door. Then he stooped down and picked up Nightingale's empty glass. The last dribble of sherry had spilt on to the dust-impregnated carpet. He rubbed the spot with the toe of his shoe. 'That family always knows how to leave its mark,' he said mildly. He sat behind his desk again. 'I'll call him later and make him see reason.'

'Is such a thing possible?' Sarah asked. She had been unsettled by the display of uncontrollable rage.

Latimer smiled. 'Oh yes. The one thing that can be predicted about the Nightingales is their unpredictability. Toby can be quite charming when you least expect it. I suppose it depends on what part of the family blood is flowing through his brain at any given moment.'

'You sound like an expert.'

'On the Nightingale bloodlines we are. My family have worked for them since before Gaudy was named. The times haven't all been bad.'

'Why did you want me here?'

Latimer swung his swivel chair to one side and looked up at the ceiling, which was yellow with tobacco smoke but patterned with fine plasterwork.

'Something *is* bothering me,' he answered slowly. Then he swung back to face her again as if he had made his mind up about something. 'Actually I'm worried about Jane Crow.'

'What about Professor Perceval?'

'That could also be the cause of my worry,' he said slowly. 'The professor seems to have disappeared. His college say they haven't seen him for over a week.'

'Has he gone away like this before?'

'Well, yes,' Latimer admitted. 'But I still have this nagging feeling of unease.'

'Why?'

Latimer held his hands out, palms up, for a moment then let them fall to the surface of the desk. 'Nothing certain; just intuition, if you like. I'm still not really happy about Silas's death. I suppose it's that dreadful creature, Pendlebury. He nearly killed me some time ago.'

'What was the matter?'

Latimer waved a hand dismissively. 'Nothing serious at first, until he prescribed the wrong drugs for me – then it could have been fatal.'

'So where do I come in?'

Latimer drummed on the desk top. 'I want you to act as Jane Crow's chaperon during the time she's here.'

'She's on her way?'

'Oh yes. I called her this morning, while you were still asleep.'

'She must have been surprised by the news.'

'She was – but she reacted well. Astonishing people, these Americans. Can you imagine anyone English getting on to an aeroplane following one call from a solicitor they've never even heard of until that moment?'

'Maybe she's as crazy as Toby. Don't forget, she has the same bloodlines.'

'I suppose anything is possible with that family. Still, she sounded sane enough. You will keep an eye on her, won't you?'

Sarah nodded. 'When does she arrive?'

Latimer glanced at his watch. 'Some time this afternoon, by Concorde. I paid the fare out of the Nightingale estate. I'd like to have greeted her myself but I have to go to see a client in Guildford this afternoon and can't get out of it.'

'Do you want me to go to the airport?'

'No, that won't be necessary, I've arranged for a car to pick her up. I've booked her into the Bryant Hotel. Meet her there. Do you know it?'

'No.'

'Charming little family place, hideously expensive. Still, Nightingale can afford it.'

'I never saw you as a Robin Hood figure.'

He smiled. 'As for Robin Hood – to be frank, I've always admired the Sheriff of Nottingham more.'

Sarah stood up. 'I shall go to the flat, collect my things and tell Polly about this new job.'

'I'm glad you've got something to get your teeth into again. And you should enjoy this more,' Latimer said with sudden enthusiasm.

'Time will be the judge of that,' Sarah said, smiling.

Latimer walked with her to the outer office. Through the window by Miss Burton's desk Sarah noticed that it had started to rain quite heavily.

'Do you have a coat?' Latimer asked.

Sarah shook her head. 'I was so close I didn't bother.'

'You'll get soaked,' Latimer said; and he turned to an overloaded coat-stand that was precariously close to the door. 'Here, take this.' He took an umbrella from the bentwood stand; it had an ivory handle. 'Don't lose it,' he said with a smile. 'It's a favourite of mine.'

Sarah strolled slowly back to Corton Court, enjoying the fresh scent of the rain-washed air.

· 10 ·

He was going to kill again, and the knowledge caused his whole body to burn as if he were touched by fire. His breath was coming fast, like that of a runner, in short panting bursts and his mouth was dry. It was as if he were aware of every atom of his being. His senses were so acute he could hear distant figures whispering, smell the coming rain and see each blade of grass beneath their feet. He touched his lips with the tip of his tongue – they were dry with a metallic taste, like an old penny. The palms of his hands began to tingle with anticipation and the muscles of his stomach trembled as if they were being stroked with a feather. This moment of waiting was exquisite, almost unbearable. It had been like this as a child. He had first experienced it when he had caught a bird trapped in the attic of the house. He had held its struggling body and felt the tiny racing heart. The same excitement flooded through him. Life at his command – then the consummate moment. Godlike, to crush out existence: a living thing reduced to lifeless, inanimate matter. Followed by an ejaculation of pleasure that exceeded any sexual encounter. After the bird in the attic there had been other creatures. Anything he could trap in the grounds: voles, rabbits, pigeons. Each time it came to the kill it gave him the same panting thrill of excitement. Now it was another human being. He blinked twice and then, with his hands striking like snakes, stepped forward and encircled the throat of his victim.

Later in the evening Sarah prepared for her new duties. She took a taxi to Park Lane and stopped first at the Grosvenor House Hotel, where she called George Conway in the Red Lion. 'No songs tonight?' she asked.

'If your story doesn't live up to expectations I may never sing again,' he answered. 'What are you up to now?'

'I'm about to meet my new responsibility.'

'What does that mean?'

'I'm babysitting an heiress.'

'Why?'

'My new boss thinks she needs a minder.'

'This isn't dangerous, is it? You know the company's policy about women staff doing dangerous jobs.'

'George, how sweet. Are you concerned for me?'

'It's the financial director's office,' he continued. 'They don't like the insurance premiums.'

'Well you can put their minds at rest. I don't think I'll come to much harm at the Bryant Hotel.'

'You're staying at the Bryant, are you? Very posh.'

'It's hell working as a private eye.'

'Down those mean streets a girl must go – keep in touch, you may be my last hope.'

Sarah rang off and made her way to her destination, which was close by, down a half-hidden cul-de-sac leading from Upper Brook Street. The narrow opening to the road looked on to a tall blank brick wall, but once Sarah turned into the street it changed character completely and widened into a cobbled roadway that was free from the boom of traffic.

It was as Latimer had described it – charming. The wide, three-storey building faced a row of stylish mews cottages that made a fine counterpoint to the hotel's grander presence. It was a solid Edwardian building, with a porticoed doorway that jutted out from an ivy-clad frontage. Window-boxes, planted with early daffodils and crocuses, stood on the ground-floor ledges.

The gusting rain had blown away by now, but there was a coolness in the air and the cobblestones still glistened as Sarah picked her way around the shallow puddles in the uneven road.

A sudden sharp stab of wind chilled her and made the bright lights of the hotel look even more welcoming.

A log fire was burning in the little entrance hall where a rather smart young woman in an elegant wool suit sat in a small cubicle faced by a wooden counter. She was reading a thick novel and looked up with a smile at Sarah. 'Oh, hello,' she said in a happy voice. It was more like the greeting of a friend than the professional manner of most hotel receptionists.

Sarah smiled back. 'I believe you have a reservation for me. I'm Sarah Keane.'

'Have we?' the girl answered in the same cheerful tone. She flipped open a large leather-covered book. 'Yes, here we are: Keane and Crow. Keane and Crow,' she repeated. 'You should go on the halls with names like that.'

'Halls?' said Sarah.

'Yes,' the girl answered. 'At least that's what my grandfather always says.' She smiled and frowned at the same time. 'Actually, I don't know what "on the halls" means.'

Sarah signed the book the girl had turned to her, with the fountain pen provided, before she answered. 'Performing an act in music halls. That's what your grandfather means.'

'Oh, dear,' the girl said. 'I do hope you're not offended.'

'Not in the slightest,' Sarah replied. 'In fact, my great-grandfather actually did perform in music halls, according to family legend.'

'Really?' the girl said. 'What did he do?'

'Just an escapologist – nothing very impressive.'

'He should have met my grandfather,' said an American voice behind her. She turned and looked into a pair of light blue eyes.

'Hi,' the woman said. 'I'm Jane Crow. I take it you're Sarah Keane.'

Sarah's first impression of the figure before her was of colour: hair that was streaked by the sun, or a very good hairdresser, in a range of tones from white to honey; skin tanned to reddish gold, and a wide, bright scarlet mouth. Jane Crow smiled and ran the tip of her pink tongue over teeth that were evenly matched and white as milk, then held out her hand.

'John Latimer told me to expect you.'

Her hand was slim. Sarah could feel the delicate bones, but her grip was firm and the skin rough and dry. This girl worked for a living, Sarah told herself.

'Why should my grandfather have met yours?' Sarah asked.

Jane Crow smiled and shrugged so that her blue button-down shirt tightened over breasts that were surprisingly full for her slender frame.

'I heard you say yours was an escapologist. Mine used to lock people up – he was a sheriff.' She plunged her hands into the pockets of her Levis: 'So, Keane and Crow . . .'

Sarah could tell she was slightly nervous; somehow it made her more attractive.

Sarah grinned and nodded towards the receptionist. 'This young lady says we sound like a music hall turn.'

A flicker of uncertainty passed over Jane Crow's face.

'Sorry,' Sarah added, 'variety act.'

Jane smile her understanding. Sarah noticed she was carrying a raincoat. 'Are you going out?' she asked.

'I was just going to grab a hamburger. I rang down to ask where the coffee shop was and they said they didn't have one.'

'We have a restaurant,' the girl at the desk said.

'I'm not dressed for anything fancy, honey,' Jane replied, gesturing to her faded Levis.

'What you're wearing is fine, really, it's not very formal,' the girl reassured her.

Jane Crow looked indecisively to Sarah.

'You'll do,' Sarah said.

'Are you sure?' Jane replied. 'I came over on Concorde. What the other women were wearing made me feel like a bag-lady.'

'I bet most of them would have killed for a figure like yours,' said Sarah, attempting to reassure her.

'Oh, I love you already,' Jane said. 'OK, let's eat in the restaurant.' She looked down at Sarah's overnight bag. 'Gee, I'm sorry, do you want to go up and dump that first?'

'Will someone put this in our room?' Sarah asked the receptionist.

'Of course.'

'You can tell I'm just a country girl,' Jane said in an unconcerned voice. 'Where I come from you tote your own bags.'

The dining room reflected the discreet Edwardian character of the hotel in its dark polished wood, glowing brass and snowy tablecloths covered with heavy silver cutlery. Clusters of glasses reflected light from the tulip-shaped gas lamps above each table. The walls displayed paintings and old cartoons, framed playbills and ancient photographs of sporting aristocrats. Green leather banquettes divided the room, giving each table its own intimacy.

Sarah noticed Jane Crow hesitating on the threshold: despite her earlier flippancy she was obviously beginning to feel intimidated.

The head waiter showed them to a table and presented them with menus. The food was very English, of the roast beef and treacle pudding variety. Almost immediately, a white-haired man wearing a long white apron appeared.

'Right, ladies, what you goin' to 'ave?' he asked in a growling East End accent.

'What do you recommend?' Jane asked.

The old man smiled crookedly. 'There's a lovely bit of lamb on the trolley, or if you fancy fish, the Dover soles are smashing.'

'So who was the escapologist?' Jane asked when they had made their selection.

'My grandfather's father,' Sarah answered. 'He could afford

to send his son to public school, so he became a doctor, and so in turn did my father.'

Jane looked at a photograph of a bearded cricketer that hung on the wall near them, then asked, 'What about your mother?'

Sarah paused. 'She died when I was at school. What about yours?'

'She went away when I was little. I guess I never knew her. My grandma raised me, but she and my daddy died a few years ago.'

She leaned back as the wine waiter appeared and asked Sarah to order. Sarah asked for a half-bottle of Chablis to go with their prawn cocktails and claret to accompany the lamb. Jane watched him depart and said, 'I guess we didn't have too many problems worrying what class we belonged to. Where I come from you were either white, Mexican or Indian.'

'Where was that?'

'A little place south of Tucson.'

'Were there many Indians?'

'Sure,' Jane replied. 'My old man worked on a reservation.'

'What are the Apaches like? I've only seen them in the cinema.'

Jane grinned. 'They're not like that any more, they don't shoot settlers now.'

The wine waiter reappeared and opened the bottle of Chablis. Sarah took a sip and nodded.

'I met some American Indians once,' she said.

'Where?'

'In the Canadian Rockies. They were called Papagos, built like the Greek Gods. They were some of the best climbers I've ever seen.'

'Even most Americans don't appreciate how many different types of Indians there are,' said Jane. 'They think they're still all like Crazy Horse, riding about the Plains shooting at stagecoaches.'

'So what did you do in Apache Point?' Sarah asked.

'I worked for a dude ranch until recently, then I moved to New York. I didn't have any family left and I wanted a change from showing kids how to stay on cow ponies.'

'You were a riding teacher?'

'No, they don't stay long enough to teach them to ride. Besides you just sit in a Western saddle, it's not like the ones they use back East. We just had to put them up and walk around with them. After a couple of days they felt like cowboys.'

Sarah felt relaxed enough now to raise a more personal question. 'Did you know about your connection with the Nightingales?' she asked.

'Not until the call from this guy Latimer, the lawyer. All I knew was that my grandma had turned up in Apache Point the day before Pearl Harbor and she had my daddy with her. He was still a baby. A year later she married Billy Bob McKay, he was the sheriff.'

'But your father never took his name?'

'No, he loved Billy Bob like a son should, and he became sheriff when Billy Bob retired; but he always insisted he was called Harry Crow; and he wanted me to use the same name.'

'What happened to him?'

'He was killed. Shot dead in a bar in Tucson last year. Some guys were sticking the joint up and he just got in the way. It was nothing personal.'

'So when did you learn about the inheritance?'

'When I spoke to Latimer, this morning.' She paused while the waiter served their next course.

Sarah looked at her with interest. 'And you just got on a plane and came here.'

Jane Crow nodded. 'Listen, honey, my daddy always used to say a rainbow only shows up in your life once. When it does, grab it with both hands. When I got the call from London I didn't wait to see if I was dreaming –' she made a motion with her hand like an aircraft taking off – 'I just packed a bag and reached for that rainbow.' She took a sip of wine and said, 'Tell me, do you know this guy Nightingale?'

'Toby. I've met him,' Sarah replied. And for the next quarter of an hour she told Jane Crow what she knew about her newly discovered relative and his lifestyle.

'Good Lord!' she exclaimed. 'He sounds like a retard.'

'I suppose he is in a way. Isn't that what happens when you interbreed too often?' Sarah said as the waiter asked if they wanted more coffee.

Jane shook her head and yawned. 'Jet lag, I guess,' she said with a quick smile. 'I'm totally bushed.'

'Would you like to turn in?'

'What I'd *really* like to do is beat up the town – but I guess that had better wait until I've had some sleep.'

Sarah asked for the bill and signed it. They left the restaurant followed by a cheery goodnight from the waiter. 'I thought the prawn cocktail was great,' Jane said to him as she passed.

There was no lift in the hotel so they climbed the stairs to the top floor. Sarah had expected a double room, but Latimer had booked an impressive suite. Her overnight bag was resting at the foot of a double bed with an ornately carved headboard; it looked a poor thing amidst such luxury.

'Pretty fancy, isn't it?' Jane said after Sarah had inspected the living room and little kitchen and now stood in one of the grandly appointed bathrooms. Jane took a soft bathtowel from the heated brass rail and held it to her cheek. 'We sure didn't have anything like this in Apache Point.'

'You'd better get used to it.'

'I still can't believe it,' Jane said. 'I don't want to go to bed in case I wake up and find out it's all a dream.' She took hold of Sarah's arm. 'Let's just have a final drink to celebrate,' she said. 'There's some cute little bottles of champagne in the refrigerator.'

Sarah didn't want any more wine, but knew that Jane would enjoy the gesture. 'Fine,' she said. 'Crack it open.'

'I'll fix it,' Jane said. A few minutes later she emerged from the kitchen with two glasses and handed one to Sarah.

'Here's mud in your eye,' she said and raised the glass. When they had finished, Jane yawned again. 'Well, I guess I'd better go to bed now, if you don't mind.'

Although Sarah had not slept for long the night before she was not yet tired: 'You go ahead, I'll watch television for a while,' she said. They said goodnight, and Sarah turned out all of the lights in the living room, except for one large lamp. In the kitchen she poured away the remains of her champagne and found a bottle of milk which she brought back into the darkened room. She switched on the television and sat on a deep sofa that was softly upholstered with dark green silk: it was wonderfully comfortable. Flicking through the channels with the remote control she settled for an arts programme on the work of an obscure French film director. It was just about interesting enough to hold her attention. Later, she could not recall at what point she fell asleep.

Sarah knew it was a nightmare but that did nothing to stop the fear which held her motionless. It was as if her whole physical being had been encased in lead. No movement was possible: she wanted to scream and struggle but the muscles of her body refused to respond to the messages from her brain. Everything was concentrated towards this one primal need, but there was no response. She could not draw breath or even shout for help. Hell – this is what Hell is like, the still rational part of her mind told her.

The heat was suffocating, but the tiny room where she was trapped was without windows, and about her the rest of the building was burning. Now there were screams that sounded barely human, and the crack of wooden timbers splitting. Suddenly the flames burst through the walls of her refuge and she knew death was near. The darkness had given way to hard, flickering light that seared her eyes. Smoke filled her lungs with molten fire. She wanted to fight, but her body remained unresponsive. Only her mind still cried out hopelessly.

Then someone was trying to pull her from the tiny room, but the dead weight of her body proved a heavy burden. An overwhelming blackness blotted out her thoughts. She knew time had passed; there was a coldness now, bitter as a winter's night and she began to shiver uncontrollably. Something was thrust over her face. She tried to push it away but devilish hands restrained her. After a time, she could breathe again: it was still cold but the fear was receding. She heard a man say, 'She's coming round.'

Her eyes slowly opened and a demon head, yellow and black with snout-like features, gazed down at her. Then the fireman pulled off his breathing apparatus and she looked up at his reassuringly human face.

'That was a close one love,' he said cheerfully, and Sarah felt a gentle rain falling on her upturned face. Jane Crow came into vision, leaning close to her so that her long blonde hair brushed Sarah's cheeks. 'It's OK,' she said. 'You're safe now.'

With great effort, Sarah struggled to raise her still leaden body to her elbows. She was lying on a stretcher on the wet cobblestones outside the Bryant Hotel, which she now saw was on fire. Two fire engines stood silhouetted against the blazing front of the building. Jane Crow crouched beside her. 'The place just went up,' she said. 'We were lucky to get out.'

'Very lucky,' a policeman standing nearby said. 'The fire chief says it began in your suite.'

Sarah looked to Jane. 'Thank God you woke up.'

Jane ran a hand through her tangled hair. 'I'm a lousy sleeper and I heard somebody moving about – I thought it was you so I decided to come out for a talk. The room was on fire when I opened the door.'

'You rescued me?' Sarah asked and when she spoke her throat felt as rough as the cobbles her hands rested upon.

'I was getting out anyhow,' Jane replied, forcing a smile, 'so I thought I'd take you with me.'

'Thanks,' Sarah answered. 'I ought to pay *you* to be the bodyguard.'

'Who said anything about a bodyguard?' Jane said. 'I thought you were just supposed to be my guide.'

'I'll tell you about it later,' Sarah answered. Gratefully she accepted the mug of sweet tea that a policeman brought her.

'Do you want to come along to the hospital now?' an ambulancewoman asked. Sarah shook her head. 'No, honestly, I'm quite all right. I'd really rather go home. I don't live far away.'

'You ought to come in for observation,' a paramedic said to her. But Sarah insisted: 'Honestly, I'm fine.'

'Suit yourself,' the man replied doubtfully and he moved on.

'Just give some details to the sergeant,' a policewoman said, 'and I'll fix up a lift for you.' She turned to Jane: 'What about you, love?'

'She's staying with me,' Sarah told her. By now she was on her feet. There was a fair crowd of people from the hotel, looking strangely incongruous in their dressing gowns. One woman carried a Yorkshire terrier, its little head bobbing from one point of excitement to the next, while a balding, anxious man in nightclothes was assuring the assembled guests that he would soon have alternative accommodation for them.

When a policeman had ticked them off his list they made their way to the WPC who had offered them a lift. A few moments later they were ushered into a police car.

Sarah looked at her watch when the police dropped them off: it was just after five o'clock. Latimer opened the door. He was wearing a dressing gown and still dazed with sleep. 'What on earth are you doing here?' he asked thickly, then he spotted Jane Crow behind Sarah.

'Forgive me,' he said. 'I didn't know you had someone with you.'

'Miss Jane Crow,' Sarah said.

'Was there a problem at the Bryant Hotel?' Latimer asked as he ushered them into the living room.

'It burned down,' Sarah replied.

'What did?' Polly asked, entering the room after them.

'The hotel.'

'Are you sure?' Latimer said. He still seemed half-asleep and unable to cope with the news.

'We're absolutely sure,' Jane Crow said. 'We almost burned down with it.' She looked towards Polly, who was hanging on every word spoken. Sarah introduced her and continued with the story: '... and Jane rescued me,' she said, bringing her narrative to an end. 'I'd have been dead if it hadn't been for her.'

'Good heavens,' said Latimer in a shocked voice. 'What a terrible start to your visit, Miss Crow. I can assure you, life is usually quieter in London, particularly at the Bryant Hotel.'

'Well it's going to be pretty damned quiet there for a while,' Jane Crow said. 'The whole place is just a heap of rubble now.'

Sarah looked towards Jane, who wore her mackintosh over a flimsy nightdress. 'What about your bags and clothes? You must have lost everything.'

Jane grinned and held up a leather handbag. 'I've got my birth certificate in here, that's all I need.'

'Well done,' Latimer said. 'That's the spirit.'

No one felt like sleeping, so Polly made some tea and Latimer built up the fire.

'Now, what did you mean by that remark about being a bodyguard?' Jane said to Sarah, when they were settled on the leather sofa.

• 11 •

George Conway sat on the news desk of the *Gazette* picking at a thumbnail with a paper clip while his deputy, Alan Stiles, prepared the morning schedule. Stiles was to attend conference in his place, as Brian Meadows had called for a meeting to discuss the plans for the television advertisements that were to begin the campaign the following week. George watched his deputy with a jaundiced eye. Stiles was a man who made no secret of his ambitions, and during the brief regime of the previous editor he had almost succeeded in ousting George from the paper. Since then he had been quiet in his machinations, but George knew he was having secret meetings with Fanny Hunter. Tony Prior, a reporter loyal to George, had seen them having lunch the day before in the wine bar in Bleeding Heart Yard.

'She had her Lady Macbeth face on, George,' Prior had told him. Conway knew the look, just as he knew that the destruction they planned was his own. Stiles brushed his thinning ginger hair and whistled tunelessly as he waited for the secretary to run off the news schedule copies. Then he began to walk towards Gordon Brooks's office, where the conference was to take place. As he passed, Conway held out his hand.

'Don't forget my copy,' he said.

'Sorry, George,' Stiles said with feigned surprise. 'I didn't think you'd be interested today.'

'I'm always interested in the news schedule, Alan,' Conway answered with a bleak smile.

Fanny Hunter left her office and headed towards Meadows's room and George followed, still holding the schedule, which he had not yet studied. Roger Mantle was with Meadows when he entered. Fanny was talking to him, standing so close that her generous breasts were brushing his silk tie. It needed no expert in body language to tell what Fanny's plans were for Mantle; and it was clear he was prepared to meet her more than halfway.

When they all sat down, Meadows said, 'You'd better start, Roger.'

Mantle outlined the first set of television advertisements for the newspaper's current promotion, Treasure Island. Each week, they claimed, it would make a lucky reader of the *Gazette* financially independent for life.

'Sixty thousand a year, tax free, for life. Is a pretty good incentive, I think,' Mantle enthused. 'Blimey, it would do for me.'

George thought about it for a moment. If he was fired from the paper he would probably get a pay-off that would keep him for a year if necessary. Then he would have to get another job. It was a long time to his pension. He had no doubt that he would find work; but in a more junior capacity, somewhere below the salt. No lifelong security for old news editors. Meadows interrupted his gloomy train of thought.

'How about you, Fanny? What are your plans for next week?'

'This is a great one, Brian,' she began confidentially. 'Dog week in the *Gazette*.'

'Dog week?'

'That's it. We kick off with interviews – stars and their dogs. The gimmick is, we ask the stars about the dogs first, then we pretend to ask the dogs what they think of their owners. Their PRs will give us the dog copy.'

Mantle was nodding his head rapidly. Meadows looked bored. Fanny continued. 'Next we do readers' favourite stories about their pets – and we've found a dog psychiatrist who is going to write on how you can tell if your family pet is heading for a nervous breakdown. There'll also be side-bars about famous dogs in history – and we get readers to nominate dog heroes of their own. Then we have an awards ceremony and we get a corgi to present the awards. Get it? We can pretend it's one of the Queen's.'

'Maybe we could get the Palace to co-operate,' Mantle interjected, his face shining with pleasure. 'Blimey, they could do with some good publicity.'

'I think not,' Meadows said gently.

'I bet they'd do it for *Hello* magazine,' he replied. He turned to Fanny. 'Anyway, we could use the dog in the commercial and a voice-over like the Queen's saying, "We are very amused." '

Meadows glanced at his book-lined shelves then said to Mantle, 'You like the idea?'

'Like it? It's bloody brilliant. There's more than six million dog owners in Britain, they'll lap it up.'

Meadows then looked towards Conway. 'What do you think, George?'

George had been glancing at the news schedule while they spoke. An item at the bottom of the page caught his attention. It was about a fire at the Bryant Hotel. 'Not everyone likes dogs, you know,' he said, looking up.

'Bollocks,' Fanny said quickly, 'What do you think we should do? "Why I Hate Dogs" week?'

George smiled without rancour. 'No, I just made the observation in passing.'

'What have you got, George?' Meadows asked.

He shrugged. 'You know what news stories are like, Brian. We've got irons in the fire.'

'Well I hope one of them is white hot by Sunday,' Meadows said ominously, and he waved to signify the end of the meeting.

George walked swiftly back to the news desk. He entered his computer terminal and called up the agency news file. Scrolling through the reports he found the Press Association copy on the fire at the Bryant Hotel and was relieved to see there were no injuries or fatalities. Then he sat back and laced his fingers behind his head. His antennae were working again, telling him that Sarah could be on to something – maybe something big.

Latimer went to his chambers later in the morning, instructing Sarah to bring Jane there when they were ready. The rain was heavy again but Sarah remembered Latimer's ivory-handled umbrella which she had put in the box room. At the entrance to Corton Court they found Colin Greaves, who was about to enter the building.

'I saw a report about the fire at the Bryant Hotel: there's an investigation. The fire brigade think it could be arson,' he said.

'There was no harm done,' Sarah replied. 'I was going to ring you later.' She paused and saw that Jane was looking at Greaves with interest. 'I'm sorry,' Sarah said. 'You two don't know each other. Jane Crow, this is a friend of mine, Superintendent Colin Greaves.'

Jane was confused by the title. 'Superintendent?' she repeated. 'Are you the janitor for the building?'

Sarah laughed. 'Colin is a Superintendent at Scotland Yard.'

'A cop,' Jane said. 'Good to know you.'

'We're on our way to John Latimer's office,' Sarah explained.

'The man I was coming to see,' he said. 'There's a couple of points I want to clear up about the Nightingale business.'

'Jane is a relative of the Nightingales,' Sarah said. 'She stands to inherit part of the estate.'

'So I understand, congratulations,' Greaves said, and he walked beside them as they skirted the playing fields in the centre of the square.

'Why are you interested in this business, Colin?' Sarah asked.

Greaves glanced at her without expression as they walked. 'Sir Silas Nightingale dies in bizarre circumstances and then one of his heirs nearly dies in a mysterious fire the first night she arrives in London? It may be coincidence – but you know how we policemen hate coincidence.'

'You think there could be something funny going on?' Jane asked.

'There's something else a well,' Sarah remembered. She told him about the missing professor.

'Curiouser and curiouser,' Greaves muttered, but made no further comment.

'All this water,' Jane said, looking up at the weeping sky. 'Why is it they call the French frogs? It should be the British.'

'Doesn't it ever rain in Apache Point?' Sarah asked as they stepped aside from the spray of a passing taxi.

'Never. We're in the desert,' Jane replied. 'It doesn't snow either.'

By the time they reached his office Latimer had been busy. He was slightly surprised to see Greaves, but listened with interest when he explained his misgivings.

'Well I'm delighted to have such eminent help,' Latimer said. 'Frankly, I didn't expect Scotland Yard to take much interest in my suspicions. After all, there isn't any concrete evidence to support my concern.'

Greaves knew he was right. The police had enough on their hands dealing with crimes that had already been committed. He could imagine what kind of reaction Latimer would have got had he turned up and told them he was worried about a crazy old reprobate like Nightingale and a professor of ancient history who made a habit of wandering off on his own for days on end.

Latimer sat at his desk and looked at Greaves. 'So you're waiting for the fire service's report before you take any further steps?'

'Officially yes, but that doesn't stop us from jumping to a few conclusions, does it?'

'No, I think it would be best if we allowed our imagination full rein,' Latimer agreed. He turned to Jane. 'But first I must go through a few formalities, if you don't mind. Can you provide me with proof that you are Miss Jane Crow of Apache Point, Arizona?'

Jane shrugged. 'My passport and stuff was destroyed in the fire, but I've still got my birth certificate.'

'May I see it?'

'Sure,' Jane replied. She handed over a folded document.

Latimer examined the sheet of paper and nodded with satisfaction. 'Excellent,' he said briskly. 'At least this part of the business is settled.' He handed the certificate back to Jane and turned to Sarah. 'Although we have no positive proof, I now believe there's a possibility that someone wishes Miss Crow harm. With this in mind, do you still wish to carry on with the commission? I would understand perfectly if you wanted to withdraw at this juncture.'

'Jane saved my life,' Sarah answered shortly. 'I'm going all the way.'

Greaves held up a hand. 'I understand Sarah's commitment,' he said carefully, 'but maybe it would be better if I was the one who stuck close to Miss Crow from now on.'

'No, Colin,' Sarah said gently. 'It's got to be my job.'

'This is no time to let emotions rule out common sense,' he replied.

Sarah continued: 'I'm using common sense. If there really is somebody trying to do her harm, they're going about it in a very devious manner – setting fire to a hotel isn't the same as hiring a hit-man armed with a sniper rifle.' She smiled. 'Besides, I don't think you know her well enough to go to the bathroom with her just yet.'

'There's one thing I want to know,' said Jane suddenly. Up until then she had seemed more interested in the poverty of Latimer's surroundings. Now she looked at each of them in turn. 'Who wants to see me dead?'

Latimer winced slightly at such plain talk. 'I don't think it would be wise to name names, Miss Crow,' he said. 'Such an action could easily be construed as criminal libel.'

Jane shook her head. 'No way, honey. If there's someone out there who wants me dead and you know who it could be, then I want to know their name – and now.'

Latimer placed his fingertips together and half closed his eyes. 'Let us examine the evidence,' he said slowly. 'You have expectations in the will of the late Sir Silas Nightingale – but so do others. One might expect Sir Toby Nightingale to be the prime suspect, but there are others who would also benefit greatly.'

'Who are they?' Greaves asked.

'Well, obviously, Toby Nightingale seems to be the one with the most to gain, but that isn't strictly true. The will states that the interest on the capital of the estate is to be divided annually, in equal amounts between Sir Toby, Professor Perceval and Miss Crow; but the estate itself shall be wholly owned by Sir Toby Nightingale and his descendants, with precedence given to the males of the line, as is customary with the accepted English practice of primogeniture.'

'Suppose they were all to be killed off, and there were no offspring of either sex?' Sarah asked.

Latimer sat up and folded his hands. 'Then Doctor Pendlebury will administer the estate for the benefit of himself, the tenant farmers and servants, with special provision made for Trooper Stone and Nathaniel Scroat.' He raised his hands and laced the fingers behind his neck. 'In fact, Scroat and Stone would do very nicely out of it – to say nothing of Pendlebury.'

'How about you, Mr Latimer?' Greaves asked evenly. 'Are you in any way a beneficiary?'

Latimer gave a wintry smile. 'Alas, not a penny, Superintendent.'

'Exactly how much is the annual income from the estate?' Sarah asked.

Latimer raised his hands: 'It's impossible to be exact, there are too many variable factors, but the average for the last five years has been a shade over three and a half million pounds.'

'That's more than I anticipated,' Greaves said.

'Yes, it's certainly a tempting sum.'

'Have I got this right?' Jane Crow said slowly. 'I'm going to get more than a million pounds a year?'

'That's right,' Latimer said. 'Of course, it's highly irregular for you to know this information before the reading of the will.'

'What about Professor Perceval, how much does *he* know about all this?' Sarah asked.

Latimer stood up and came from behind his desk to stand on the scruffy carpet at Sarah's feet before he answered her. 'I really can't say. Very little, I would imagine,' he replied thoughtfully. 'I rang his college to inform him of the reading of the will, but they did not know his whereabouts. Naturally I wrote a letter immediately, but as yet I have received no reply.'

'Perhaps I should go up and make a personal call,' Greaves suggested.

'I do wish you would,' Latimer said with sudden enthusiasm. 'We only have a few days, and if he doesn't attend the reading of the will it could cause all sorts of complications in his claim to the revenues of the estate. If you go and make thorough inquiries there can't be any repercussions if he is dissatisfied later.' Latimer paused and walked back to his desk, where he picked up three white oblongs of thin board. 'By the way,' he said, looking at Sarah, 'Sir Toby did calm down after I spoke to him. We have been invited to attend Gaudy today – and stay for the revels. Scroat, Nightingale's servant, called and delivered these earlier.'

'What about Jane?' Sarah said. 'She doesn't have any clothes to wear. Nor do I for that matter.'

Latimer smiled. 'A very practical problem, but an easy one to remedy.' He sat down at his desk again and produced a chequebook. 'I shall make this out for £5,000,' he said as he wrote. 'I'll ring my bank in Fleet Street and instruct them to open an account in Miss Crow's name immediately. If you go there with her, she can sign the necessary papers and draw whatever she needs. Then the both of you can go shopping. Your purchases will be charged as expenses to the estate, so please keep all the bills you acquire.'

He was about to hand her the cheque, when he thought better of it. 'No, I shall come with you. I don't want you to think I take less than a keen interest in your personal arrangements, Miss Crow.'

He ushered them from his office and Jane stood for a moment against the coat-stand next to Miss Burton's desk.

'We're all going out, Miss Burton,' Latimer announced as if telling a child of an exciting expedition in which she were not to take part.

'Then I do hope the weather doesn't inconvenience you, sir,' she replied.

Latimer looked out of the window at the pounding rain. 'Damn,' he said lightly. 'I shall need an umbrella.'

Sarah reached for the overloaded coat-stand and one of her sleeves hooked on a curling peg. Tugging it free, she pulled the whole stand over. Jane just stepped out of the way before it clattered to the floor. As she was nearest, she rummaged among the jumble and handed Latimer his ivory-handled umbrella.

'This weather really is foul,' Latimer said. 'Shall we cheer ourselves up with a splendid lunch?'

'I'm game,' Sarah answered. Jane and Greaves agreed.

'Any requests?' Latimer asked.

'Don't look at me, I'm the new kid on the block,' Jane said with a smile.

'Langan's would be handy for your shopping later,' Latimer

said. 'I think I can get a table. How does that suit you, Superintendent?'

'Fine,' Greaves replied. 'I have my car here so I'll drive there and go on to Oxford later.'

'Langan's it is,' Latimer said. 'Please make the booking, Miss Burton.'

It took longer at the bank than Latimer anticipated, despite the courtesy of the frock-coated attendant who ushered him and Jane into the hushed network of corridors and offices behind the counter screens of bulletproof glass.

Sarah had not entered with them; she found a sandwich bar opposite the Law Courts and stood at the counter drinking coffee. It was nearly eleven o'clock when Latimer and Jane Crow finally joined her. The mood of celebration seemed to affect Latimer even more than Jane. He hailed a taxi, instructed the driver to take them to the restaurant, then turned to the others. 'I think a bottle of champagne would start the lunch off in a suitable fashion,' he added with satisfaction. When they climbed aboard, Jane smiled as she took out her new chequebook and examined the elegant typography. 'Is it true?' she asked. 'Does the Queen of England have one just like this?'

'She certainly banks there,' Latimer assured her, 'so perhaps she has the same sort of chequebook.'

In the bar of the restaurant Latimer ordered a jeroboam of champagne. After the usual ceremony with ice-bucket and napkin he took his first sip. 'I think so,' he said to the waiter.

'It's kind of dry for my taste,' Jane said and made a wry face.

'Oh, dear,' Latimer replied. 'What would you prefer.'

'I'll try a little cassis in it,' she suggested.

The waiter took away her glass and returned a few moments later; the champagne now was tinged a delicate rose hue. Jane took a sip and smiled. 'That's just great,' she said. 'We call them purple togas in Phoenix.'

'We call them a kir royale,' Latimer said.

'Does that mean the Queen of England drinks them?'

'Perhaps,' Latimer answered thoughtfully. 'Making cocktails with Dom Perignon is certainly a regal enough gesture.'

As Sarah sipped some champagne, Greaves entered the bar. He slid into an empty chair and nodded his agreement to the waiter, who had reappeared with an additional glass. 'Cheers,' he muttered after taking a sip.

'Did you have trouble parking?' Latimer enquired. Sarah noted that it was a question frequently asked by men of each other, as if the act involved a demonstration of virility.

Greaves shook his head: 'Actually a friend let me leave it on his forecourt.'

'Most convenient,' Latimer answered, as if to imply that Greaves had been caught in some shady act of police malpractice. Sarah felt some kind of undertow in the conversation but she was used to the strange manifestations of male rivalry. She had often watched reporters striving to outsmart each other, even when they weren't working on stories. Jane seemed oblivious to their edginess and quite at home in the fashionable surroundings.

· 12 ·

When the others ordered coffee, Sarah excused herself, saying she wanted to find out what later news there was about the fire at the Bryant Hotel. The rain had stopped, so she walked to the street vendor at the corner of Dover Street and bought an *Evening Standard*. At a telephone booth she rang George Conway, but he was away from the desk.

'What do they say?' Latimer asked when she got back to the table.

Sarah scanned the news pages and found a report. 'Police are treating the case as arson,' she read aloud. 'A London Fire Brigade spokesman says there is evidence that the fire was started deliberately and the sprinkler system had been sabotaged. He also stated that it was a mircale that there were no fatalities. The police do not believe it was an act of terrorism but the work of an individual who is in a very disturbed state of mind. The Bryant Hotel is one of London's most favoured –' she glanced up. 'The rest is about the history of the place.'

A silence descended on the table as they thought about the implications of what Sarah had just read. The waiter, who appeared with the bill, freed them from their introspection.

'Oh God, an afternoon shopping,' Jane said with mock dismay. She turned and nudged Sarah. 'How do we get to the places where Princess Di buys her clothes?'

'I can drop you at Harvey Nichols,' Greaves answered. 'I'm heading for Oxford now.'

'I must go back to my office,' Latimer said as he signed his credit card slip, 'but I shall meet you at Paddington station at six o'clock. Don't worry about tickets, I'll fix those. We can all go down to Gaudy together.'

While Greaves drove them on the short journey to Knightsbridge, Jane Crow listed her requirements aloud. 'Underwear, make-up, shoes, stockings, evening dresses . . .' the litany began.

'Better get some country clothes,' Greaves suggested.

'What kind of country clothes?'

'Tweeds, cardigans, that sort of thing.'

'How about a dog as well?' Jane suggested with a grin.

'Well there's a pet shop in Harrods if you really feel the need.'

'How are we going to manage all this?' Jane asked.

Sarah gave the question some thought. 'If we get a taxi driver who will stay with us for the rest of the afternoon, we can get what we want and leave it in the cab. At the end we can buy the luggage to pack it all in.'

'Smart girl for a bodyguard,' Jane answered, as Graves drew up outside the first department store.

Sarah had never spent quite so much money on clothes in one day before, and in normal circumstances she would have felt guilty at her extravagance. Despite Greaves's money and her own salary, she had not lost the prudent habits she had developed in her year of marriage to Jack – he had spent every penny that came his way. But now, she told herself, she could afford it. She used her own credit card, determined to pay for her purchases herself.

The taxi driver they hired was a cheerful young man in a stylish shirt and a bomber jacket. He entered into the spirit of the occasion with relish. When the question of some particular item arose, he would take them to a shop or store that had only existed for Sarah in the pages of fashion magazines. The area of activities was foreign to Jane Crow, but she seemed to have an instinct for finding the right items.

'I think that could be considered record time,' Sarah said, when Jane had bought her last items of underwear in an elegant establishment in Beauchamp Place.

'They always said at home I'm part truffle-hound,' Jane answered.

They arrived at Paddington with only five minutes to spare. They even managed to find a porter.

Latimer was impressed when he saw the heaped set of matching luggage. 'You have exceeded my wildest expectations,' he said, and they loaded the purchases on to the train with some difficulty.

'What else have you discovered about England?' he asked Jane when they were settled in their seats.

'Twilight,' she answered. 'It just gets dark quickly at home. The day seems to linger on here.'

Latimer talked about England for a time, taking pleasure in pointing out aspects of British life that often puzzled visitors.

'You make a great guide, Mr Latimer,' she said finally.

'John, please,' he replied, while Sarah looked from the window into the rushing darkness of the Thames Valley.

They were the only passengers to alight on the dimly lit little station. Natty Scroat was waiting for them: he was dressed in riding breeches, stock at his throat and a brown bowler hat set over one eye. He eyed the mounting pile of luggage and gestured for a pair of footmen to load them on to a cart.

'I've only brought the pony and trap,' he explained. 'The others'll manage this lot.'

Leaving the footmen to bring up the rear with the baggage they set off, legs wrapped in rugs against the cold wind. Around the station there were a few straggling houses built in Cotswold stone, but nothing that could be described as a village. Natty

Scroat kept the pony at a brisk trot and the paraffin lamps cast a weak light on the narrow lanes ahead of them. The countryside they passed through consisted, for the most part, of gently rolling hills. In the darkness Sarah could just make out the masses of woods. The high banks of hedgerows might have been sinister but for the comforting click of the pony's iron-shod hooves that caused an occasional spark as they struck the scattering of gravel along the lanes.

They had travelled for some time when Sarah began to feel there was something odd about the surrounding countryside. Eventually she realised what it was. 'There are no lights at all,' she said. 'Doesn't *anyone* live around here?'

'No,' Scroat answered without further comment.

'Why not?' Jane asked.

'The Nightingales own all this land,' Latimer answered. 'Sir Silas's father wouldn't have modern conveniences on the tenant farms. No electricity, no piped water, no gas. The tenant farmers wanted the land, but they didn't want to live on it. So nowadays they all live in the village on the other side of the river. They drive to work every day. At night the place is deserted. Peaceful, isn't it?'

'How long have we been on Nightingale land?' Jane asked.

'Since you left the station,' Natty replied. 'Course this isn't what we call the estate proper, that's all behind the Gaudy walls, but he owns it all the same.'

Another wood stretched out each side of them now, but through the bare branches Sarah could make out two sets of flames burning in the treetops. The lane curved again then widened and ahead she could see a gatehouse set into high walls. The fires were from leaping gas jets that burned fiercely in high brackets on the walls.

'This was why Sir Silas's father wouldn't allow any electricity on the farms,' Scroat explained. 'The old man wanted the gaslights of Gaudy to be the brightest in the countryside.'

145

'Gas?' said Jane. 'Isn't there any electricity here?'

Natty Scroat laughed and spat again. 'You're at Gaudy now, Missy,' he answered as the great gates swung open. 'You can say goodbye to the twentieth century.'

· 13 ·

Greaves looked through a wide hatch into the dimly lit porter's lodge of Professor Perceval's college and cleared his throat. An old man who sat at a battered desk drinking from a large china mug glanced up at the second cough, and with agonising slowness rose to his feet and shuffled to the other side of a counter.

'I've come to see the Master,' Greaves said in a loud clear voice. 'I telephoned, he's expecting me.'

'What name . . . sir?' The porter asked, with enough of a pause before 'sir' to indicate contempt for Greaves and to establish his own authority.

'Superintendent Colin Greaves,' he replied, with a slight bark, knowing instinctively that the man was an old soldier and would react to an authoritative manner and the imposing title. It was an effective ploy. Immediately the porter's manner altered and he reverted automatically to responses instilled in him some distant time in the past.

'Yes, sir,' he replied in deferential tones, and consulted a list. 'If you would care to cross the quadrangle past the last staircase on the right, you'll find the Master's house, the one with the red door. It should be open.'

Greaves thanked him and stalked away. There was a deep silence in the enclosed quad he now crossed, his footsteps soft on the grass. Cracks of light showed at the shuttered windows and there was even a slight mist in the cold damp air. Greaves, who had known the college in his undergraduate days, remembered visiting a friend's rooms nearly twenty years ago. Nothing seemed to have changed much – that was the idea of Oxford, he supposed, although there were women undergraduates at all the colleges now.

He found the red door ajar as the porter had predicted and entered a stone-flagged hallway hung with portraits of ancient academics. He could hear music playing. Unsure of where to go, he paused for a moment and glanced up at a particularly ferocious bewigged face who he judged dated from some time in the seventeenth century.

'Ugly-looking customer, isn't he?' said a high, cultivated voice behind him and Greaves turned to see that he was being observed by a portly gentleman wearing a large, light-blue bow tie and a three-piece tweed suit.

The figure stepped closer and Greaves noticed the matching silk handkerchief in his breast pocket, and the fact that tie and handkerchief were the same tone as the brightly searching eyes that now studied him. The man's face was a healthy pink; white hair fringed his head in a wispy halo.

'Guy Landis,' the man said, holding out his hand, 'Master of this college. You must be Superintendent Greaves. Come and have a drink.'

He led him into a room off the hallway that was warmed by a large open fire. Apart from one small desk lamp in a far corner, the room was illuminated only by flickering flames from the fireplace that threw vast moving shadows. A woman sat in a wing chair to one side of the mantelpiece: she was listening to the last notes of a piece for the French horn that was being played by quite a small girl.

'My wife, Lydia – and my granddaughter, Clare, is the musician. This is Mr Greaves.'

The young girl looked at him for a moment and said, 'Do you think it's silly for girls to play the French horn, Mr Greaves?'

'Not in the slightest,' he answered. 'I have a friend who plays the same instrument and she's not the least bit silly.'

'Now, Clare, what can you tell me about Mr Greaves?' Landis asked.

The child cocked her head to one side and glanced him up and down once more before she replied. 'Six feet tall, fit, and he stays in training. Public school, and this university . . .' she paused. 'Time abroad – somewhere in the colonies perhaps.' She thought again and then said, 'He could be a detective!' with a certain admiration in her voice.

Greaves looked questioningly to Landis, who beamed with pleasure. 'No, Mr Greaves, she knows nothing of our telephone conversation.' He turned to Clare: 'Tell him on what you based your description.'

'The accent is too correct for England, that's what suggests he's been abroad, mixing with old-fashioned people. The ruling classes at home are much sloppier these days. It comes from imitating pop stars.'

She looked towards her grandfather, who nodded for her to go on. 'He walked across the grass of the quad. Only Oxford graduates do that.'

Greaves smiled and she continued. 'I could tell that from your shoes: there's no dust from the gravel and it was only raked this afternoon. Also your shoes are well polished, and the cut of your suit looks military. You stand very upright, even when you're relaxing. That means you're used to working in some kind of hierarchy.'

'Why did you think I was a policeman?'

The little girl smiled. 'I heard grandfather call you Superintendent when he talked to you on the telephone earlier.'

'Well done,' Landis said. 'You're forgiven for the last confession.' Then he turned to Greaves. 'Forgive our little game, I know it's deplorably rude; but as you have come here to ask me questions I didn't think you would mind.'

'Not at all,' Greaves replied. 'I'm deeply impressed.'

'Our little hobby. We have a club, you know, all sorts of people belong. I'm sure you can tell that we have studied the methods of the great Holmes with devotion.' Landis turned to his wife. 'If you would be so kind as to leave us now, my dears, Mr Greaves and I will discuss our business.'

When they had departed, Landis offered Greaves a drink. He accepted a whisky and a seat by the fire.

'As I said on the telephone,' he began, 'I'm trying to trace Professor Perceval. I have some information for him that will be greatly to his advantage.'

Landis sipped some of his whisky and looked into the fire. 'I'm afraid Edwin Perceval is not in the precincts of the college at present,' he replied.

'Do you have any idea where he may be?'

Landis shrugged. 'Mere conjecture – he is a solitary man, not given to sharing the details of his movements with others.'

'But you have some idea?'

'A few hunches.'

The word 'hunches' sounded very foreign coming from Landis, rather like the Archbishop of Canterbury greeting visitors with a 'howdy, folks', but it gave Greaves a clue to Landis's behaviour. 'My visit is like a game for you, isn't it?' he asked.

Landis nodded. 'And a very enjoyable one. You see, Mr Greaves, as you have no doubt already gathered, detective stories are my passion. When the real-life article rings me up and says he wants to question me on the whereabouts of a colleague who has mysteriously vanished – well, you may be able to understand my excitement. An opportunity to match my skills with a professional. How could I resist?'

'So you're not going to tell me anything?' Greaves said.

'Not directly,' Landis replied, 'but in other ways I shall offer every conceivable co-operation. You may stay in the college and question anyone you wish, including myself. Start tonight by dining as my guest at high table.'

'You do know where he is, don't you?'

Landis smiled and put down his tumbler. 'I have a pretty good idea, Mr Greaves, no more. I do hope we come to the same conclusions.'

'I'm afraid I don't have a dinner jacket with me.'

'Don't worry, my son keeps his evening clothes here. I would say you are of almost identical build – except perhaps for the shoes; but your own will suffice.'

After he had changed, Greaves accompanied the Master to the part of the college where the dons and their guests had assembled for drinks before dinner. Mostly they were men, but there were two women in the party: a formidable chemist called Hilda Marks who had a crushing handshake, and the pretty young wife of a visiting American academic, introduced as Natalie Weedle. Her husband, Curtis, hovered edgily around her, but appeared to wish he was in another part of the room. After some desultory conversation dinner was announced. The Master led them in procession to the high table in Hall.

'Over here, Mr Greaves,' Landis called out. 'Between me and the bursar. Any clues yet?' he whispered, before an undergraduate in the body of the hall had finished racing through a Latin grace. They sat down to the scrape and clatter of chairs before Greaves answered.

'Nothing,' he replied, glancing down the long room and observing that the phrase 'high table' was still literally true. The elders and betters, with whom he now associated, were raised above the main body of the room on a stone plinth at the warmer end of the vaulted hall, while the undergraduates took their lowlier places at long tables that did not glitter with silver.

The bursar, who sat on Greaves's left, was a cadaverous, ashen-faced man called George Glossop. After a few minutes of stilted conversation, Greaves deduced that he was a physicist and his particular interest was the wavelength of certain types of light. At least, he thought that's what the man had said. Glossop had a peculiar habit of allowing his sentences to die away to an almost inaudible whisper.

'Do you know Professor Perceval well?' Greaves began after they had dispensed with the customary civilities.

'Edwin Perceval and I were undergraduates together at th . . .' Glossop trailed away.

'So you're old friends?'

'On the contrary, I could never stand the man. In my opinion, he is an insuffra . . .'

'Bore?' Greaves asked hopefully.

'Prig,' Glossop corrected. Then he continued: 'His frequent absences from this college stand as the highlights of my . . .'

'Life?' Greaves hazarded.

'Scholastic calendar.'

Greaves looked away and saw that Landis was smiling mischievously at his discomfiture. He decided that to pursue his present line of inquiry could be more misleading than informative and cast his mind around for another avenue of conversation. After a few false starts they landed on cricket and Greaves managed to battle on for the rest of the meal.

Landis rose to his feet after the savoury and Greaves thought the meal was finished; but the Master muttered to him to keep his napkin when they left the table. They walked from the hall and through a cloistered part of the quad before climbing a staircase to a darkly panelled room that sparkled with candlelight. Leather chairs and small tables were arranged in a semicircle about a log fire. There were decanters of port and Madeira on the tables, bowls of nuts, dishes of hand-made chocolates and Turkish Delight. Greaves sighed and tried to listen politely to a conversation on his left about Elizabethan candlesticks, but his eyes roamed around the room as if hoping to spot the elusive figure of Perceval in the encircling gloom.

· 14 ·

Once Sarah and the others had passed through the gates of Gaudy, the darkness of the night closed in again and she could make out little of the estate that lay about them; just the wide, curving tree-lined drive of fine-chipped gravel that glowed whitely ahead. The only sound was of the iron-clad wheels and the clip of the pony's hooves. Then the clouds parted and moonlight revealed woods to their right and a broad expanse of water rippled by the gusting wind.

When the great house came into view Sarah's memory of the burning Bryant Hotel returned. The sweeping Georgian façade was illuminated by flaring gas lamps that momentarily gave the impression that the house was on fire. As they drew closer, she could see that the wind-blown torches were held aloft by painted statues of blackamoor footmen spaced along the frontage. Although the lighting was primitive, the effect was quite beautiful, and the delicate tracery of decoration made the house seem as fragile as a piece of Dresden china.

Although Sarah knew of the Nightingale fortune, somehow she had anticipated that the house would be a crumbling ruin encrusted with grime and ancient ivy. Any such thoughts were immediately dispensed when they entered the elegant hall. The butler and housekeeper who greeted them were a middle-aged couple who emanated efficiency and competence.

'Welcome to Gaudy,' the butler said smoothly. 'If you ladies will follow my wife she will show you to your rooms.' And then, to Latimer, 'And you are in your usual quarters, sir. The footman will bring up your luggage.'

As they followed the woman, Sarah looked about her with fascination. Behind the Georgian frontage of the great house were the remnants of much older buildings. Stone walls, part of a Norman keep, merged into Elizabethan panelling; a minstrels' gallery had been added to a wall decorated with Saxon wall paintings. Corridors widened and narrowed: they walked on rich carpeting, then stone, then polished wooden floors. There were paintings that ranged across the centuries and the weapons and ancient banners that filled the high walls bore testament to the Nightingales' warrior past.

After a longish walk, up staircases and along corridors, Sarah and Jane were shown to rooms with a connecting doorway. This part of the house seemed to be Jacobean, Sarah thought, judging by the barley-twist furniture and pastoral tapestries. Two footmen, dressed in the same sky-blue livery as the torch-bearing blackamoor statues, brought their luggage, and when they had withdrawn, the housekeeper introduced them to Karen, a short girl in a black uniform who was to act as their maid.

'Dinner will be served in one hour,' the housekeeper said.

'How should we dress?' Jane Crow asked the maid when the woman had left.

'The gentlemen will be in evening clothes, Miss,' replied the maid.

'What does that mean we wear?' Jane asked. 'A cocktail dress or an evening gown?'

'Either would be fine, Miss.'

'Do you work here all the time?' Sarah asked Karen.

'Yes, Miss,' Karen answered. 'The Nightingale family have a lot of lady visitors.'

'Do you like the work?' Jane enquired.

'Oh yes, Miss,' she replied. 'My sister works in a biscuit factory in Oxford, I'm much happier here.' She held up one of the dresses she was unpacking and said, 'This is lovely.'

'It's got creased,' Jane said anxiously.

'That's all right, Miss,' Karen reassured her. 'I'll pop it down to the kitchen and give it a good press.'

'I bought a travelling iron, you could do it here,' Sarah said.

Karen laughed. 'Not unless it's gas-powered, Miss,' she answered.

'Of course – no twentieth century. Don't you miss television?' asked Jane.

Karen shook her head. 'There's enough goings-on here to keep anyone interested,' she said. 'When I go to my sister's on my day off, they don't want to watch television. They just turn it off and listen to me telling 'em about Gaudy.'

'What about bathing?' Jane asked with sudden concern. Karen crossed to an oak door and opened it to reveal a vast Edwardian bathroom, complete with a contraption fired with gas jets, for the provision of boiling water.

Jane and Sarah selected their dresses and Karen took them to the housekeeper's room.

When they were alone, Jane, with no concern for modesty, took off her clothes and stood quite naked before a cheval glass. Sarah could see, from the tiny sections of untanned flesh she now revealed, how pale her skin actually was. Her breasts were burned the same gold as the rest of her body. When they had bathed, they took turns in towelling each other's hair.

'How the hell did anyone manage before hair-driers?' Jane asked when Karen returned with their dresses.

'Hot brushes, Miss,' Karen answered. 'I'll show you.'

Finally, Karen led them once again through the bewildering maze of corridors into a reception room where Sir Toby Nightingale was entertaining his other guests.

Sarah recognised Doctor Pendlebury, but there were three

other people whom she had not seen before. Latimer was talking to a bony, sharp-faced woman seated on a chaise-longue. A younger version, who could only be her daughter, was standing close to a weakly handsome young man who had shifty eyes and wore an elegantly cut tailcoat which he kept tugging into minor adjustments, like an actor seeking to perfect a newly donned costume.

There was no sign of Scroat or Stone. 'Ah,' Nightingale said, pushing himself from the mantelpiece. 'The ladies.' He gestured about the room. 'This is Doctor Pendlebury and his wife, Sylvia.' The elder of the bony women inclined her head frostily. 'And this is their daughter, Iris Broome and her husband, Edward.' He waved again. 'Jane Crow, and her companion.'

Sarah realised that he still did not know her name, despite their brief meeting in Latimer's office and the encounters at the Corinthian Club. Nor did Pendlebury. She had imagined that in his case it was because she no longer wore a wig but she couldn't be certain: there were some missing parts to Gaudy, like an incomplete jigsaw puzzle.

She accepted a glass of champagne from a footman and looked around the room once the conversation had resumed. This part of the house was evidently part of the Georgian additions. The fireplace Nightingale stood against was intricately carved with flowers and cherubs and a magnificent Venetian glass chandelier, festooned with candles, illuminated the room, which was delicately frosted with exquisite plasterwork. The walls were covered with pale blue-green silk interspersed with landscapes and portraits that Sarah imagined were of great value.

'Do you hunt?' a voice said. Sarah turned to see Edward Broome, who had left his wife and come to join her.

Up to that point in her life, Sarah had never really held an opinion on the subject, but a note of condescension in Broome's voice immediately caused her to side with anything he might consider a quarry.

'Neither the slipper nor the thimble,' she replied sweetly.

A deep furrow creased Broome's brow and he thought so hard about her comment, she imagined she could hear his mind whirling like a clockwork toy. 'I say, you're not against field sports, are you?' he asked at last. Remembering the company, and the purpose of her visit, she decided it would be unwise to start an argument, so she smiled again and said: 'My father brought my up to eat everything I killed – and I don't fancy the taste of foxes.'

'Your father's a hunting man, eh?' Broome asked.

'He used to be.'

'Where?'

'The North African desert, long before I was born.'

The crease returned to Broome's forehead. 'What did he hunt in the desert?' he asked.

'Germans and Italians,' Sarah said.

'You can't eat Germans and Italians,' Broome said, puzzled.

'That's why he was a pacifist by the time I was born.'

Edward Broome sensed he was not being taken seriously. 'Look here, are you trying to be funny?' he bridled.

Feeling she might have gone too far, Sarah nodded, but still couldn't take Broome seriously. 'I'm sorry, it's my job. I'm a professional comedian, you see. Sometimes I find it difficult to get away from my work.'

'Comedian!' Broome answered. 'That's a rather coarse job for a woman, isn't it?'

Sarah feigned innocence. 'Do you think so?' she asked. 'It always seems quite ladylike to me, providing the jokes I tell aren't dirty, of course.'

The butler announced that dinner was served and they walked to another part of the house. The dining room they now entered appeared to be Elizabethan, its wood panelling blackened and warped with age. Early Nightingales glowered from their frames, their severe features somehow incongruous against the ruffs and frills of their elaborate costumes. Sarah noticed that no women graced the walls.

They were seated at one end of a long polished table with a surface and edges that were worn uneven by time. Heavy, almost primitive, silver glowed dully in the candlelight. Sarah found that the constantly changing features of the rooms, each of which reflected the style of a different century, gave a certain dreamlike quality to the events of the evening: it was as though Gaudy caused her memory to be confused and disjointed. Already, her first impressions of the flame-lit front of the house and the Jacobean bedroom seemed to belong to distant and quite separate occasions.

Nightingale, seated at the head of the table flanked by Sarah and Jane, now seemed to be the epitome of a caring host, urging them to enjoy the wine that was served with the first course, a delicate soup laced with truffles.

'Damn fine silver, this, Toby,' said Pendlebury when the fish was served. Sarah looked up and saw that he was holding the figure of a woman that served as part of the condiment set.

'Best of its kind in the whole of England,' Nightingale replied without arrogance. 'The British Museum have been trying to buy it from us for years.'

'Why?' Jane asked.

'Most silver of this quality owned by the aristocracy was melted down during the Civil War,' replied Nightingale. 'Only the Kremlin has anything comparable from this period.'

'The American Civil War?' Jane enquired.

Nightingale burst into laughter, and the Pendlebury party joined in with rather forced heartiness.

'The English Civil War,' Latimer answered.

'Which side were we on?' Jane asked, undaunted by the

mocking laughter and determined to show Pendlebury and his relatives that she had some claim to be seated at the table.

'The winning side, of course,' Nightingale answered. 'At first we backed Cromwell, then when the Restoration seemed inevitable we were all for the return of Charles II.'

'I hear the family used to be on pretty good terms with royalty,' Jane continued. 'Do you still keep in touch?'

Nightingale did not reply, as he was paying attention to an enormous joint of beef that had just been brought to the table. After a close inspection he nodded his approval to a footman, who began to carve at the sideboard. He returned his gaze to Jane.

'We gave them up when that German princeling, Albert took over,' he said flatly. 'The whole business turned into a damned farrago of Christmas trees and kilts.'

This comment led to a dreary conversation about the state of the monarchy that Sarah did not wish to enter. It was hard for her to remember Nightingale's behaviour on previous occasions: the rage in Latimer's office and his murderous anger when he had threatened the girl at the Corinthian Club. Now he seemed perfectly rational; even a little dull. Sarah's attention was drifting away from the table when Nightingale sat straighter in his chair and said: 'What time is it, Pendlebury?'

The doctor consulted his watch. 'Almost twelve,' he replied.

Nightingale reached into his pocket and produced a silver case. 'Time for another pill, eh?' He opened the container and took a round capsule, the size and texture of a smallish cherry; as he did so another of the pills rolled from the case and rested beside Sarah's wine glass. She picked it up and placed it before Nightingale.

'Don't you find them hard to swallow?' she asked.

Nightingale shook his head and gulped the capsule down with a mouthful of wine. 'No,' he answered when he'd refilled his glass. 'They slip down a treat.' Then he stood up. 'Excuse me ladies, nature calls.'

When the door closed behind him, Sarah looked to Pendlebury: 'Does Sir Toby have to take those pills very often?' she asked.

The doctor waved dismissively. 'When I think it necessary,' he answered.

'What are they for?' she pressed. 'They look like something you'd give to a horse.'

Pendlebury gave a short laugh. 'I can assure you they're quite safe. I made them up myself.'

'You did?' Sarah said.

He leaned forward and smiled easily. 'You may know that Sir Toby can be . . . what? erratic from time to time. The pills are quite simple concoctions. Just measures of a common tranquilliser sealed in layers of gelatin coatings of various strengths. The first coating melts quickly and releases the desired quantity of medication. The second and third coatings are of greater strength and consequently take longer to dissolve. It keeps him calm for several hours at a time.'

'And you actually prepare them yourself?' Sarah asked.

Pendlebury nodded.

'My husband is a brilliant doctor,' Mrs Pendlebury said in a hushed voice, as if he had just announced the cure for a major disease.

'I'm sure he is,' Sarah answered. Then she turned to the doctor again: 'Have you been prescribing them for long?'

Pendlebury shook his head. 'No, Sir Silas didn't approve of the idea when I put it to him. He always said Toby was just highly strung and pills and potions weren't the answer. I started the medication today as a matter of fact.'

Toby returned just then and the conversation continued with a discussion on hunting. Lost in her own thoughts she heard a clock chime midnight just as she was being offered a glass of port with her cheese, and her thoughts turned to Colin Greaves.

On the last stroke of the hour, Landis led his party across the darkened quadrangle, back to the Master's Lodge. The group consisted of the American, Weedle, and his wife Natalie, the lady chemist, the bursar, George Glossop, and Greaves. Landis walked a few yards ahead, talking earnestly with Weedle and Glossop, while Greaves brought up the rear with the two women.

'Another filthy British night,' Natalie Weedle said, looking up at the patchy clouds half obscuring the moon. 'It's going to rain again.'

'Don't you like English weather?' Greaves asked.

'I wouldn't mind so much if they paved the entire country,' she replied sharply. 'But the mud and gravel of Oxford are destroying all of my decent shoes.'

'I will carry you if you wish, darling,' her husband said in a maudlin voice. Graves had noticed that he'd drunk most of a decanter of port before they had finally departed from the common room.

Natalie ignored his offer and took hold of Greaves's arm.

'Do either of you know Edwin Perceval?' he asked.

'No,' Natalie answered.

'Yes you do,' said her husband. 'That historian you described as a capon when you sat next to him the first dinner of term.'

'Oh, that one,' Natalie said. 'I'd hardly say I knew him. The last conversation we had was about his allergy to a certain brand of washing powder.'

'He talked to you about washing powder?' Greaves asked.

Natalie released his arm as they entered the Master's Lodge. 'He told me his manservant washed his walking socks in a new brand and it brought his ankles out in a rash. I think he was probably the dullest man I've ever met – and that includes the entire faculty of the Halford Wolstan College of Divinity.' She paused, as if thinking, then said, 'I did see him recently, now you mention it, all kitted out to go walking.'

'Did he say where he was going?'

'Maybe, I didn't take much notice – now what the hell was it he told me?'

'I would be grateful if you could remember.'

'It may come back later,' she said, then was edged away from him by Mrs Landis, who had been waiting in the living room with a tray of sherry.

George Glossop leaned across Greaves and took one. 'Oxford is a maelstrom of social activity at this time of year,' he said apologetically. To Greaves's surprise, Glossop now seemed able to complete his sentences without fading away. His voice now boomed around the room.

'How's the throat, George?' Landis asked, pouring him another glass of sherry.

'Better, I think.'

'The bursar coaches our second boat,' Landis explained. 'A testing exercise for the vocal cords.'

Glossop downed the second sherry in one gulp and handed his glass to the Master. 'I'm off, Guy. Back on the towpath at eight. Goodnight,' he announced to the room and departed.

The rest of the guests continued talking in a desultory manner for another quarter of an hour until the host addressed them all.

'Well, I won't keep you from your beds any longer,' said Landis with one of his beaming smiles, which somehow made the command a treat rather than an instruction. 'You remember where you're sleeping, Mr Greaves?'

'I think I can find it,' he replied, and after saying his goodnights, made his way to the top of the house. As he undressed, he thought about the events of the evening. It was clear to him that Landis was enjoying himself with the charades he was orchestrating; there was more to the game than just playing detectives. Greaves was slightly irritated by the necessity to indulge the pastimes of an overgrown schoolboy, but he needed to know about Professor Perceval; and if this was the price – so be it.

He was not tired so he settled down to read for a while.

The little room was sparsely furnished but comfortable enough. A single bed, nondescript rugs on polished boards, a huge Victorian wardrobe and a small button-back chair next to an old and elaborate gas fire that had been lighted earlier to warm the room. There was a good reading lamp and a selection of books on the side table. Greaves was satisfied: he realised it might be some time before he could sleep. He deliberately chose the dullest book he could find – a collection of Victorian sermons – and began to read. Just as he was starting to feel sleepy he became aware of the distant but distinct sound of 'Moonlight in Vermont' being played on the French horn. Slipping on the dressing gown provided, he left the room.

Halfway down the staircase he found Landis's granddaughter sitting on the second landing. She saw him but continued her recital with 'Autumn in New York'. After the final bars she laid the instrument aside and looked up at him. 'I'm hyperactive,' she said in a matter-of-fact voice. 'I'm only staying here because my mother is having a rest cure at a health farm.'

'Is it an inconvenience?' he asked.

'My mother being at a health farm?' She shook her head. 'Being hyperactive is: I tend to wear people out. Grandfather only allows me to play popular music in my own time,' she volunteered, noticing Greaves's enquiring expression.

'Do you enjoy it here?'

'Oh yes,' she replied. 'Some of the dons know a great deal, it helps to fill in the time. I'm writing a history of the college. I know the names of all the masters since 1259.'

Greaves could see she was about to recite them, and held up his hand. 'Clare,' he began carefully, 'if you know everything about his college, do you know the name of Edwin Perceval's manservant?'

'Ned Randell,' she answered briskly.

'And where can I find him?'

'He lives at Woodstock, but he'll be on duty at Professor Perceval's rooms at 8.30 tomorrow morning.'

Thanking her, he bade her goodnight and Clare resumed her playing.

'So tell me,' Nightingale asked as he selected a Havana cigar. 'How do you like Gaudy?'

Sarah realised he was talking to her. 'I don't think I could apply the word "like" to it at all,' she replied. She was now seated on a deep leather sofa against a panelled wall covered with Edwardian sporting prints. Nightingale had led them from the dinner table to a smoking room, where the ladies had opted to remain with the gentlemen, who were now taking their brandy and cigars.

Nightingale raised his eyebrows. 'Am I to take your reply to mean that you don't like it at all?'

'Not in the least,' Sarah answered. 'Some parts are beautiful, others quite sinister. "Like" would be a totally wrong word to use. One might as well say one *liked* the weather.'

'So I gather you don't actually disapprove.'

'Not at all. Your ancestors must have been remarkable men, Sir Toby.'

'By, God, they were,' he replied with enthusiasm. 'Men of bottom and fine judgement. Any damned fool can build a house that conforms to a particular period; the Nightingales decided on this Chinese puzzle. Each generation has to do its bit, you know.' The words came naturally from the young man, although Sarah knew he was simply reciting something he had been told as a boy by his uncle. She wondered which of the

Nightingales had originally made the speech that had been passed from generation to generation.

'What do you mean: your ancestors were men of bottom?' Pendlebury's wife asked.

Nightingale answered the question with passion. 'Bottom is a term for men of courage and quality, Mrs Pendlebury,' he said.

'Quite right, quite right,' Pendlebury said.

Nightingale now seemed more than pleased with Sarah's company. He turned to her again. 'It doesn't stop with the inside of the house, you know,' he continued. 'There are splendid aspects to other parts of the estate.'

'What kind of thing?' Jane asked.

Nightingale did not answer her immediately. 'Natty, Trooper!' he bellowed. The two men must have been lingering nearby, because they entered the room almost at once.

'Get the torches,' Nightingale instructed. 'And tell Mrs Hunter to find some coats for the ladies, we're going to the Whirling Pool.'

'Must we?' Latimer suddenly protested. It was the only thing Sarah had heard him say for hours. 'The night is foul, Toby, and the ladies are exhausted. Can't we leave it until some other time?'

'I would like to see it,' Pendlebury's daughter said in a pleading voice.

'So would I,' the doctor's wife added. She turned to Sarah and Jane. 'My daughter and I aren't allowed to stay for the revels, you know, you two must feel very privileged.'

Jane was not to be intimidated. 'Well, I guess it's a family matter,' she said. Then to Nightingale: 'I'd love to take a look outside.'

'That settles it then,' Nightingale said firmly. 'I'm afraid you're outvoted, Latimer.'

A quarter of an hour later, they were dressed in a variety of waterproof clothes taken from the gun room. Nightingale led them to the front of the house where Natty Scroat and Trooper Stone stood waiting on the gravel drive, each carrying a pair of blazing torches. Only Nightingale ignored the falling rain: he had not bothered to change from his velvet dinner jacket and elegant dancing pumps.

'This way,' he called out. He led the group across wet grass towards the edge of the lake that lay beyond the wide lawns spreading out from the drive.

Sarah could make out very little beyond the circles of wavering torchlight, but even though she could only occasionally see the reed-fringed bank of the lake, she could somehow feel the dark body of water they skirted. Gradually the rain began to drift away, leaving a sky patched with clouds. In the sudden moonlight, two clusters of fountains appeared at the far end of the lake, some distance away from the house. Monumental figures from Greek mythology entwined and spurted water into gigantic bowls shaped as scallop shells that spilled their overflow into the dark waters.

Nightingale led the party beyond the fountains and Sarah noticed they were now close to a dense wood. Finally, he stopped and in the torchlight Sarah saw they stood before a deep brick pit about the size of a squash court. She stepped closer to the edge and looked down into the depths.

Despite the flickering torches, the bottom of the pit was still in darkness, but she could make out huge pieces of cast-iron machinery, great wheels and cogs linked with spindles. It looked like the inside of a gigantic clockwork toy.

Sarah shivered involuntarily. There was something repellent about the obscured depths of the pit.

'What's that sound?' Jane asked and through the wind they could hear a chorus like the squeaking of a thousand distant gates.

Nightingale laughed and threw his torch into the depths. Striking various parts of the vast machinery during its descent, it finally came to rest at the bottom, and they saw the reason for the strange noise: the floor of the pit was covered with a moving carpet of rats that scurried from the flame in panic.

A feeling of revulsion engulfed her and Sarah stepped back from the brink.

'Don't you like rats?' Nightingale laughed. 'In that case, Trooper will deal with them.' He turned to the silent giant who had accompanied them and said, 'Trooper, operate the wheel.'

Stone handed his torch to Scroat and strode to a contraption that Sarah had not noticed. It was another piece of cast-iron equipment, set at the head of the pit: a great wheel with a curving handle. She was reminded of the household of some family of giants. This piece was like part of an old-fashioned clothes mangle.

Sarah watched as Trooper Stone spat on his hands and reached down to seize the handle. His shoulder muscles bulged as he slowly began to turn the great wheel. Gradually his action became faster; and with each turn there came another noise above the squeaking of the rats: the sound of rushing water.

Moments later, the floor of the pit was filled by a roaring torrent that gushed into the depths with enormous force. The water began to rise from the depths unusually quickly; but instead of overflowing, as Sarah anticipated, the surface suddenly formed a great whirlpool that turned with increasing speed. The rushing water was alive with the swirling bodies of rats. The force of the whirling water caused Sarah to step back even further. There was something compelling about the gaping black hole in the centre of the pool, as if the massive vortex was drawing her forward. It began to create a sensation of vertigo, and Sarah felt both fear and a desire to throw herself into the depths.

'How do you like this part of Gaudy, Mrs Keane?' Nightingale called above the sound of the rushing water.

'What purpose does it serve?' Sarah answered.

'It empties the lake,' Nightingale explained. 'There is an underground stream that fills the lake up and the overflow runs into the river. But if we wish to drain the lake, this machinery diverts the stream. The whirlpool, which is artificially created by the shape of the pit, draws off the water into drainage pipes that flow out of this pool, and beneath the walls of the estate. They empty into the Thames below the waterline on the embankment.'

'Are we close the the river?' Sarah asked.

Nightingale gestured behind him. 'Beyond those woods is the wall of Gaudy. It runs beside the Thames.'

Just then Pendlebury called out: 'I say, I think she's fainted.'

They turned to see that Jane Crow, who had wandered away from the pool to look into the lowering waters of the lake, had now moved towards the wood and suddenly collapsed on the wet ground. They hurried to her side and Pendlebury crouched over her.

'I'm all right,' she said in a dazed voice. Then she smiled weakly and tried to make a joke. 'It was just the sight of all that water. We girls from Arizona aren't used to it, I guess.'

'I shall assist you back to the house,' Nightingale announced and he bent down to help her to her feet. After a few steps he paused and called back, 'Trooper, make sure to restore the water level of the lake before you come in.'

Jane seemed to have recovered by the time they reached the hall. 'I feel such a damned fool,' she said to Sarah when they climbed the staircase to their bedrooms. 'I've never passed out in my life before.'

'You've had a hectic few days,' Sarah replied. 'It's nothing to be ashamed of. I nearly fainted too when I looked into the whirlpool.'

Karen ran baths for them both. After a long soak, Sarah

returned to her room and called out goodnight to Jane through the half-open door; but there was no reply.

She was about to take off her dressing gown when she heard a voice shouting from below. Opening the window she saw that it overlooked the cobbled stableyards. Two figures were standing in the moonlight: Natty Scroat and Trooper Stone.

Sarah could just make out Stone shouing: 'I seen her, Natty, I tells you I seen her.' He sounded terrified. Then Scroat led the shambling figure into one of the stables and she could hear no more. Sarah remained, listening intently for a few minutes, then turned away and closed the window.

The bed was comfortable, but despite her tiredness she had difficulty falling asleep. Eventually she drifted off; but was disturbed by memories of the whirling pool. She dreamed that all the guests and servants at Gaudy held tightly on to each other's hands and were drawn one by one into the gaping black darkness. She awoke with a start, to see that Karen had left an oil lamp turned down low on a table by the fireplace. The soft light was comforting, but as she turned to sleep again, she could hear a distant howling coming from somewhere in the surrounding countryside.

· 15 ·

Now he was the only one awake in the great house. It was as if he could feel the others; knew that their weak, sleeping bodies had given up to the night. But he did not need to rest. In the cold of the early hours, stone and wood contracted, causing the fabric of the building to creak and groan softly like a ship under sail; but he made sure that his footsteps were light.

He stood for a moment in the great hall, where the embers of the fire still glowed through the white ash, and listened. There was a distant howling that rose and fell on the wind. They were calling him – wanting what only he could provide.

The elation came again, and a sense of supernatural power that flowed through his body, warming him to his duties. All this was his, he told himself – no one would ever share it. Like the others, who had come before him, he would enjoy it alone, untroubled by the rules of good and evil that lesser beings imposed upon themselves.

Soon it would be time to kill again: the tingle of anticipation burned through his body, as he slipped into the darkness and hurried towards the distant, insistent calling of his friends.

Early the following morning, Greaves was up before the rest of the household. He decided to avoid Landis and, slipping from the lodge, made his way to the Riley which he had parked next to the college vegetable garden. He sat behind the wheel making notes for some time until he looked up and met the suspicious stare of a gardener who was pushing a wheelbarrow. The next figure to stride into his line of vision was the bursar, clad in a thick tweed overcoat and college scarf. He paused when he saw Greaves and took the pipe from his mouth. Greaves got out of the car and bid him good morning.

'Eventful night?' Glossop asked, and Greaves thought he could detect a note of sympathy in his voice.

'It had its moments,' he replied.

Glossop nodded. 'Guy has a unique sense of humour. Complicating matters is one of his most endearing characteristics.'

'He certainly succeeded. I only came to ask him a simple question.'

'Anything I can do to help?'

'I want to catch somebody. I'd appreciate somewhere to wait other than the Master's Lodge,' Greaves replied, glancing at his watch. There was still some time before Randell came on duty.

Glossop looked at his own watch. 'I'm due on the towpath in ten minutes,' he said, 'but you're welcome to use my rooms.'

'Are they anywhere near Edwin Perceval's?'

'Almost next door.'

'Do you share a servant?'

'Ned Randell. He's due in my rooms in a few minutes.'

Greaves smiled. This was a better start to the day.

He took the key Glossop offered and watched him march away, emitting little clouds of fragrant smoke. A few minutes later he let himself into Glossop's rooms. The study and living room were extraordinarily neat, with no careless piles of papers or littered books. Everything was crisply squared away among furniture that Greaves judged to have been manufactured during the age of austerity following the Second World War.

He sat down on a spindly chair with a copy of *The Times* and waited. As soon as Ned Randell opened the door, Greaves relaxed. The wizened old man was of a type he recognised instantly. One who knew all the dodges: cheerful, cunning and conspiratorial. Greaves held out a £10 note, which Randell's eyes fixed on like a stoat watching a field mouse.

'I'm a friend of the bursar's,' Greaves began, deciding that Glossop might be a more reliable name to use than the Master's.

'Yes, sir,' Randell replied. Still concentrating on the £10 note, he opened the door even wider. 'And how can I be of service to you?'

'I'd like to take a look at Professor Perceval's room. I lent him a book a few weeks ago and I need it back.'

Randell looked at him with disbelief; his left eyelid flickered but didn't quite wink. 'Just follow me, sir,' he said.

The surroundings Greaves was ushered into were in total contrast to Glossop's quarters. Each clearly bore the stamp of the bachelor, but the spartan qualities of the bursar's rooms stood in sharp contrast to the fussy comfort Professor Perceval favoured. Victorian furniture was crammed into the small room: sofas, armchairs, tables and cabinets crowded each other and all available surfaces were cluttered with boxes, pottery figures, china ornaments and framed photographs. A small brassbound desk stood under the window, which overlooked an enclosed garden of bare fruit trees. The walls were covered with ancient framed maps that barely left enough space to see the ornately patterned wallpaper.

'I'm just going to make a nice pot of tea, sir,' Randell said. 'Would you care for one?'

'If it's no trouble,' Greaves answered.

A few moments later, Randell emerged from the kitchen with a mug and handed it to him. 'There's cups and saucers, sir, but I thought you'd prefer a mug.'

Greaves sipped gratefully at the strong sweet mixture.

'I could tell there was nothing fancy about you, sir,' Randell said.

'Really,' Greaves replied. 'How?'

Randell chuckled. 'Blimey, sir, it only takes one look. These academic types never know how to keep their chins up. It's filling their heads with rubbish – weighs them down, I suppose.' He gestured to one of the chairs and sat down himself. 'Take a seat, sir.'

Greaves sat facing him, still holding the £10 note. 'I've been asked by a friend of Professor Perceval's to find him as he's wanted on urgent business,' Greaves began. 'I wonder if you'd mind answering a few questions about him?'

An uneasy expression passed across Randell's face. 'Well, that depends, sir,' he answered. 'These gentlemen are very particular about gossip. I wouldn't want anything I said to get back. It's more than my job's worth.'

Greaves took another banknote from his pocket, and held on to it. 'I can assure you, Mr Randell, anything you tell me would be in the greatest confidence. You have my word I shan't mention your name.'

'Well that's all right, sir,' said Randell, as he closed his fist on the money. 'Seeing as you're a gentlemen, your word's good enough. What do you want to know?'

Greaves drank some more tea before he began. 'What sort of a man is the professor?' he asked, placing his mug on a table by his chair.

'Very particular, sir,' Randell said without hesitation. 'He likes everything just so. Comes from not being married, I suppose. A married man has to put up with things he don't like; bachelors don't have to.'

'In what way is he particular?'

Randell paused. 'Everything has to be in its proper place. Clothes in the right drawers and cupboards, Indian tea in the morning and Chinese in the afternoons, and I have to dust all around his stuff. "Don't change anything, Randell," he says. And he really goes mad if a book is moved, he does, straight up.'

'Does he have many friends?'

Randell shook his head. 'He don't have *any* friends, sir, and that's a fact.'

'None?'

'No friends and no family, at least none I've ever heard of, and I've known him thirty years . . . Lots of enemies,' he added as an afterthought.

'What sort of enemies?'

'Oh, you wouldn't believe these college people, sir. They can make a row over a Christmas pudding last until midsummer. But Professor Perceval – well he's something special. The Reverend Cranshaw hates him because he objected to the choir practising in the Library annexe. Now they have to go over to St John's. Professor Burke hates him because he's twice voted the wrong way on the wine committee, and Professor Burke says they'll run out of decent clarets within twenty years. Mrs Landis hates him because he objected to her lectures on female emancipation to the new lot of women undergraduates. You've got to hand it to him – there isn't a single solitary soul he hasn't rubbed up the wrong way.'

'I understand he goes away a lot,' Greaves said. 'Do you have any idea where?'

Randell gestured to the walls. 'He goes about Oxfordshire, making himself objectionable to the landowners.'

'How?'

'Ancient rights of way,' said Randell. 'That's his passion in life. He finds out where there's a lost footpath – then he goes and opens it up again. There was a time when he used to do it with his Boy Scout troop, but they disbanded.' Randell noticed Greaves's expression and shook his head. 'No, there wasn't any of that sort of thing. The boys just couldn't stand any more of him, like everybody else. But that doesn't stop him wearing all the stuff. Off he goes with his little tent and knapsack, and in a few days, somebody else hates him as well.'

'Do you think that's where he's gone now?'

'Most likely, sir. He's a man of very regular habits.'

Greaves handed over the other banknote. 'Do you mind if I look around the room while you're here?' he asked.

'Help yourself, just as long as you don't disturb anything.'

Greaves began a slow exploration of the room. As Randell had told him, the framed maps all showed ancient footpaths that Professor Perceval had reopened to an indifferent public. Each bore a precise caption in tiny copperplate handwriting giving the date of its liberation. Finally Greaves arrived at the brassbound desk. In the centre of the blotting pad was a book, exquisitely bound in dark blue leather and tooled with gold leaf. The embossed title read: *Notes on the Methods of Sherlock Holmes*. He turned the cover and found a folded sheet of heavy, hand-made paper which, with an apologetic glance at Randell, he opened. As he did so another smaller piece of paper fluttered to the ground. Greaves retrieved it and read the hastily scribbled note: 'I think this may be of help, Guy Landis.'

Greaves now studied the larger sheet of paper: it was an old map of Oxfordshire showing the area of Gaudy. He could see a footpath clearly marked that ran beside the walls of the estate, next to the River Thames.

After breakfast, Latimer announced that he had to go up to town on urgent business. Sarah and Jane Crow stood on the gravel drive before the great house and watched him climbing aboard the pony-trap that was to take him to the station. 'Any messages you want delivered?' he asked, 'or is there anything you'd like me to bring you from town?'

Jane looked up at the overcast sky. 'Some sunshine would be nice,' she answered with a smile.

'I'll be back before six o'clock,' he said. 'But I can't promise sunshine.'

'You'd better be, guvnor,' Natty Scroat said briskly. 'There's no way of getting in or out of Gaudy tonight.'

'What do you mean?' Sarah asked.

Scroat gently played the end of his whip over the hindquarters of the pony and then looked up. 'The Gaudy revels commence at six o'clock this evening, Miss. After that there's no way of leaving the estate and no way of getting in. That's always been the rule.'

He flicked his whip and the pony-trap pulled away with a final wave from Latimer. They watched until it passed out of sight along the curving drive. Rain was beginning to drift down like a soft mist. As they were about to re-enter the house, Toby Nightingale and Trooper Stone appeared in the doorway dressed in tweeds and carrying shotguns.

'They've made up the fire in the library,' Nightingale told them. 'Or you might find it pleasant in the conservatory.' He looked up at the weeping sky. 'I shall be out for a couple of hours.'

'Is there anything I can ride in the stables?' Jane asked.

Nightingale looked her up and down for moment. Then he glanced at Sarah. 'Do you ride as well?' he asked.

'After a fashion,' said Sarah.

'Then the grooms will fix you up. Lavender and Achilles could do with a run. Tell them I said so.'

He began to walk away, and then paused and turned. 'My fellow Corinthians will begin to arrive this morning,' he said. 'It would best if you tell them right away that you're my special guests. They can be rather boisterous with unattached females.'

The two women made their way to their rooms.

'Did you notice anything odd about Nightingale just now?' Sarah asked when they were changing into the riding costumes they had bought on Latimer's instructions.

'Yes, he seemed quite sane,' Jane answered lightly as she struggled to get into her new riding boots. 'Why do you ask?'

Sarah paused. 'No dogs. He was going shooting, but he didn't have a gun dog with him.'

'Maybe he doesn't like dogs.'

'I think not. Usually it's only lesser mortals people like Toby Nightingale can't abide. Dogs and horses count as members of the family.'

Jane stood up and stamped her feet. 'Perhaps Natty Scroat and Trooper Stone are enough for him – he certainly treats them like dogs.'

Sarah laughed. 'That could be the answer,' she said.

When they left their rooms, Sarah pointed to her right along the corridor. 'The stables are that side of the house,' she said. 'Perhaps there's a quicker route than going all through all those corridors again.'

'Don't get me lost,' Jane said as they turned in the direction Sarah had indicated. 'I don't want to die in this house and have to haunt it for ever.'

Sarah's instincts proved right. After a short distance the corridor merged with an older, stone-built part of the house and they found themselves in a passage that led to a narrow winding stairway.

'Jesus, these are arrow slits,' Jane said softly, pausing for a moment at an aperture in the wall. As they were about to descend, a clear, quavering voice came to them. 'Have you got my butterscotch?' It seemed to come from all around them, as if from the stones themselves. The women exchanged glances, each wondering if the other had spoken. 'It wasn't me,' Sarah said, in reply to Jane's questioning glance.

'I *said*, have you got my butterscotch?' the voice repeated, more petulant than angry.

'This way, I think,' Sarah said after a moment's hesitation; and they began to climb the worn stone steps. The staircase ended at a massive blackened door bound with strips of iron.

'I'm in here,' the voice commanded, and Jane lifted the latch.

They entered a small round room with walls of rough stone. What little light there was came from a tiny mullioned window decorated in stained glass with the Nightingale coat of arms. The meagre light fell on an ancient four-poster bed, casting blue and magenta colours over the figure of a tiny hunched old woman, dressed in a white nightgown, who watched them with a suspicious gaze.

'Well, have you brought my butterscotch?' the old woman demanded again. As she spoke she ran a withered hand through the strands of white hair that framed a face seamed with wrinkles.

'I'm afraid not,' Sarah answered and as they grew closer the scent of age came to her: a dry musty smell of old flesh and ancient linen.

The woman pursed her mouth so that the chalk-white face seemed even more narrow, and clapped her hands together. 'It's that Natty Scroat,' she said peevishly. 'He's keeping it for himself. My Tobias wouldn't ever forget.' She fumbled in the bedclothes beside her and produced a pair of wire-framed spectacles. 'Who are you two?' she demanded. 'New maids, I suppose. Why aren't you dressed properly?'

'We're guests of Sir Toby,' Jane answered.

'Master Tobias, to you, Miss,' she corrected. 'I won't have him called Toby, that's a name for a jug or a pug dog.'

'Who are you?' Jane asked.

'Who am I?' the old woman said. 'I'm Nanny Parsons, of course. Didn't anyone tell you not to ask personal questions, Miss?'

'I'm afraid I didn't have a nanny,' Jane replied.

'Well anyone can see that,' the old woman said with a sniff. 'Ladies didn't wear a gentleman's riding clothes in my day.' She glanced at them with sharper eyes then said in a wheedling voice, 'If you don't have any butterscotch, what about a piece of chocolate?'

Sarah looked about the room and saw a box on a small table

by the door. She opened it and found a hoard of hand-made confectionery. 'Will this do?' she asked.

The old woman snatched the box from her with surprising speed and crammed two of the pieces into her mouth.

'So you two are friends of my Tobias?' she said, when she had finished the sweets.

'Yes we are,' Sarah said.

'But you haven't known him as long as I have.'

'No we're recent acquaintances.'

'Old friends are the best friends,' she said, her hands scrabbling through the box of chocolates again.

Jane tugged at Sarah's sleeve and moved her head in the direction of the door. The woman saw the gesture and looked at her sharply. 'Would you like to see how Tobias looked when I first knew him?'

'Sure,' Jane said after a moment's hesitation.

The old woman fumbled among the crumpled bedclothes again and this time produced a large leather-bound book. They stood closer as she turned the pages.

Inside the cover was a thick curl of blond hair sealed beneath plastic, facing a large picture of Toby Nightingale as a baby, held in the arms of the woman who sat before them. 'I raised three generations of Nightingales,' she said. 'But Tobias was my darling.'

She turned the page and they saw him dressed in the miniature uniform of an officer in the Brigade of Guards. 'He was a pageboy there, that was just before his mother and father were killed,' the old woman said, then suddenly thrust the book towards Sarah. 'Here, there's no reason for me to do everything.'

Sarah turned the pages slowly and they saw Toby Nightingale's life unfold before them. Each picture was captioned and dated in a clear copperplate hand. Natty Scroat holding him on a pony; Sir Silas teaching him to fish on a riverbank; birthday parties where he was the only child present; Christmas mornings surrounded by lavish gifts, but no one with whom he could share them. There was a large picture of him standing next to Trooper Stone, holding up a brace of pheasants; it was a melancholy record of a spoilt and lonely life.

A later set of pictures showed the boy, now grown into adolescence, with a rather severe, emaciated little man. The photographs were taken in what Sarah guessed was the library. Toby Nightingale sat at a desk and the man leaned over his shoulder as if to indicate something in a book. The figure looked somehow familiar to Sarah; she read the caption with a slight shock: *Doctor Horace Hostler, MA instructing Tobias in Latin.*

'What happened to Dr Hostler?' Sarah asked. 'We haven't met him.'

'And you won't,' the woman said. 'Nasty, bossy little man, he took my Tobias away from me, you know.'

'Where is he now?'

The old woman turned her head away like a child that didn't want to answer an adult and began to hum a nursery rhyme.

'Nanny,' Sarah coaxed. 'Where is he?'

'Wouldn't you like to know?' she replied in a voice that was now childlike. 'It's all in my book, all in my book.'

Sarah saw that after the photographs there was a diary, written in the same bold hand; but as she turned to the entries for recent years the handwriting began to degenerate until it became an indecipherable scrawl. She closed the book and looked down at the old woman, who had now withdrawn into her own lost world.

The door opened behind them and Karen, the maid, entered the room carrying a tray.

'I'm sorry,' she said. 'I didn't expect to find anyone with her.'

'Nanny has been telling us about the family, Karen,' Sarah said. 'What happened to Doctor Hostler?'

'Don't know, Miss,' she answered as she began to spoon-feed

the old woman. 'He just went away. He was the boys' tutor. Sir Silas wouldn't allow Tobias to go away to school.'

'What happened to his parents?'

'That was terrible,' the maid said in a suddenly hushed voice. 'They drowned on Gaudy night, twenty years ago. It was after the ball. Master Tobias's father was a wild one, like all the family. He went swimming in the lake for a bet. He just vanished. They say Tobias's mother was mad with grief. She wouldn't take off her dress for two days, then she went missing. They searched everywhere for her. But it was no use. They think she threw herself after him. They drained the lake but they never did find her body.'

There was a silence, and to Sarah the room now seemed distinctly colder.

Then the old woman suddenly spoke in a brisker tone: 'I'm going to have my nap now,' she announced. 'If you see Scroat, tell him I know where my butterscotch has got to, he's been feeding it to his horses as usual.' And she lay back and closed her eyes.

Sarah and Jane left the room and descended the stone staircase. As Sarah had thought, it did lead into the stableyard. When they stood in the cold wet air, Jane took a deep breath. 'My Lord. I don't believe this place is real. For Lord's sake let's go riding.'

After a few minutes' searching, they found two grooms in a whitewashed little room that was hung with harnesses. They sat in a warm fug created by a paraffin stove and cigarette smoke. Both had pinched faces and greasy hair, and one had two missing front teeth, as they could see when he leered at them. 'Are you some of the crumpet come for the revels, then?' he asked.

To Sarah's surprise, Jane Crow now became rather grand. 'I am Sir Toby Nightingale's cousin, Miss Crow, and this is my companion,' she said sharply. 'Sir Toby told me you would provide us with suitable horses.'

The effect of Nightingale's name on the two men was impressive. They scrambled to their feet and almost cringed before them.

'Sorry, Miss,' the one with all his teeth said humbly. 'We didn't know as you was part of Sir Toby's family.' They made curious motions with hands and hair and then scurried off. The horses they eventually led out into the yard were a pair of magnificent bays.

'Sweet Jesus, you can see the Arab blood in them,' Jane said with awe.

'Achilles can be a bit skittish, Miss,' the toothless one said to Sarah, when she was mounted. 'Better show him who's boss right away.'

Sarah gathered the reins closer. She had taken lessons in her youth but had never been mounted on a horse of this quality before.

'Where's the best place to ride?' Jane asked.

The toothless one scratched his head. 'Sir Toby's shooting the wood down by the river,' he answered. 'Best to stay over to the south-west part of the estate.'

'How do we get there?' said Jane.

The groom pointed in the direction of the yard gates. 'Take the bridle path to the right as you go out of the yard, that'll lead you to a long meadow. Cross that and you'll come to the steeplechase course. Anywhere to the right of that's fine.'

They followed the instructions and halfway along the bridle path heard the distant coughing bark of Nightingale's gun.

Once into the meadow, Jane Crow spurred her horse and Sarah had to concentrate hard to keep close behind her. Despite her anxiety it was an exhilarating gallop, and she caught up with Jane when she had stopped to canter alongside the railed steeplechase course.

'How are you at fences?' Jane called out.

'I only take them when I have to,' Sarah answered.

Jane leaned forward and patted the neck of her mount. 'I could jump over the moon on this baby,' she said with more enthusiasm than Sarah had heard in her voice before. 'I'm going to take a few,' she said. 'Do you want to try?' and she wheeled her horse away some distance then came back at a gallop to clear the railings easily.

Sarah was tempted, but common sense prevailed. 'I'll just watch,' she called out.

Turning, Jane leaned forward. With a whoop she shouted 'Let's go!' and urged her horse forward.

Sarah cantered beside the course and Jane started to draw ahead. They had gone at least a mile and a half before Sarah could see the ground rising steeply to a winning post positioned on the crest of a hill. Sarah's horse had more left in him and she was closing fast on Jane as they thundered past the finish. Although the wind rushed past her ears Sarah heard a shout of 'Bravo!' and caught a glimpse of Nightingale and Trooper Stone standing at the railings next to the winning post.

They turned the horses and trotted back to the two men. 'Splendid, truly splendid,' Nightingale called out at their approach. 'What capital sport – you ladies must ride in the steeplechase tomorrow.'

'I don't think I'm quite up to the jumps,' Sarah answered when she had recovered her breath.

'But she is,' Nightingale laughed, gesturing towards Jane. 'This is all too delicious. None of those fat rascals will match you.' He slapped his thigh. 'I say, what sport, what sport. Let me lay the bets – we shall clean up.'

'Isn't that cheating?' Jane said.

'No, no,' Nightingale said eagerly, like a child planning a trick. 'It's not cheating, all part of the sport.' He turned to Stone:

'Not a word to a soul, now Trooper, we won't even tell Scroat. Oh, what a splendid lark.'

Sarah looked at Trooper. He looked deeply troubled. His battered face was grey with fatigue and his shoulders were slumped. There was a bovine sadness about him that reminded Sarah of an ailing bull. Remembering the scene below her window the night before, Sarah said, 'Trooper doesn't look too bright this morning.'

'He's all right,' Nightingale answered. 'He had a bad dream last night – thought he saw a ghost.' He handed Stone his gun and game bag. 'Take these back to the house and sleep for a time; ask Pendlebury for one of his sleeping draughts. I'll walk back with the ladies when they've rested.'

Nightingale leaned against the railing when Trooper had set off and took a hip flask from the pocket of his shooting coat. He was about to drink when he remembered Sarah and Jane. 'Sloe gin,' he said, offering them the flask. Sarah smiled and shook her head, but Jane took a long pull and then looked at the flask as if she were trying to see the contents through the silver casing. Finally she handed it back and Sarah saw that Nightingale took another of Pendlebury's pills which he swallowed with the gin. Another several hours of peaceful behaviour, she thought.

When they reached the house once more they found a scene of bustling confusion. The drive was crowded with expensive motor cars and horseboxes; men and women milled about, calling out greetings and embracing one another. Sarah and Jane dismounted, and Nightingale took the bridles of the horses.

Sarah recognised several of the Corinthians and most of their companions, who seemed to be treating the event as office girls would a works outing. Natty Scroat was supervising the unloading of the horseboxes and shouting instructions to the two scurrying grooms who took the horses from their master.

One of the girls was standing with the politician who, Sarah recalled, had hidden his wristwatch. She recognised Sarah.

'Hello,' she said. 'I didn't expect to see you here. Mr Purse told us you was a writer after you'd left the other day.'

The politician glanced at her wearily. 'Not a journalist, are you?' he asked, a smile failing to concealing his evident unease.

'Nothing like that,' she replied. 'I'm writing an historical romance.'

'Well, you've come to the right place,' he said with relief. 'Lots of good material here.'

'So I've noticed,' Sarah answered as she moved away.

She spotted Wedge in the chaos, his emaciated frame clad in a baggy tweed suit: he was ordering two footmen to be careful with the provisions they were unloading from a caterer's van. The butler and his wife were greeting everyone with their customary efficiency and directing other footmen who were weighed down with luggage.

A cheer went up when Nightingale shouted: 'Champagne and a cold buffet are waiting in the hall.'

'No hot dinners, Toby?' a member called. 'Can't you afford a bit of roast beef for your chums now?'

'We're roasting an ox just for you this evening, Paxton, you fat fool,' Toby called back. 'Everyone else will have to make do with your leavings.'

Sarah and Jane stood beside Nightingale now. He put his arms about both of their waists in a proprietorial manner, once more the Regency buck. Sarah could see that the guests were already taking the events in the spirit of a fancy-dress party – but for Nightingale it was real life.

'What do you think of my two beauties?' he asked of the Corinthians who stood nearby.

Another of the girls who recognised Sarah from the Bawdy House leaned forward and whispered: 'Blimey, you've fallen on your feet, haven't you?' Then she winked and said, 'Or maybe it's your backside.'

· 16 ·

Greaves turned from the arterial road and, after a long winding drive, approached the village of Gorton along a narrow lane that cut through a deep gully topped with ancient hedgerows. He knew from his road map that the Thames snaked through this part of the countryside and that when he reached the village the estate of Gaudy would lie close by, just across the river.

The first houses to appear were plain and ugly, faced with pebbledash and separated from the road by scrubby gardens, but the older part of the village was much prettier. The tallest building was a grey stone church with a sharply pointed spire, flanked by horse-chestnut trees. The walled graveyard spread along one quarter of a square-shaped village green. Bigger houses lay to his left, facing the road; the other sides were fringed with cottages. He could only see one public house: it also looked over the road, which now dipped down to the river.

Parking by the church, he found his raincoat and a tweed fishing hat, then set off in the gentle rain to explore. He paused at the public house but after a moment changed his mind and continued walking to where the road made a steeper descent to the river. There was a row of shops here, which he glanced at. The general store did not look promising, but between an off-licence and an antique shop there was a small place that sold sporting goods.

Greaves stopped before the window and studied the rows of fishing rods, river waders, shotguns and a general clutter of country sports equipment. He became aware of a thickset, bearded figure who watched him from inside. The man sat at a little workbench in space cleared to give him a good view of the street. He was shaping the butt of a shotgun, held in a vice, with deft strokes of a spokeshave.

Greaves smiled at the man, who nodded cheerfully in return, and entered the shop to the tinkling of a little bell. He edged through the crowded showcases to the workbench.

'Good morning,' Greaves said.

'Good morning to you,' the man replied in a curious flat monotone.

'I'd like to buy a clasp knife.'

'For any purpose in particular?'

Greaves shrugged. 'Just a good general knife with a locking blade.'

'How much do you want to spend?'

Greaves smiled. 'Money is no object.'

The man laughed, and that sound also had a curious quality. He turned away to look into a display case in the window and Greaves craned over his shoulder. The man's hand roamed over a knife that Greaves like the look of and he said 'How about that one?'

But the man ignored his question and reached for another.

'May I see the one with the bone handle as well?' Greaves asked before the shopkeeper turned round, but he still ignored the request. As Greaves had suspected, the man was quite deaf.

'This is German,' he said, handing over the knife. 'Wonderful steel. It will hold an edge even if you're cutting through stone.'

Greaves nodded his agreement, and paid with a credit card. When they had completed the transaction, the man said, 'Now, what is it that you want to know?'

'Know?' Greaves repeated. 'What makes you think I want to know anything?'

The bearded man smiled. 'You didn't come to Gorton just to

buy a knife; and you're not a tourist, because there's nothing here to see.'

'What else can you tell me about myself?' Greaves asked easily, and for a moment he was reminded of the little girl at Professor Perceval's college. The man cocked his head to one side and scratched his beard with stubby fingers. 'I'd say you were looking for somebody, but not somebody who lives around here.'

'Why?'

'You would have gone to the village policeman if it had been a resident.' He shook his head. 'No, you're looking for someone who passed through.'

Greaves was interested. 'What kind of person, would you say?'

The man smiled again. 'A man, but a bit of a killjoy.'

'What makes you say that?'

'You paused before the pub: that means it was probably a man. Women don't usually go into pubs on their own. But you changed your mind, so you thought he wasn't the type who'd stop for a casual pint.' The man hesitated for a moment, then said, 'Then you looked at the general store, but you saw that the girl on the checkout till sat with her back to the window, so you made up your mind she wouldn't notice anyone who passed the store unless it was a rock star. Well – how am I doing?'

'Fine until now, go on.'

'Then you saw me, and you really cheered up. There's a nosy bugger, you thought. If anyone noticed him, he would.'

'And did you?'

The man stood up and looked at his wristwatch. 'Buy me a pint and I'll think about it some more.'

'It's a deal,' Greaves answered, noticing that his new companion was at least six and a half feet tall.

'I'm Jack Potter,' the man said as he locked up the shop.

'Colin Greaves.' They shook hands and walked the few yards

to the public house. Potter led them into a comfortable bar with a blazing fire, spoilt only by three noisy youths who were playing pool and, until Jack Potter stood at the bar, dominating the space with their loutish behaviour. Greaves glanced at them and saw they were fairly common types: slack faces, tattooed arms, the beginning of beer bellies bulging from their T-shirts, but bodies made powerful by hard farm labour. He was first at the counter and he saw that their eyes narrowed at the sight of a stranger. But their reactions to Potter were different.

'Out,' he said in his flat voice.

'Just having a game of pool, Jack,' one of them whined. 'No harm in that, is there?'

'Out,' Potter repeated.

They made no more protest, but replaced their cues in the rack and filed from the bar. 'Fucking deaf cunt,' one of them said loudly to Potter's broad back.

'I'll forget you said that, Billy Fisher, just this once,' Potter said, watching the youths' reflection in the mirror behind the bar. The door banged quickly behind them.

Greaves took his first swallow and then held the pint up to the light.

'Good stuff, isn't it?' Potter said.

Greaves agreed. Potter reached out and lifted the receiver of the telephone that rested on the counter and dialled a number. The display panel showed when the call was answered, and Potter said: 'I'll be home for lunch at two o'clock, love.' He replaced the receiver and turned to Greaves. 'A man came through here three weeks ago. Obnoxious little fellow. An outdoor type.'

'Did you speak to him?'

'Twice. The first time he bought some fuel for his portable cooker; the second time I sold him a boat.'

'What kind?'

'A lightweight folding canoe. Nice piece of work, made in Taiwan.'

'What did you deduce from that?'

Potter grinned. 'That he was going boating.'

Greaves bought another round. 'What's the lay of the land around here – on both sides of the river?'

Potter dipped his finger in his beer and traced a map on the counter.' This is the village, with woods and farmland each side of us,' he began. 'There's a narrow bridge at the bottom of the road. When it crosses the river it runs due north, inland, alongside the west wall of the Gaudy estate. About a mile downstream, the river widens and there's a little island in the middle of the stream.'

'What's on the north side of the river down here?' Greaves asked, pointing to Potter's beer map.

'That's all Gaudy, there's nothing but the south wall of the estate.'

'And what's the embankment like on that side?'

'Narrow, rough, overgrown with brush and bramble.'

'Not a place you'd choose to camp?'

'No,' Potter answered. 'This is the best place,' he replied, and he put his finger in the circle that represented the island.

'And you'd need a boat to get there.'

'Definitely,' Potter agreed.

Greaves took another swallow of his pint and then looked up at the clock. It was just after 1.30. 'Tell me, do you happen to know a man called Guy Landis?' he asked.

Potter nodded.

'You're a member of his club.'

'That's right, but his granddaughter is the clever one – best detective I've ever played.'

'Played?'

Potter drank some beer. 'You've heard of war games?'

'Yes.'

'We do the same with crimes. Landis sets them up and we have to solve them. I take it you're a new recruit. Landis always makes new members solve one of his puzzles before he allows them to join.'

Greaves laughed. Then he said casually, 'Do you have any of those Taiwan canoes left in the shop?'

If it had been summer, Greaves would not have been able to see where Professor Perceval had landed his boat, but winter had not repaired the crushed reeds where he had pulled his canoe ashore. Stepping carefully, Greaves traversed the little spit of land, making sure he left no marks himself. It was a pear-shaped island, with the tapering end pointing downstream, about eighty yards long and thirty across at its widest part. Luckily there had only been two other visitors in recent weeks. Greaves could read the signs quite clearly. Perceval had camped in the middle of the island. He'd pitched a tent beneath the only oak tree, and cooked on a primus stove. There was no sign of a camp-fire. From the trails he'd made in the long grass, Greaves could see that he had kept to a regular routine: backwards and forwards to where he had dragged his boat ashore on the south side of the island and some trips to the place where he had concealed himself while he watched the walls of Gaudy.

Greaves could also see that another figure had approached Perceval while he lay concealed. The signs of their struggle were evident – more broken reeds, and despite the recent rain the mud of the bank was still churned by Perceval's clawing hands. He now stood close by the spot, puzzled by the little landing stage that was set, without apparent reason, against the high, blank walls of the estate. 'I don't like this, Sarah,' he said softly to himself after a time. 'I don't like this at all.'

Without actually consulting each other, Sarah and Jane had both decided to avoid the other guests who had been arriving all day at Gaudy. They chose the library as the place in the great house where they would be least likely to be disturbed. They settled down in comfortable chairs before the fire with a selection of books, only raising their heads from time to time when the sounds of baying laughter and breaking glass drifted faintly in their direction.

Sarah was absorbed by an illustrated volume on dog-breeding but after a time she became aware of Jane's restlessness.

'What's the matter?' she asked, when Jane had got up for the third time and poked at the log fire.

'I don't know,' Jane said with a shrug. 'This place gives me the creeps, I guess.'

'Well, it won't be for long.'

'What are you reading?' Jane asked.

'A book about dogs. There's quite a lot of books on the subject. Strange considering there are none in the house.'

'I used to have a dog,' Jane said, 'but it didn't live in the house either.'

'What kind was it?'

'A Rhodesian ridgeback,' Jane answered in a distracted fashion. Then she stood up again. 'I think I'll get off the estate for a while,' she said. 'Do you fancy coming with me?'

'Whither thou goest, I will go,' Sarah replied.

'We don't have to if you don't want to,' Jane said hurriedly. 'I don't want to be like Nightingale, ordering the help around.'

'Don't worry,' Sarah said. 'I feel a little claustrophobic myself. Let's go and find the village.'

'What village?' Jane asked.

'There's always a village if you're in the country in England,' Sarah explained. 'Then there's a nearest town. Going into town is a big occasion; going into the village is for ordinary things – like meeting a lover or buying some more postage stamps.'

'Let's hope we meet lovers,' Jane grinned. 'I've got enough postage stamps.'

The rain had stopped when they got to the stableyard. But their expedition was soon thwarted.

'Natty's taken the pony-trap, Miss,' the toothless groom said apologetically. 'To pick up Mr Latimer from the station.'

'How about us borrowing one of the cars?' Sarah asked.

The groom shook his head, 'It ain't hardly worth it. Takes nearly half an hour to get to the village. By the time you got back, the gates would be locked up.'

'That's all right,' Sarah said. 'Just give me the key, we'll let ourselves back in.'

The groom laughed as if he was dealing with wayward children. 'You can't have the keys to Gaudy, Miss,' he said, amused by their presumption. 'Only Sir Toby has them. Besides, no one comes in or out of the estate during the revels, everybody knows that.'

'What happens if someone insists?' Jane asked.

The groom shook his head. Clearly such an eventuality was beyond his comprehension.

Slowly the two women walked away from the stables. When they reached the front of the house, they found Latimer dismounting from the pony-trap dressed in a suit of particularly lurid tweeds. Both the women were glad to see him.

'Have you heard from Colin Greaves?' Sarah asked as they entered the house.

'Not a peep,' Latimer answered. 'God knows what he's up to.'

Then they heard Natty Scroat calling out: 'Mr Latimer.' When he had his attention, he said, 'Will you tell Sir Toby I've had to go into the village.'

'I thought that wasn't allowed?' Sarah said.

Scroat looked at her with an unblinking expression, like a lizard contemplating an insect. 'It's an emergency,' he said without taking his eyes from Sarah. 'Tell him I found out at the station that we haven't got a match for Trooper Stone any more. His opponent broke his back in Croydon last night. I've got to go

195

into the village to telephone, so as to see what can be fixed up in a hurry.'

It was quite dark when Greaves returned to his car and stowed the little boat he'd bought from Jack Potter. The rain had begun to fall again, with greater force than earlier in the day. He suddenly realised that he was very hungry, not having eaten since the night before. Remembering that the public house served food, he walked back and, as he stood in the brighter light at the doorway, saw that his shoes were thick with mud from the riverbank.

He paused to wipe them with a handkerchief and then entered a different bar from the one he had visited with Potter.

A friendly young woman drew him a pint of bitter; but shook her head when he enquired about a meal. 'It's still a bit early for anything cooked,' she said sympathetically. 'But I think I could get you a sandwich if you don't mind eating it in the Old Tap Bar.'

'Anything will do,' said Greaves. 'I don't mind eating it on the doorstep.'

'What would you like then?' the barmaid asked. 'I can do you ham, ploughman's and I think there's some cold sausages.'

'One of each would be fine.'

'Well, you just go and sit in the Old Tap, love, and I'll bring it through presently.'

'Which room is the Old Tap?'

'Next door but one, where the pool table is.'

Greaves entered the bar he had been in with Potter and, as he had anticipated, found that the only occupants were the three youths who had been ejected earlier.

They stopped their game when he entered, watching to see if he was accompanied by Potter. When they were sure he was alone they gradually began to torment him, like three cats with only one mouse to share. Greaves went to sit on one of the bar stools.

'Don't sit there,' one of them ordered. He wore a studded leather jacket and gave the command without taking his eye from the ball he was about to strike. Greaves marked him as the leader. Although he was not as tall as the other two, his neck was thicker and there was more bulk around his shoulders.

'Where do you wish me to sit?' Greaves answered quietly.

'Where do you wish me to sit?' the leader mimicked to his companions. 'Where shall we tell him to sit, Arnie?' he said to one of the others, who wore a black T-shirt and heavy silver rings on each hand.

'Fucking yuppies don't deserve a seat,' the third one interjected. Greaves noticed he had a dagger tattooed on his forearm.

'That's right, Brian,' the leader continued as he took another shot at the pool table. 'We don't like yuppies coming around here, buying up our cottages.'

Greaves drank some beer before he addressed them again. 'I assure you, I have no intention of settling in your village.'

Just then the barmaid entered with his sandwiches. She saw the three youths grouped close to Greaves, who now stood against the bar, and said, 'Are you behaving yourself, Vince? We don't want any trouble in here.'

'No trouble, Shirl,' Vince replied. 'We're just having a chat like with this yuppie.'

'Would you like to eat in the other bar?' she whispered to Greaves. He smiled and shook his head. Shirl glanced at the youths for a moment and then shrugged and left the room.

Vince turned back to the table and this time missed the shot. 'Bollocks,' he said angrily, then turned to Greaves who was now eating a ham sandwich: 'You put me off my stroke.'

'I'm very sorry,' Greaves replied. 'Perhaps I can buy you a drink to compensate.'

'You can buy me a large Bacardi and Coke; and one for my mates here,' Vince said, but there was no friendliness in his voice.

'As you wish,' Greaves said, turning to gain the barmaid's attention. She came from the other bar and served the order. 'And some crisps,' Arnie said. 'Salt and vinegar.'

'I want prawn flavour,' Brian ordered.

'Shall I buy a selection?' Greaves suggested, taking off his raincoat and placing it on the stool beside him.

Vince laughed. 'Don't you yuppies have no pride?'

Greaves considered the question, then shook his head. 'Pride goeth before a fall,' he answered.

'You're yellow,' Arnie said as he crammed beef-flavoured crisps into his mouth.

'Somewhere between the shades of canary and daffodil,' Greaves agreed.

'Fucking London pansy,' Vince said in disgust and he turned back to the table. 'I'm going to eat you with my packet of cheese and onion when I've won this game.'

Just then the bar door opened and Natty Scroat entered. 'Evening, Natty,' the youths chorused. Scroat nodded and ordered a large whisky.

'How's everything over at Gaudy?' Vince asked.

'None of your fucking business,' Scroat answered. 'I know who's been taking pheasants this winter.'

'We ain't been on the estate, Natty,' Arnie called out. 'We can't help it if they fly over the walls.'

'Just as long as you lot don't fly over the walls,' Scroat said.

'Fat bloody chance of that,' Vince replied. 'The last three lads who tried climbing into Gaudy ended up in hospital.'

'Did you know them?' Scroat asked.

Vince paused and chalked his cue. 'I know Danny Woods. He showed me the scars he got from the spikes. Nearly killed him, they did.'

Scroat ignored them and went to the telephone. He dialled a number and it was answered immediately.

'Cohen, it's Natty Scroat here. I need a match for Trooper tomorrow night, have you got anybody?' He listened for a few moments and then said, 'Well I can't help it if he fractured his skull last time. It was a fair fight. What about that Jamaican kid? He looked useful ... Oh, inside is he, well haven't you got anybody?' There was a pause and then Scroat hung up the receiver.

He turned to the room and looked at Greaves, who had just finished his sandwiches, then at the youths who had been listening to his conversation. 'Do any of you want to earn five hundred quid?' he asked. The youths laughed. 'What, fighting Trooper Stone?' Vince answered with another snigger. 'He ain't human. I'll fight him if I can use a tractor and a shotgun.'

'How about all three of you then?' Natty pleaded. 'I'll give you five hundred each, now that's reasonable.'

'Jack Potter will be in any minute,' Vince said. 'Why don't you ask him?'

'That's an idea,' Scroat answered. 'What time does he get here?'

'Six-thirty on the dot,' Brian answered.

Greaves looked at his watch. He had only ten minutes in which to impress Scroat. 'I think I'd like you to buy me a drink now,' he said to Vince.

The youth turned with an incredulous expression on his face. 'Are you talking to me?' he answered.

'I don't mind which one of you buys it,' Greaves answered. 'You all smell equally bad.'

Vince put down his cue and walked slowly over to Greaves, his arms hanging loosely at his sides.

'Now that's your first mistake,' Greaves said pleasantly, leaning back against the bar, with his elbows resting behind him. 'You would probably have found a weapon useful.' At the edge of his vision Greaves could see Natty Scroat in the corner, watching with rapt attention. Vince stood so close to him now that Greaves could still smell the onion crisps on his breath.

'I could take you, with my little fucking finger,' Vince said. And he began to raise his fists.

Greaves had a complicated decision to make. In normal circumstances he would have finished the job as quickly as possible, but he needed to put on an impressive display for Scroat so he was going to have to make this look flashy and spin things out a bit.

As Vince lumbered towards him, adopting a clumsy fighting posture, all the vulnerable spots at the front of his body were exposed. Greaves could have put him down quickly, but he ignored his training; instead he struck forward with his upper body so that his forehead smashed into the bridge of Vince's nose. Painful; but not a finishing blow.

Vince reeled back, slightly stunned, until he sprawled against the pool table. He shook his head and looked down at the blood he had wiped from his nose. Slowly his expression changed from amazement to sheer animal rage. 'I'm going to fucking kill you for that,' he said thickly and pushed himself forward again.

Greaves called on the boxing he had been taught at school, rather like a ballet dancer recalling how to waltz. Vince swung a haymaker at him, which he side-stepped. Remembering to use his fist rather than an open hand, Greaves punched him in the kidneys then stepped back. Vince grunted in agony and swung again. Greaves swayed away to avoid the flailing fists and then came forward to deliver two straight lefts which drew blood from Vince's mouth.

Roused like a fighting bull now, Vince advanced again, trying to kick Greaves with his heavy leather cowboy boots. But Greaves caught one of the legs and, with a twisting heave, threw him on to his back. His companions stood by, open-mouthed at the turn of events, until Vince called out, 'Come on, give me a hand with this fucker!'

Greaves saw that they both took a firm grip on their billiard cues before edging towards him. It was time to drop the Marquess of Queensberry rules.

He had chosen to fight at a point in the room where tables narrowed the area so that they had to come at him one at a time. Arnie was first, and to Greaves's relief he saw that he had chosen to wield his cue like a club, rather than a rifle with a bayonet, which was much more difficult to counter. Greaves picked up a chair, and when Arnie aimed the first vicious swing at his head he blocked the blow easily. Arnie attempted to swing again, but was too late. Greaves kicked with careful precision and dislocated his opponent's kneecap. Arnie collapsed like a tower of playing cards and rolled away screaming.

The kick had been delivered with such speed that Vince and Brian could not see why their friend was out of the action. They paused, puzzled, and then Brian edged forward, muttering, 'You cheating bastard.' He held his own cue ready to swing and expected that Greaves would fall back, but he was sadly misguided. Before Brian could use his weapon, Greaves dropped the chair and delivered an open-handed thrust to his solar plexus. The intense pain shocked Brian's entire nervous system: the cue fell from his hands and he rocked, wide-eyed, the breath suddenly driven from his body. Greaves pushed him over by cupping his hand under his chin. Vince was the only one left standing now and he was filled with fighting madness, which made him a much more dangerous opponent.

He looked around wildly and snatched Greaves's empty beer glass. Holding the handle, he smashed it against the counter and held the jagged remains out before him. Two writhing bodies lay on the floor between them. It was not the best surface for fancy footwork, Greaves decided.

'Come on!' Vince shouted. 'Come on! I'm going to fucking gut you.'

Greaves had to lure him back on to safer ground.

'You couldn't gut a rabbit with that,' Greaves answered contemptuously and he turned his back on Vince and stood facing the door. With a scream of hatred, Vince leaped at him, aiming the broken glass at the back of Greaves's neck. As Potter had earlier in the day, Greaves turned his head slightly and used the mirror behind the bar. With careful timing he moved his head just before the jagged edge was about to rip into him. The hand holding the glass smashed through the window in the top of the door and Greaves swung his body with full force, ramming his elbow into Vince's exposed belly. Then he hit him once on the jaw. Vince went down heavily, his hand dragging on the broken glass of the window. Blood from his lacerated wrist spurted in a fountain across the floor of the bar. Greaves moved quickly. He took the muddied handkerchief he had used to clean his shoes, snapped one of the pool cues and fashioned a tourniquet. When he looked up, Natty Scroat was standing over him.

'How would you like to earn a thousand pounds?' Scroat said.

'I thought you'd never ask,' Greaves replied.

'Come on,' Natty said, 'The Old Bill will turn up in a minute. They've already phoned.'

'Hold on to this until an ambulance arrives,' Greaves instructed Vince, who was now coming around. He placed the youth's hand on the piece of broken cue.

'Have you got a car?' Natty asked when they got outside.

'Over here,' Greaves answered.

Scroat patted the pony that was waiting in the darkness, then quickly unhitched it from the trap. He slapped its rump twice, and the pony ambled on to the village green. 'I'll be back for you later,' he called out and they made their way to the Riley.

'So how much fighting have you done?' Scroat asked as he directed Greaves across the bridge and into the lane that ran alongside the walls of Gaudy.

'None here,' Greaves improvised. 'But I worked on the West Coast of America for a couple of years.'

'Funny your face hasn't been messed up,' Scroat continued. 'Street fighters gets a worse battering than regular boxers as a rule.'

'I was careful,' Greaves continued. 'That was my gimmick. Gentleman Johnnie, they used to call me. They even made bets on when I'd finally get my nose broken.'

'Well it could be tomorrow night, lad,' Scroat said in satisfaction. 'You'll be matched against Trooper Stone and he ain't like one of those farm boys back there.'

'I'll take my chances.'

'That you will, lad, that you will,' Scroat agreed, and he sat back happily in the passenger seat until they reached the gates of Gaudy.

A footman had been posted to allow Natty Scroat to re-enter the grounds. Greaves watched with interest as they drove through the great gates. 'I don't suppose you're bothered by burglars,' he observed, when he had noted the locking of the gates.

'They can't come through here and they can't get over the walls neither. There's razor wire up there and rolling spikes. Plenty of experts have tried to burgle Gaudy. They usually ends up in the hospital.'

'Who owns all this?' Greaves asked innocently.

'Sir Toby Nightingale,' Scroat replied. 'A real sporting gentleman.'

'I know the type,' Greaves answered as they approached the house.

When they had parked in the stableyard Scroat sat scratching his chin. It was clear that he was struggling with some inner decision.

'What's the problem?' Greaves asked.

'It's like this,' Scroat said awkwardly. 'I'm not sure how you should be treated while you're here.'

'How about with common courtesy?' Greaves suggested helpfully.

Scroat looked at him again. 'Are you real gentry, or is that just the airs you put on?'

'I once held the Queen's commission, and that stated officially I was an officer and a gentleman,' Greaves answered.

Scroat was still unsure, 'I'd better let Sir Toby decide,' he said. 'Until then you can consider yourself one of the hired help.'

Having made that decision, Scroat let Greaves carry his own bag into the house. As they crossed the entrance hall they saw a stream of men in dinner jackets descending the staircase, led by Nightingale, who stopped when he saw the pair. 'Who the devil is this, Natty?' he called out sharply.

'The man to fight Trooper Stone, Sir Toby,' Natty replied. Greaves looked up at the sea of faces that stared down at him, and saw Latimer among them. They exchanged glances; but Greaves showed no sign of recognition and Latimer followed his example.

'The hell he is!' Nightingale bellowed. 'What about the Medway Mauler?'

'Broke his back in Croydon last night, sir, but this lad is as good as I've ever seen.'

'You've watched him fight?' Nightingale demanded. 'Where?'

'In the Fox and Goose, Sir Toby, just now. He put down three of them, and they was using billiard cues.'

'Yokels in the Fox and Goose don't sound like much opposition.'

'He's good, sir, on my word.'

'Your word, you blackguard,' Nightingale said softly. 'I'll decide this matter. Bring him to the hall in ten minutes.'

'As you say, Sir Toby.'

Scroat led Greaves into the servants' quarters, where footmen, maids and kitchen hands moved about with hurried efficiency, preparing food and drink for the guests. No one took any notice of him when he dumped his bag on a table in the corner and sat down while Scroat lit a cigarette.

'Where were all the women upstairs?' Greaves asked.

'It's the Corinthian dinner tonight,' Scroat explained. 'Just the men. The women have their meals in their rooms.'

'Don't the men and women ever get together?'

'Oh, they do some of that right enough,' Scroat said. 'But it comes later.' He glanced at his watch and said, 'Right, let's get upstairs again, Sir Toby will be ready to see you now.'

The Corinthians were gathered in the great hall when they ascended. Greaves looked around the ancient walls at the rows of weapons and ragged battle flags while Scroat walked ahead of him across the stone-flagged floor to where Nightingale stood warming himself before a vast fireplace. He was chatting to a group of fellow Corinthians and ignored Greaves until he had finished telling of his dark horses for tomorrow's race. Then he turned and looked Greaves's slim frame up and down slowly before he spoke again.

'Trooper's got at least six inches on him, Scroat. He won't last one round,' he said dismissively.

'He's very fast, sir,' Scroat pleaded.

Nightingale looked Greaves over again. 'Trooper must go at least sixty pounds heavier.'

'He's very strong,' Scroat replied.

'And endowed with the divine gift of speech,' Greaves added, growing tired of being examined like a farmyard animal.

'You don't talk like a professional prize fighter,' Nightingale answered sharply.

'I wouldn't claim it as the major preoccupation of my life.'

'So how would you describe yourself?'

Greaves thought he was gaining the measure of Nightingale and knew he needed to display some flashy accomplishment that would intrigue his host. 'Poet, sportsman, soldier of fortune – and latterly gentleman of leisure,' he answered.

'So you consider yourself a poet?' said Nightingale, and he turned his head as he spoke as if it were a question asked by all of the Corinthians who now crowded around them.

'Others have,' said Greaves.

'Then give us some of your verse,' Nightingale ordered.

Before he began, Greaves stepped behind Nightingale and took a long poker from the corner of the great fireplace. He plunged it into the hot coals, then dusted his hands and turned to address the room. Gradually the great hall fell silent and Greaves bowed towards his host. 'To be a Nightingale,' he announced. A ripple of comments passed among the crowd. They fell silent when Sir Toby held up a hand. Greaves began:

> 'Some birds chatter, some birds steal,
> some birds live in cages,
> but the strangest bird is the Nightingale,
> that's lasted through the ages.
> This cunning bird can't fly or sing,
> and its hand it never turns,
> for it built its home
> in a house of stone
> and lackeys catch the worms.'

There was a heavy silence in the great hall when Greaves finished his piece of doggerel. It was as if all the Corinthians were holding their breath in anticipation of their host's reaction. As they watched, Nightingale stood with his hands plunged into his pockets, a deep frown of concentration on his brow.

Finally he spoke, almost to himself: 'By, God, that's clever,' he said at last, in a soft voice that was filled with admiration. Then he shouted: 'Have you ever heard anything as clever as that, Pendlebury?'

'Never in my life, Toby,' Pendlebury agreed.

Nightingale gave a chortling laugh. 'Lackeys catch the worms! By my coat and trousers, that's what I call smart. The strangest bird is the Nightingale, eh, eh,' he repeated, nudging Greaves in the ribs. 'You're a capital fellow, pity to knock out your brains on Trooper's fists. That's a precious gift you have. House of stone, brilliant I say – brilliant.'

He took a glass of champagne from a footman's tray and handed it to Greaves. 'But have you got the bottom to put up a good fight with Trooper? That's the big question.' He gestured about him. 'After all, we can't disappoint these chaps, can we? Takes a lot of guts to go up against my man, you know.' He appealed to his fellow Corinthians. 'Does he have the bottom?'

None of the men in the room seemed prepared to give an opinion on the subject, so Greaves decided to answer the question for them. He turned to the fireplace once again and drew out the long poker he had thrust into the hot coals. About four inches of the iron rod now glowed white hot. Swinging it in an arc, which caused several Corinthians to step quickly aside, Greaves raised it to his mouth and then deliberately ran the tip along his tongue. A small puff of steam rose where the white-hot metal made contact with flesh, accompanied by a satisfying hiss.

'My, God,' Nightingale said in astonishment, 'What kind of trick is that?'

'It's no trick,' Greaves answered casually. 'Anyone can do it.'

'Anyone?' Nightingale repeated.

'Anyone with guts.'

'Is that so, Pendlebury?' Nightingale asked. The doctor nodded as he pushed forward through the crowd by the fire. 'It's the same principle as walking on coals. I've heard it's done, but never witnessed it until now.'

'So it's just a trick?' said Broome, Pendlebury's son-in-law.

'Will you do it then?' said Nightingale. Broome laughed uneasily. 'I think not. I've no desire to work in a circus.'

Nightingale pushed the poker back into the fire and turned to the rest of the Corinthians. 'Who will be the first to emulate our friend?'

As Greaves expected, there were no volunteers. 'No one?' Nightingale said. 'Not one man bold enough to match the stranger?'

The silence continued. Nightingale pulled the poker from the coals, held it up to the others and drew it along his own tongue, producing the same hissing puff of steam. Then he cast it aside to clatter in the grate and seized a glass of champagne, which he drank in one draught, to the cheers of his guests.

'By, God, this man is matched against Trooper Stone,' Nightingale shouted. He turned back to Greaves and, linking arms, led him across the room. 'You must understand that if you fight tomorrow night you must stay until the end of the Gaudy revels. There's no leaving the estate. Are you prepared to stand by the rules?'

'I am.'

'Splendid,' Nightingale said jovially. With his arm around Greaves's shoulder, he went on: 'Come and sit with me at dinner, I want you to teach me that verse.' On their way to the dining room Nightingale asked, 'What's your name?'

'Colin Greaves.'

'You know, a fellow like you should join us in the Corinthian Club,' Nightingale said. 'There's no need to worry, I shall make sure Pendlebury gives you the very best of medical attention when Trooper's done with you tomorrow night.'

Nightingale sat Greaves to his right at dinner and insisted he repeat the verse several times so that he could learn the words.

Greaves managed to conceal how little he was drinking and noticed that halfway through the meal the quality of the wine changed. The other members did not seem to realise. As the butler came to Greaves's side and poured more claret into his glass the two men watched each other. Greaves knew that the butler was now serving an inferior vintage, and no doubt pocketing the difference, but somehow he seemed to know that Greaves was there under false colours as well. The two men continued looking impassively into each other's eyes until the butler slowly winked.

When the long meal was over Scroat was sent to summons the ladies. Greaves took his opportunity to slip away and went to a lonely bed, escorted by a silent footman. His room had a balcony and he stood for a few minutes in the darkened night looking south, where the river flowed beyond the walls, and listened to the childish commotion the Corinthians made when they were at play.

He was about to turn back into the room when two high wailing howls echoed around the sleeping countryside. It was a strange sound, almost plaintive, yet it seemed to chill him more than the night air. With a slight shudder he turned away from the window and stood quite still in the darkness. The sound had ceased now. There was nothing but the distant sounds of the Corinthians below and the nearby ticking of a clock.

· 17 ·

The following morning Sarah was ready for her breakfast; she had eaten lightly the night before. Going down ahead of Jane she made her way to the hall where to her astonishment she found Colin Greaves sitting alone at the vast table. A footman at least fifty yards away was presiding over the food which was kept warm beneath vast silver salvers.

'What on earth are you doing here?' she asked when she sat beside him.

'Aren't you glad to see me?'

'Of course I am, but how did you get in? This place is like a prison camp.'

Greaves looked about him. 'Nice cells,' he answered, and just then Jane descended the staircase. She was equally surprised to find him there.

'Our fellow guests don't appear to be early risers,' Greaves noted, looking around the empty hall. Then he explained the sequence of events that had brought him to the table.

'Did you say you fought three of these guys in the public house?' Jane asked when he had finished. Greaves had skimped the details of the fight.

'One at a time,' he answered. 'They weren't very big.'

'So you think you can take on this Trooper Stone?'

'I have no intention of finding out,' Greaves replied. 'I want us all to get out of here – this morning.'

'You think this guy Professor Perceval was murdered?'

Greaves glanced around, but there was no one in the room except for the distant footman at the table of silver dishes. 'I can't be sure if he's dead or not,' he said quietly, 'but I don't think it's safe here. Nightingale is as unstable as mercury. Anything could happen.'

Jane looked down into her coffee cup. 'You guys go, I'm staying,' she said.

'Why, Jane?' Sarah asked. 'Colin has told us how dangerous it is here. If he says so, we ought to get out.'

'This family owes me,' she replied firmly. 'Whatever happens, I'm not going until I hear the will read tomorrow morning.'

'The will,' Sarah said. 'Damn, I forgot that.'

Jane looked up at them. 'There's no need for you to take the risk. Why don't you both take off now?'

Sarah and Greaves exchanged glances. 'We stay,' Sarah said, then she forced a smile. 'Besides, I want to see if you can win the steeplechase.'

Greaves looked to see if she was serious. 'Are you riding in a race?' he asked.

Jane nodded.

'What an active lot we are,' he said drily. 'You taking part in the sport of kings and me taking part in the sport of idiots.' He slapped the table. 'That's settled then: we stay until the will is read – but then we clear off. While you two are racing, I'm going to find a way out of here, just in case we want to leave in a hurry. From now on we'd better not look too chummy.'

Sarah looked over his shoulder. 'Here's Latimer,' she said.

The solicitor saw them and hurried over. 'I looked in your rooms to tell you Greaves was here,' he said, 'but you'd already come down.'

'Do you know what happened to him yesterday?' Jane asked.

'No. It was impossible for us to speak last night,' he said.

'We'll go and change. You can tell him all about it,' said Sarah, and told him where their rooms were located.

Greaves poured more coffee when they had departed. He retold his story, while Latimer consumed a substantial breakfast. When they had both finished, Latimer looked thoughtful and said, 'I think that finding a way out would be a wise precaution.'

'Do you have any suggestions?' Greaves asked.

Latimer stirred his coffee while he answered. 'I'm afraid not.'

'I thought you were familiar with the place?'

Latimer smiled. 'Oh, I've been here plenty of times, even as a child. But there's a line between employee and master that one doesn't cross. At least, the Nightingales always made that clear to my family.'

'It's a shame they weren't a little more friendly.'

'I'm beginning to think I should have gone to the police with my doubts now,' Latimer continued. 'It all seems to be getting even more dangerous than I envisaged.'

'What would you have told them?' Greaves asked. 'It's all pretty circumstantial. Even now I've got no real proof.'

Latimer speared a final piece of sausage that Greaves had thought he was going to leave. 'It may be as you say,' he added with a sigh.

'So you're sure you don't know any weak spots in the walls?'

Latimer shook his head. Then he thought again. 'Wait a minute,' he said slowly. 'There may be a way off the estate I don't know about.'

'Go on.'

'It's just something coming back to me.' He looked up at the high ceiling and tapped lightly on the table. 'I know Sir Silas used to go bathing every morning of the year, no matter what the weather was like.'

'Yes?'

Latimer looked at him. 'He always used to say he swam in the river, not the lake; something about preferring moving water. It's a long way to the river if you go via the main gate. Perhaps there is a gate or some other way.'

Greaves remembered the little wooden jetty. 'Of course,' he said. 'And I thought it was for a boat. It's for bathing.'

'What is?' Latimer asked. Greaves told him of his discovery the day before.

'It may be the solution,' Latimer said sceptically, 'but it's a bit of a long shot.'

Greaves smiled grimly. 'No, that's it. There must be a way out to the river near there. I'll find it.'

'Do you want me to help?'

'No,' Greaves answered. 'Better to go on my own.'

'If you think that's best,' Latimer replied, but his voice was still full of doubt.

Greaves decided to consult a map of the estate before he set out, but was unlucky when he searched the library. Despite the excellence of the index, no information on the grounds was to be found. Disappointed, he made his way to Sarah's room and sat on the end of her bed while she changed into her riding clothes.

'I shall just have to go tramping off about the grounds,' he said rather grumpily, 'and hope I can find it by dead reckoning.'

'There's a blue silk shirt in the wardrobe,' Sarah called out. 'Will you pass it to me.'

Greaves did as he was asked. He failed to secure the door latch and the wardrobe door swung half open. When he took his seat on the foot of the bed again he saw Sarah's naked form reflected in the mirror set in the door. He took no more than a cursory glance; no point in yielding to temptation just now. Sarah struggled into her tight breeches and, buttoning up her blouse, turned to see his back reflected in the same mirror. 'So it's true,' she said with a smile. 'You really are a gentleman.'

He turned round and said ruefully, 'Looking is all I get to do these days.'

Sarah had a sudden thought. 'Why not try Nanny Parsons?'

'For sex?'

'Don't be silly, she's about a hundred years old.'

'Who is?' Greaves asked.

'Nanny Parsons,' Sarah said. 'Up the staircase at the end of this corridor. She's lived here for ever. I bet she knows everything about Gaudy.'

'I suppose it's worth a try.'

'Give her some sweets if she's cantankerous,' Sarah warned. 'They're in a box by the door – and don't forget to refer to Nightingale as Master Tobias.'

Greaves followed her directions and found himself before the iron-bound door. He knocked and a voice called for him to enter.

'Who are you?' the old woman demanded.

'A friend of Tobias, Nanny,' Greaves replied, remembering Sarah's instructions.

'Tobias doesn't have any friends,' the old woman said suspiciously. 'Sir Silas won't permit him to play with the children from the village.'

'I'm not from the village.'

'I thought not. You don't sound like them. How did you meet Tobias?'

'In London.'

'Well I'm glad he's getting out more. It's not good for him to spend so much time at Gaudy. He won't meet a nice girl in this house.' She looked about her in a distracted fashion. 'There were two young women in here recently, but they weren't the right type. Both of them were dressed like grooms. Girls like that would be a bad influence.'

'I shall bear that in mind,' Greaves answered.

The old woman looked up sharply. 'You're not laughing at Nanny, are you?'

Greaves shook his head and looked around for the box Sarah had told him about. 'Would you care for one of these?' he asked.

This time she made a careful selection before putting a chocolate into her mouth.

'I want your help to give Tobias a nice surprise,' Greaves said.

'What kind of surprise?'

'Do you remember where Tobias used to bathe with Sir Silas when he was a little boy?'

'Of course I do. I can remember everything, you know.'

Greaves sighed. 'I wish I could, Nanny,' he said. 'I've forgotten how to get through the wall.'

'Ha,' she exclaimed. 'Then you're a silly boy, aren't you?'

'Yes, Nanny.'

'What can you remember?'

'Nothing.'

'Silly boy, you recall the kennels, don't you?'

'In the stableyard?' Greaves guessed.

'No, no,' she scolded. 'In the woods, close to the wall.' Her old hands gripped the bedclothes. 'That was a naughty thing to do, building kennels to look like a chapel . . . Still, the Nightingales always were up to mischief.' She looked at the box and Greaves offered it again.

'Now, where was I?'

'In the kennels.'

'The lever is behind the altar, where it always was.'

'Thank you, Nanny,' Greaves said. He offered her the box again before he left.

The guests had roused themselves by now. Almost half the men, already dressed in riding silks, were milling about the hall while footmen served punch. The women were dressed in country clothes, but were much too glamorous to be taken for gentry; they looked more like the extras in a costume drama.

Greaves was beginning to feel a little frowsy: he had been wearing the same tweed suit since he left London. He found Natty Scroat in the crowd and drew him to one side.

'Are there any clothes about the house that would fit me?' he asked.

Scroat eyed him up and down as he would a racehorse.

'Old Sir Silas was about your size when he was young,' he said. 'The weight fell off him when he got older.'

Greaves gave him the last of his £20 notes.

'I'll take you up now,' Natty said, pocketing the money.

Scroat was right: the clothes in Sir Silas's changing room fitted Greaves pretty well. Rack after rack of them hung in wardrobes scented with sandalwood. Greaves made his selection while Scroat opened cupboards and dressing tables to reveal layers of shirts, socks and ties, rows of hat-boxes, containing headgear for every conceivable occasion and enough pairs of hand-made shoes to equip half a regiment. He felt quite the dandy when he descended the staircase, dressed in a dashingly cut whipcord suit with a canary yellow waistcoat. He had almost worn a curly-brimmed bowler, but eventually left it behind.

The weather had cleared, leaving a washed, pale blue sky. The air was crisp and fresh as spring water. While Nightingale and Wedge inspected the course, the guests moved in chattering groups from the hall towards the paddock close to the starting line. There were only footmen in the hall now, collecting glasses.

No one paid any attention to Greaves. He strolled out of the house and instead of following the bridle path towards the racecourse he cut across the lawns and beside the lake, heading for the part of the woods where he calculated the bathing spot would be located. Passing the Whirling Pool, he glanced down into its shadowy depths; and for a moment felt a sensation similar to the one Sarah had experienced when she'd looked into the same pit.

Now Greaves became aware of the distant voices of the racegoers. They came faintly on a sudden wind that was spotted with a flurry of raindrops. He hurried on and entered the wood by an overgrown footpath. It wound crookedly through the dense undergrowth deep in the shadow of the trees. After some time he emerged in a clearing, before a little Gothic chapel. Ivy wound about the arched windows and curled across the slate roof. Through the bare branches of the trees he could see the great wall at the edge of the estate.

He entered the little chapel and stood in the gloomy silence looking about him. Instead of pews there were rows of empty stone-built kennels, facing an altar. The place smelt musty and unused. He walked forward and found that there was a hollow space behind the raised dais. Reaching into the dark hollow he felt a lever, which he pulled. With a gentle rumbling sound, a section of the floor behind the altar pivoted upwards to reveal a flight of stairs. The motion was so easy, Greaves guessed the mechanism was controlled by a series of gears and counterweights concealed in the walls of the chapel.

When he descended the staircase into darkness he felt the atmosphere change. It was warmer down here, but there was another quality about the surroundings. Greaves could feel the danger.

In the gloom he saw a gas mantle close to his head. He lit the mantle and it cast a light some way along the length of the tunnel in which he now stood before fading into darkness. Greaves examined the walls that curved above his head: they were brick and very old. Eighteenth-century work, he guessed. They looked sound enough apart from deep indentations where the ancient mortar had crumbled away to powder.

He walked further and found another mantle, which he lit. This light revealed carcasses of meat hanging from hooks in the ceiling, and he saw that the passageway was blocked by a massive iron cage. The air was warm and gagging, with a scent like the part of a zoo that houses mankillers; the smell of wild beasts mingling with the smell of raw flesh.

Two huge creatures slowly emerged from the shadows cast by the hanging meat, and Greaves felt his flesh crawl.

At first, he was not sure they were dogs, so great was their size. As he drew closer, a low snarl came from both of them and their mouths opened to reveal jagged rows of massive teeth. Caught in the gaslight, their eyes gleamed with an eerie, phosphorescent quality. The black coats of the creatures shone like jet, and Greaves could see the great muscles on their shoulders and haunches move as they criss-crossed each other in prowling movements behind the bars of the cage. All the time he watched, they never took their eyes from his face.

Like some primitive man wishing to make a placatory sacrifice to a feared spirit, Greaves looked about him for a way to prepare an offering. At one side of the tunnel he saw a butcher's block with a long knife stuck into it. Hacking a large strip of meat from one of the carcasses, he threw it into the cage.

The dogs leaped on it in a frenzy and in moments tore the flesh to shreds. So violent were their actions that some particles of meat escaped the ravenous jaws and were thrown about them. Greaves stepped back at the terrible sight and his eye was caught by something small and white on one side of the tunnel wall. The object was lodged in a gap between bricks that was left by the crumbling mortar. He was about to reach out and touch it but drew back in sudden horror. It was a human finger; starting to wither, but still recognisable.

A wave of nausea swept over him. Some time recently, the dogs had been fed with a human cadaver. Fighting back his revulsion, he looked beyond the cage and saw that on the other side another flight of steps led up from the tunnel. He hurried away from the hellish place, not stopping until he stood in the woods outside the chapel once again. He breathed deeply in the cold, damp air.

Greaves had known fear before; he had encountered savage enemies; but nothing in his experience equalled this barbaric discovery. Even taking account of the creatures' great size, they would have needed time to eat a whole body. Someone must have butchered the corpse and fed it to them piecemeal. He had no doubt now what had happened to the remains of Professor Perceval – and it meant that Jane Crow was in terrible danger.

Still turning the events over in his mind, Greaves emerged from the wood and distant cheers reminded him of the steeplechase that evidently was now in progress. It didn't seem possible that so little time had passed since his descent into the tunnel, but he now realised it had only been a few minutes.

He set out at a good pace for the course, glad of the fresh air, and soon saw a crowd of spectators grouped around the winning post. By the time he had joined Sarah, the runners had entered the final furlong, and Pendlebury, equipped with a large pair of binoculars, was shouting out the progress of the race to Wedge, who was acting as steward.

'Bradbury and Vehane are in the lead coming to the final fence,' he shouted. 'Closely pressed by McGrath and Haig, but this group is falling back as Nightingale comes to take up the lead. Nightingale is ahead now, but he's being pressed by the woman. Nightingale is drawing away, but no, the woman is staying with him.'

Greaves could see the riders quite clearly. Nightingale was laying his whip on his labouring horse, but Jane Crow was with him every inch of the way. They passed the winning post with nothing between them. Greaves joined in the cheers. Others who had watched the race from other parts of the course were arriving on foot and in a variety of motor cars. The rest of the runners who had survived the race straggled past the winning post, and the crowd ducked under the railings to surge about the tired horses.

'Capital run, by God!' Nightingale shouted out as he accepted a silver mug of champagne from one of the crowd. 'This should go to the winner.' He spurred his mount forward to make a path through the spectators, and handed the cup to Jane Crow.

'I thought you had it,' she answered, taking the drink gratefully.

'You by a nose I think, but at least the horse was mine.'

'Are you sure?' Jane asked, and she handed the remains of the champagne to Sarah who was now standing with Greaves beside them.

'I'm sure,' Nightingale replied, 'but we can ask the chief steward for a ruling, if you wish.' He bellowed to Wedge: 'What did she win by?'

'At least a short head, Sir Toby,' he answered, knowing quite clearly the result his host desired.

'Splendid,' Nightingale shouted. 'A bath now and then a celebratory drink in the hall. You can all pay me my winnings there. And no Bawdy House money – at Gaudy it's coin of the realm.'

Sarah was pleased with Jane's performance in the race. For a time it had blown away the curious claustrophobic atmosphere that hung about her both in and out of the house. But it returned when Jane asked her to come back to the room and choose the clothes she would wear for the rest of the day. The heavy Jacobean furniture and faded wall-hangings somehow depressed her high spirits and she began to long for the time when they would be able to leave.

After choosing suitable tweeds she looked into the bathroom where Jane was soaking in the tub, reading a copy of *Country Life*.

'I thought only schoolteachers and librarians wore that kind of outfit,' Jane said, examining the clothes Sarah had selected. Then she glanced down at her own ample breasts and said, 'If I wear a tweed jacket on top of these, I'll look like an overstuffed sofa.'

'I think the men would know the difference,' Sarah said drily.

'Men!' Jane said. 'They've been looking at these since I was thirteen. The boys used to follow me around calling out: "The cow with big tits and no milk".'

'Boys?' Sarah asked.

'The boys on the reservation,' Jane said and she cast the magazine aside and stepped out of the bath. There was a knock on the door and Greaves called out: 'May I come in?'

'Just a minute,' Jane answered. She wrapped herself in a towel before opening the door.

When Greaves entered the room Sarah noticed his worried expression. 'What's the matter?' she asked.

He hesitated and nodded to Jane. 'I'll wait until you're dressed,' he said. Crossing the room, he opened the door to Sarah's bedroom. The two women exchanged puzzled glances and while Jane put on her clothes, Sarah joined Greaves.

'Is it bad?' she asked softly.

Greaves smiled quickly, without humour. 'I think so,' he replied. 'If you can bear to wait a few more minutes, I'd like to tell both of you at the same time.'

'Is there a way out?'

'I think you and I might manage something on our own, but we're not the ones in danger. The problem is Jane.'

'Why am I a problem?' she asked from the doorway.

'I'm pretty sure someone is planning to kill you,' he answered flatly. 'That's why I think it is imperative that you stay close by us until we can all get away later tonight.'

Jane shook her head. 'Look, I've already told you, I'm not budging from this place until the will is read.' She sat down on the bed and held her hands up appealingly. 'It's not because I'm greedy – believe me. It's just as I said: I feel this family owes me something – something they took away from my grandmother. Now the debt's due for payment, and I've made myself a promise I'm going to collect.'

Greaves stood up and plunged his hands into the pockets of Sir Silas's whipcord jacket. 'I didn't want to show you this,' he said, drawing out a spotted handkerchief. They watched as he unrolled it between them on the bed. It contained the finger he had discovered in the tunnel.

'Dear Lord,' Jane said quietly.

'Where did you find it?' Sarah asked, looking at the gruesome object.

Greaves described the passageway to them and they both looked at Jane who now sat, head lowered in dejection. 'Of course you're right,' she said finally. 'I'll go with you tonight. What's the plan?'

'It will need courage and a lot of nerve,' Greaves said, 'and you're going to have to do it without me.'

'Where will you be?' Jane asked.

'I'm afraid I shall be fighting Trooper Stone,' Greaves said. He began to explain his plan.

Half an hour later Sarah and Jane joined the rest of the guests in the great hall, where the drink was flowing freely. 'Here comes my spitfire,' Nightingale shouted enthusiastically and he put down his silver cup and held Jane around the waist. 'By God, I almost think we ought to bend the rules of the Corinthian Club for this one,' he called out to the other members. 'What do you say?'

The assembled group raised their glasses and shouted various pledges of agreement.

Nightingale would not be parted from the two of them now. He insisted they sit next to him at lunch and Sarah had to be careful not to succumb to the amount of wine he pressed upon them.

'You've got all afternoon to sleep it off,' he urged when Sarah had refused yet another glass of claret.

'I would sleep for a week if I drank the amount you've managed, Sir Toby,' Sarah said coyly. 'You really are a rascal.' As she spoke, she noted that she was automatically slipping back into the techniques taught to her during her brief employment at the Bawdy House.'

'And what costume are you wearing to the ball tonight?' he asked.

Jane leaned towards him, and when she spoke Sarah realised she had been less successful in avoiding the wine. 'Sarah's got a Fifties-style ballgown,' she said with a slight slur. 'I'm more up to date.'

Nightingale shook his head. 'Oh, dear, that won't do – won't do at all.'

'Why not?' Sarah asked.

Nightingale turned to her. 'It's a Regency ball, didn't anyone tell you?'

'No,' Sarah answered, without much concern. She did not plan to be around for much of the night's festivities.

'Never mind,' Nightingale said happily. 'There's masses of dresses upstairs. The housekeeper will fix you up after luncheon.' Then he leaned forward so that his head rested on the table and soon was sound asleep.

'I think I'd like to go up now,' Jane suddenly said.

'Do you want me to come with you?' Sarah asked.

'No,' she answered, standing up and gripping Sarah's shoulder. 'Stay here, please. I'd rather manage on my own.'

Sarah did what she asked, but watched anxiously as Jane, with slightly unsteady steps, crossed the hall to the staircase.

Like the Dormouse at the Mad Hatter's tea party, Nightingale suddenly raised his head from the table and said in a clear strong voice: 'Scroat, feeding time, see to it.' Then he lowered his head to the table once again. Only Sarah and Greaves noticed the remark; the other guests were now becoming noisy and amorous, pledging love toasts to the ladies or openly fondling their partners.

Sarah could feel the atmosphere changing from cheerful

exuberance to something gamier: the same pervading decadence that had seeped about the rooms of the Corinthian Club. Seeing that couples were now drifting away towards the bedrooms, she caught Greaves's eyes and nodded briefly. They rose and made their way to the staircase.

'Have you seen Latimer?' Greaves asked softly.

'Not all day,' Sarah answered.

As if in answer to his question, they found Latimer with Jane in her room. They were talking when Sarah and Greaves entered. Latimer stood up and looked worried. 'Jane has told me everything,' he said. 'I agree with you completely. The women must leave tonight. I'll go with them.'

'How do you feel?' Sarah asked Jane.

'I'm fine, but I do want to sleep for a time.'

'I'll stay with them,' Greaves offered.

Latimer nodded. 'If you wouldn't mind. I really have to do some work in my room,' he smiled apologetically. 'Life must go on – even the weary business of being a solicitor.'

Sarah had not thought she could sleep, but she drifted off quite quickly. When she awoke again it was quite dark, apart from the gentle glow of gaslight from one corner, where Greaves sat by the open door to Jane's room. He was reading and the effect was somehow peaceful and comforting. It seemed a long time since he had watched over her.

He glanced up when she stirred. 'How do you feel?' he asked.

'All right,' she answered. 'I dreamed a lot.'

'I know,' he replied. 'You moved about quite a bit.'

'How's Jane?'

'Fine. She's still sleeping.'

Sarah glanced at her watch. 'I suppose we ought to see the housekeeper about the correct dresses for the ball.'

Jane entered the room as they spoke, rubbing her eyes. 'Did I hear you say we ought to be getting a move on?' she said.

'I think so,' Sarah answered. 'We'd better find the housekeeper.'

Jane went to a bellrope and pulled. 'Karen will do that,' she said with another yawn.

The maid entered a few minutes later and Sarah explained about the dresses.

'That's all arranged, Miss,' Karen said. 'Mr Latimer's already had a word with the housekeeper. I'm to take you to Sir Toby's rooms.'

'Is Sir Toby there?' Sarah asked.

'I think he's out visiting different guests, Miss,' Karen answered innocently. 'If you'd like to follow me.'

She led them on another bewildering journey, along more corridors and flights of stairs, until they reached a part of the house Greaves recognised. 'These are Sir Silas's rooms,' he said.

'That's right, sir,' Karen answered. 'Sir Toby's just along the corridor. This one here,' she said, stopping before a door.

'I'm going to sort out something to wear myself,' Greaves said. 'I'll join you when I'm done.'

'Where will you find a costume now?' Sarah asked.

Greaves nodded in the direction of Sir Silas's rooms. 'I'll find everything I need in there.'

Toby Nightingale's quarters were surprisingly feminine. The delicate Georgian furniture was upholstered in pastel colours to match the beautiful Chinese carpets. Bowls of flowers stood on practically every surface, and for the first time in the house Sarah saw portraits of women on the walls.

'I would never have taken this for Sir Toby's room,' Jane said.

'These were his mother's rooms once, Miss,' Karen explained. 'The Nightingales never change anything from the past. They just build a new bit on, but everything anyone had before has to go on like that for ever.'

'For ever?' Jane asked.

Karen nodded. 'This wallpaper had to be replaced last year,

Miss. They brought in a man from London to make it by hand. Even the flowers have to be the way Sir Toby's mother wanted them.'

'What about these dresses?' Sarah asked.

'Through here, Miss, in the changing room.'

Four vast tulipwood wardrobes ran the lengths of three of the changing-room walls. There were long cheval glasses that could be adjusted to examine a full-length figure from all angles, and a dressing table covered with beautiful crystal and silver perfume decanters and make-up jars. The room also contained four large leather-bound trunks, that Sarah and Jane could have climbed into together.

Sarah looked into the wardrobes. The fashions stretched back, decade by decade, through the century. 'Look at this,' she said to Jane, holding up a short flapper's dress from the Twenties that was beaded with crystal and pearls. 'It must be worth a fortune.'

'Everything's worth a fortune at Gaudy,' Karen said. 'The Regency period clothes are in the trunks.'

Jane hurried to the first and opened it. It was lined with rose-coloured silk and the fragrance of sandalwood came to them. The dresses were protected by layers of silk and each had a matching cloak, gloves and delicately embroidered slippers.

'This is the one for me,' Jane said firmly as she held up the first dress from the trunk. It was a white Empire-style ballgown, full length with puffed sleeves. Simple, and quite lovely.

'Are you sure?' Sarah asked. 'There's masses more.'

'I'm sure,' Jane answered. She held it in front of her and looked into the mirror. As she did so, a soft cloud of dusty white powder billowed from the dress.

'What's that?' Sarah asked.

'For the moths, Miss,' Karen answered. 'These dresses are all brought out and cared for at least once a month.'

Jane lifted the long white gloves and slapped the dress a few times. Even more powder came out. 'How do you wear a bra with this?' she asked. 'You don't,' said Sarah. 'That was the fashion – some of the more daring ladies of style even went topless.'

'You're kidding?'

Sarah smiled. 'They were liberated times,' she said. 'Both here and in France. When Napoleon was defeated in Russia, he wanted the Paris Ballet to perform without panties to take people's minds off his problems.'

'And did they?'

'The *corps de ballet* drew the line at that.'

Jane continued to hold her dress in front of her while Sarah searched. Eventually she settled on one in the same style, but in the palest of lemon.

'How shall we do our hair?' Jane asked.

'I know the style,' Karen said. 'Yours will be easy. And I can fake something for you, Miss,' she added, looking at Sarah's short mop.

'You know,' Jane said in a sudden, animated voice. 'This might be fun – after all. It's kind of like an adventure, isn't it?'

'I suppose so,' Sarah agreed; but her thoughts kept returning to Greaves's grisly find.

Two hours later they were seated before Jane's dressing table adding the final touches to their make-up when Greaves and Latimer knocked on the door. 'Just a moment,' Jane called out, and they rose to stand before the fireplace. 'Let them in,' Jane told Karen. The maid opened the door and the two men entered and stopped in admiration.

Karen had arranged Sarah and Jane's hair in the correct Grecian style, with soft ringlets about their faces and used some trickery to give the impression that Sarah's matched Jane's in length.

'You both look wonderful,' Latimer said. 'Quite wonderful.'

'You don't look so bad yourselves,' Jane answered. Sarah agreed. The dramatic Regency evening dress suited them both.

'I hired mine from a theatrical costumier's,' Latimer said. 'It isn't quite as splendid as Greaves's.'

'I've even found a snuff box,' Greaves said, taking a beautifully enamelled little container from a pocket in his waistcoat.

'You look angelic with that big white bow tie,' Sarah told him.

'You should have seen me dressed as a choirboy,' he replied, and held out his arm. 'Shall we go down?'

Despite the brooding danger that hung over them, they laughed and chatted easily as they walked the corridor to the grand staircase. As they approached the great hall they heard the sound of an orchestra; it made the sense of anticipation grow even stronger.

Turning at the top of the staircase they looked down. The sight filled Sarah with sudden awe. Thousands of candles illuminated the ballroom, their soft light bringing a unique quality to the scene. Liveried footmen passed among the crowd of guests, who chattered animatedly while the orchestra played a stately air. The men were, for the most part, dressed in the black Regency evening dress of the style Latimer and Greaves wore, but there was a good sprinkling of dress uniforms. Latimer identified Hussars, Lancers, Guardsmen and Rifle regiments.

'You should have worn your dress uniform,' Sarah whispered with a nudge. Greaves laughed. 'The Metropolitan Police didn't exist in Regency times,' he answered.

'I thought you were in the army as well?'

'For a time.'

Sarah looked at the great hall again. She was pleased to see that most of the women wore darker colours; some even had elaborate ostrich-feather head-dresses that swayed gently as they talked. Latimer asked Jane to dance when the bandmaster announced a quadrille.

'I don't know any of this stuff,' Jane replied. 'I can just about manage a waltz.'

'No waltzing at the time of Waterloo, I'm afraid,' Latimer answered. 'Come on, it's quite easy, you just have to watch everyone else and you'll soon pick it up.'

Greaves offered an arm to Sarah. 'Shall we?' he asked.

Latimer's prediction was correct. The girls from the Bawdy House had been well schooled in the dances. With ease they formed rows and patterns, and the movements within these structures came quite easily to the beginners.

Sarah was surprised to find that she was enjoying herself. Perhaps because of the grandeur of their surroundings, the splendid costumes and the gaiety of the music, the Corinthians and their partners were actually behaving like ladies and gentlemen. For the first time since she had been at Gaudy, Sarah didn't half expect to see guests tear off their clothes and begin rutting on the floor. She even liked the punch that Greaves brought her during an interval.

'Delicious,' she said appreciatively. 'I much prefer it to champagne.'

'Take it easy,' he warned. 'It's stronger than you think.'

'What's in it?'

'Fruit juices and some tasteless spirit, I would imagine.'

'Why aren't you having any?'

'Being drunk's all right if you want to go in fighting mad and slug it out,' Greaves answered. 'But Trooper Stone would murder me if I tried that. I shall have to move and think fast if I want to survive.'

Latimer and Jane had come to sit by them on one of the clusters of chairs spread around the edge of the dance floor. Sarah noticed that Jane seemed to be even more exhilarated than she was. She had danced enthusiastically and a sheen of perspiration now showed on her breasts as she continued to gaze about the dance floor, as if she wished to leap to her feet once more. Catching the end of the conversation, Jane said, 'He can only knock you out, can't he? Surely that's not so dangerous.'

'On the contrary,' Latimer said drily. 'If you stood still, on the flat of your feet, facing a trained boxer and let him hit you with all of the power he could muster, the first blow would quite probably kill you.'

'Surely not?' Jane said, looking from one man to another to see if they were jesting.

'It's a fact,' Latimer said without smiling.

'Then why don't boxers get killed all the time?'

'That's the skill of it,' Latimer answered. 'Not getting killed. And managing to hit your opponent while you're defending yourself.'

Jane was not entirely convinced. 'But I've seen the ranch hands fighting on a Saturday night in Apache Point,' she said. 'They go at each other like hell – and they knock each other out. But no one gets hurt really bad.'

'It's not the same,' Latimer answered. 'Believe me.'

Just then, Nightingale appeared before them promenading around the edge of the dance floor at the head of an entourage consisting of the Pendlebury family and Natty Scroat. There was no sign of Trooper Stone. Nightingale examined them through a quizzing-glass he was affecting for the occasion. 'Ah, my sporting set,' he exclaimed, then turned to Greaves. 'But will you win the prize tonight?' he asked. 'I'm offering five to one against you, old boy. What do you say to that?'

Greaves looked at Nightingale's challenging expression. 'I get my purse, win or lose, don't I?' he asked.

'That's the arrangement.'

'In that case I wager it all on myself at five to one.'

'Splendid,' Nightingale replied. 'Did you note the bet, Scroat?' he asked without turning round.

'I have it, Sir Toby,' Scroat answered, as he scribbled in a little book.

Nightingale looked down at Jane and noticed her exhilaration. 'And you, Miss Crow, are you looking forward to the match?'

'I am, but where's your fighter now?' she asked.

'Resting,' Nightingale answered.

'He needs his rest, does he? Just how strong is he, would you say?'

'Oh, I wouldn't bother to say at all,' Nightingale answered with a wave of his quizzing-glass. 'But perhaps I may be permitted to show you something.' He turned his head. 'Scroat, have a footman bring the Edgehill breastplate.'

They waited in silence until Scroat returned with a footman bearing a piece of chest armour, which he held out for inspection. They could see a dent in the surface.

'This was worn by one of my forebears during the Civil War. It's made of steel, and shaped to deflect sword thrusts and musket balls,' Nightingale explained. He tapped the deep dent with his quizzing-glass. 'Last year one of my guests was foolish enough to put this on and challenge Trooper to hit him.' Nightingale laughed and gestured for the footman to take the breastplate away. 'Trooper broke three of his ribs.'

He turned to Greaves again. 'Are you sure you still want the wager to stand?'

Greaves smiled. 'I take it the man in the armour wasn't hitting back?'

'That is correct.'

'It makes a difference, sometimes,' Greaves answered lightly.

'Capital, capital,' said Nightingale. 'I would expect nothing less.' Again he looked at Jane. 'One more set of dances, Miss Crow, then you can watch battle commence.' He was about to depart, but stopped and said, 'By the way, Greaves, who is going to act as your second?'

'I really hadn't given it much thought,' Greaves replied.

'Well, you must old chap, you must. Someone's got to be

there bringing you up to scratch. We must conduct the business in the proper fashion.' He turned to Latimer. 'You must do the honours, my dear fellow.' Latimer started to protest but Nightingale shook his head. 'No, really, I insist. A chap must have a second. Spirit of the sport and all that.' He walked away and Greaves looked at Sarah.

'We can manage,' she said.

Despite the nearness of their escape, Jane did not seem preoccupied with its potential danger. Instead she danced with enthusiasm until a fanfare was blown by a musician, and footmen with blazing torches formed a corridor across the centre of the dance floor.

'Is your man ready?' Nightingale asked Latimer.

Latimer nodded. Nightingale turned to the rest of the assembly and announced: 'Ladies and fellow Corinthians, the prize fight will begin in ten minutes. I advise you to wear your cloaks. The night air is somewhat chilly.' He turned to Latimer. 'Lead your man out,' he instructed.

Along with the others, Sarah and Jane collected the hooded cloaks that they had found in the chests. Jane still seemed elated. 'Can't we just watch a couple of rounds?' she asked when they stood in her room, but Sarah shook her head.

'I want to keep my thoughts clear,' she answered. 'If I see Greaves taking a beating, I shan't be able to think.'

Latimer entered the room. He took a battery-powered torch from beneath his greatcoat and handed it to Sarah. 'I took the precaution of bringing one of these,' he said. 'I think it may be useful.'

As he turned to leave, Sarah caught hold of his arm. 'If Colin is being damaged by that zombie, I want you to stop the fight,' she said urgently.

'I understand,' he answered. He paused and looked at the two women again. 'For God's sake be careful,' he said. Then he hurried from the room.

Sarah looked from her window down into the stableyard at the extraordinary scene being played before her. A ring had been formed by footmen holding blazing torches aloft. Beyond them, high seats had been arranged for the crowd to watch over the heads of the footmen. The flaring torches threw deep shadows in the far recesses of the yard. Sarah could see servants leaning from other windows, craning to gain a good view of the match.

Trooper Stone now stood in his corner with Natty Scroat. His great white body was so huge that he seemed to be in different proportion to the other men below, like a toy from a bigger box. He was stripped to the waist and wore old-fashioned black athlete's tights. When he moved, massive slabs of muscle rippled ominously.

Greaves had just pushed his way into the ring. He had also stripped to the waist, but still wore his evening trousers and dancing pumps. It seemed absurd that he was going to fight the giant facing him. Sarah tried to think of David and Goliath, but Greaves did not have a slingshot.

Now Nightingale stood in the centre of the ring and held up his arms.

'Ladies and Corinthians,' he shouted. 'You are about to witness a bare knuckle prize fight. The contestants will come to the middle of the ring and stand toe to toe at the scratch line.' He pointed to the cobbled surface that was now slick with rain and Sarah could just make out a thin line painted on the ground. 'They will continue fighting until one is knocked down. That will be regarded as the end of the round. If a contestant cannot return to the scratch line at the end of a round, he shall be deemed the loser.' Nightingale looked in turn to Scroat and Latimer. 'Gentlemen, are your men ready?'

'Ready,' they called out.

Sarah turned from the window. 'Time to go,' she said. As she spoke, a sudden roar came from the crowd below.

· 18 ·

Greaves stood in the ring of flaring torches and looked over Latimer's shoulder. 'Have you seen him fight before?' he asked.

'Once,' Latimer answered.

'How does he move?'

'Like a mastodon, but he can't be hurt.'

'We'll see about that,' Greaves answered grimly.

'Gentlemen, come to scratch.' Nightingale called out, and Greaves walked to the line. Trooper Stone towered over him, his little eyes gazing implacably into Greaves's face.

'You commence when I drop my handkerchief,' Nightingale instructed tersely. 'Understand?' Both men nodded.

Nightingale stepped back and his arm flashed down. Trooper Stone immediately struck out with his right and the crowd roared. Greaves swayed away just in time, but Stone caught his shoulder. The speed and power of the blow spun Greaves around and he tripped on one of the raised cobbles. A groan of disappointment arose from the crowd. It didn't look as if it were going to be much of a match.

Trooper returned to the scratch line and Latimer helped Greaves to his feet.

'I thought you said he was slow,' Greaves muttered.

'He moves slow, but he punches like lightning,' Latimer replied. Greaves flexed his shoulder: it felt as though he had been hit with a sledgehammer.

'I'll remember from now on,' he answered.

When they stood toe to toe once more, Greaves waited for Trooper Stone to signal his next move. From the direction in which his eyes flickered, Greaves saw he was going for a repetition of the first attack.

This time Greaves easily evaded the blow and jabbed Stone twice in the stomach. It was like punching a concrete wall. Stone smiled at the lightness of the blows and Greaves noted his opponent's confidence that he could take any amount of punishment in his midriff that Greaves would try to hand out.

Stone now lumbered towards Greaves, his massive arms pumping out like pistons but only striking air as Greaves danced back. Deciding to see if he could make the giant angry, Greaves jabbed out at the scarred flesh above his eyes and saw Trooper blink as the blows landed. Proud of his stomach but worried about his eyes, Greaves noted, and jabbed twice more at the same spot. With satisfaction he saw that his third blow had opened up a tiny cut in the battered flesh. Trooper Stone, roused by the dribble of blood, pressed forward again and managed to land a punch, leaving the mark of his great fist on Greaves's chest. It hurt badly and Greaves wondered how long he could keep going. One lucky blow from his opponent would give Trooper Stone the opportunity to pound him into oblivion.

Sarah and Jane hurried through the darkness with the flashlight playing on the ground before them. They skirted the empty Whirling Pool and were soon in the woods, following the footpath that Greaves had described. In a few minutes they found themselves outside the little Gothic building. 'This is like something from a horror movie,' Jane whispered as they entered the curious dog kennels.

Sarah had no difficulty finding the lever, as Greaves had instructed. The trapdoor opened smoothly and they descended into the tunnel. She lit the gaslight and they caught their breath at the smell that was in such contrast to the clear night air above.

They were prepared for the cage and the sinister atmosphere, but nonetheless the sight of the dogs shocked them. Both stood in silent horror. Despite Greaves's description, they were not ready for such monsters.

'I can't believe it,' Jane whispered finally, 'I can't believe it.'

The dogs, roused by their presence, began to emit low throaty growls and prowled restlessly behind the bars.

'Wait here,' Sarah told Jane. Steeling herself, she walked resolutely towards the cage. The dogs stopped prowling and watched her with glowing eyes.

She found the knife and paused to examine the latches on the doors of the cage. Once inside, it would take about six paces for them to reach the far gate. Sarah took the knife and began to hack off large strips of meat from the nearest hanging carcass. When she judged she had prepared enough, she called Jane.

'Help me to throw the meat into that far corner,' she said. 'Greaves says they're ravenous. When they start to eat, we've got to make a dash for it.'

She started to throw lumps of meat into the spot she had indicated and the dogs began to snarl and tear at the chunks in a frenzy, but when Jane approached the cage, a strange thing happened: suddenly the dogs ignored the bloody flesh and began to throw themselves at the bars before Jane. It was as though the meat no longer existed. Sarah was sure she could have walked past them without effort, but they would have torn Jane to pieces. It was a terrifying sight.

'It's not going to work,' Sarah said eventually. 'We'll have to go back to the house.'

'Ugh,' Jane exclaimed. 'This is disgusting.'

Sarah looked and saw that Jane's cloak was covered with flecks of bloody meat and saliva from the slavering dogs.

They hurried from the tunnel and Sarah suddenly said: 'God, I wonder how Colin is doing?' as they emerged into the chapel.

The fight had continued for some time, but it was not the sort of match the crowd wanted. They would have been happier to see two bruisers stand and batter each other until one was felled. This contest did not live up to their expectations. Trooper Stone shambled around the ring, constantly in pursuit of Greaves, who continued to dance backwards, jabbing at Stone's head. He had opened up another cut above Stone's other eye and the trickling blood irritated the giant and slightly impaired his vision.

Then the accident happened. Some of the spectators had crowded closer to the footmen, and when Trooper Stone hedged Greaves into a corner they thrust forward vigorously and pressed against the men holding the ring. One of them went down and his torch fell upon the cobblestones. As Greaves danced back his foot came into contact with the handle and he became unbalanced. It was only for a split second, but Stone's left fist caught Greaves a devastating blow. He felt as if dynamite had exploded inside his head. Reeling back into the crowd, he was thrust forward again and fell to his knees. Stone was ordered to his corner as Latimer hurried forward to squeeze a sponge over his head.

'How many fingers am I holding up?' Latimer asked anxiously.

'Four – I think,' Greaves replied. His vision was slightly blurred by Trooper Stone's blow and the flickering light of the torches.

Still groggy, Greaves came forward again and Trooper Stone scented the kill. With a grunt of satisfaction, he crowded in and hit Greaves twice in the body. After the humiliations he had been made to suffer he was not going to put Greaves down quickly: he had a score to settle and he was going to take his time.

Greaves managed to shuffle away. Stone came after him and landed three more punches to the body, then decided to concentrate on the face, determined that Greaves would remember this fight for the rest of his life – every time he looked in a mirror.

The first right he aimed landed on Greaves's forehead and rocked him back. He was expecting another blow when suddenly Stone froze. His jaw slackened and his chin came up. 'It's her,' he croaked, a look of sudden horror on his face. The hardened features seemed to dissolve, as though the muscles had turned to melting wax. Unaware of his opponent now, Stone gazed across the ring, eyes transfixed by something beyond the fight. It was long enough for Greaves. He brought back his arm in a jerking motion then struck forward with an open hand, like a snake, to jab his splayed and stiffened fingers into Stone's eyes.

Roaring with pain, the big man reeled back. Blinded, he stumbled forward and began to flail helplessly with his fists. Greaves avoided them easily and changed his target. Bringing his fingers together and using his hand like a spear, he jabbed into Trooper's solar plexus, just beneath the breastbone. Stone's stomach muscles were no protection against this form of attack: it was a heart-stopping blow. The giant stopped flailing and stood, sightless and stunned, his jaw exposed. Greaves put all his weight and strength behind the punch he now delivered. It snapped Stone's lolling head back with such force that his brain smashed against the top of his spine, the massive shock causing an instant blackout. But Stone still stood, swaying as if his vast body had not yet ceased to receive the message. Then he fell forward like a knackered horse, cracking his skull on the cobbled yard.

Greaves stood over the still form for a moment, then turned to hobble back to his corner. As he did so, he saw the figure that was the cause of Stone's fear and nemesis. A woman stood out among the crowd of people who were wearing dark greatcoats or cloaks. She alone wore a white dress that seemed to glow in the torchlight. It was Jane Crow, who had discarded the cloak that had been fouled by the blood and saliva of the great dogs.

'Let's get him upstairs,' Latimer said to Jane and Sarah.

Once in Jane's room, they ran a bath for Greaves while he sat in a chair and laid his head back to rest.

'We couldn't get past the dogs,' Sarah explained, when Latimer asked why they were still inside the walls of Gaudy. 'They kept making for Jane as if they wanted to eat her.'

Greaves managed a weary smile. 'Well she looks good enough in that dress,' he managed to say.

Jane took his face in both her hands and looked into his eyes. 'That was a pretty brave thing you did for us,' she said.

Greaves smiled, then he suddenly took hold of Jane's hands and buried his face in her palms. He raised his head again. 'Cocaine!' he exclaimed.

'What do you mean?' Latimer asked.

'There's cocaine on her gloves,' Greaves said.

'How do you know it's cocaine?' Latimer asked.

'There's no doubt.' He leaned forward, gathered the loose folds of her dress and held them to his face. 'You're covered in it,' he said.

'I think that's why the dogs were interested in you,' Greaves said, looking from one to the other. 'It's my belief someone has hooked them on the drug.'

'Can dogs become addicted?' Jane asked.

'Oh, yes,' Greaves answered.

'But why would anyone wish to do it?'

'Maybe to encourage their appetites,' he replied bleakly.

Latimer left the chair he sat in before the fire and examined Jane's gloves himself. Then he said: 'I think we should all stay together in these rooms tonight. I'm sure it will be the safest course of action.'

'I'll buy that,' Jane said wearily. 'I've had enough excitement. I could do with an early night.'

'What about tomorrow?' Sarah asked.

Latimer returned to the fire and said, 'I read the will at ten o'clock, then there's a shoot in the grounds. After that everybody goes home. Most people don't even stay for the end of the shoot; the gates open at three o'clock.'

'Does Nightingale provide guns for those who haven't brought their own?' Greaves asked.

'It's customary,' Latimer replied.

'That settles it, then,' Greaves said. 'We stay together until the reading of the will. If we can can get our hands on guns we might be able to shoot the dogs and get out of here. Not particularly subtle – but it should prove effective.'

'I'm ready for that,' Jane said. 'Come to that, I wouldn't mind shooting my way out of the main gate.' She looked down at her costume. 'I guess I'd better take this off. You know, someone should market this idea. Wear one of our happy dresses. A good time guaranteed for all.' Her voice changed and she suddenly sounded vulnerable. 'Do you think someone is still going to try and kill me?'

'I must say the evidence is pretty powerful,' Latimer said as gently as he could. 'Up to now, I had the feeling it might be that charlatan, Pendlebury – but it was Nightingale who guided you towards the dresses.'

'But how could he know we would try and escape past the dogs?' Jane asked.

Latimer shrugged. 'Mad people are often capable of enormous ingenuity. Perhaps we've just been manipulated in some gruesome plot he devised.'

'If I get my hands on a twelve-bore shotgun tomorrow morning, he can plot all he wants,' Greaves said grimly.

· 19 ·

Knowing that Greaves and Latimer were still in the room, Sarah slept well enough, with Jane beside her in the wide bed. Sarah woke at first light. Climbing down, she stepped over Greaves's legs, where he lay stretched out asleep in a chair, and went to the window. The weather had changed: the sky was a hard, bright blue with no sign of rainclouds. There were still some hours to go before the will was due to be read in the library. Latimer stirred in his armchair by the burnt-out embers of the fire. There was a hush of peace about the quiet house.

Sarah stood at the window thinking for a few minutes. Taking a pen from her bag, she began to write notes on some headed paper she found on a desk in the room; it was a way of clarifying her thoughts. She examined them carefully and then went to the fireplace. A few coals still glowed in the grate. She placed the pages upon them and waited until they caught the fire before she rose again and looked about the room. Greaves stirred and opened his eyes; but Latimer slept on.

'How do you feel?' Sarah asked.

'I think I could manage some breakfast,' Greaves said in a soft voice.

'Me too,' Sarah said. 'Just give me a few minutes to get changed.'

'I've never known a woman get ready so quickly,' Greaves said as they descended the staircase.

'It comes of not wearing make-up.'

Greaves rubbed his unshaven cheeks. 'Well, you look a lot fresher than I feel.'

'How are the lumps?' Sarah asked when they were seated at the table.

'I'll survive,' he answered, his grin made lopsided by a bruised jaw.

After they had eaten, Greaves suggested they collect Latimer and Jane, find the gun room and select their weapons. Back in the bedroom the others were now awake and ready to begin the business of the day.

Natty Scroat was already on duty in the gun room, finishing his instructions to the footmen who were to act as beaters. He was explaining the timing of the sweeps the footmen had to make.

'Ah, Mr Greaves,' he said when they entered. 'I've got something for you.'

As the footmen filed out, Scroat searched his pockets and then produced a cheque, which he handed to him.

'This is more than I expected,' Greaves said, examining the amount.

Scroat shook his head. 'No, that's right: £1,000 fee, which you bet on yourself at five to one, that's £6,000, plus the prize money of another £5,000, making £11,000 in all.'

Greaves looked at the cheque again. 'Good Lord,' he exclaimed. 'I wasn't expecting prize money.'

'Your lucky day, sir, in a manner of speaking. I thought Trooper had you finished at one point.'

'So did I,' Greaves replied.

Scroat turned to Sarah and Jane. 'How can I help you, ladies?' he asked.

'We want guns for the shoot,' Jane answered in a rather grim voice.

Scroat scratched his chin and made a humming sound as he

243

examined them both. 'Have you shot before?' he asked eventually.

'Sure,' Jane answered.

'How about you, Miss?' he said to Sarah.

'Only clay pigeons.'

He hummed again and turned to unlock one of the glass-fronted cabinets that lined the room. Taking a gun, he broke it to check it wasn't loaded, then snapped it shut and passed it to Jane. The moment she held it, Sarah could see she was used to firearms; there was an assurance in her manner that told of familiarity.

'A bit long,' Jane said, 'but it'll do.'

Scroat went to another cupboard from which he produced a game bag and a box of cartridges. Then he repeated the process for the others.

'What's the plan for today, Scroat?' Latimer asked, and was told that they were to shoot the woods where the Gothic chapel was concealed.

'Almost time for the reading of the will,' Latimer said when they had returned to Jane's room and waited restlessly for the last minutes to tick away.

'I want Sarah with me,' Jane answered. 'Is that all right?'

'I don't see why not.'

Leaving Greaves in the bedroom, they made their way to the library, where they found Nightingale sitting before the fire. He was drinking a dark concoction that Sarah guessed was some kind of hangover cure, but rose to his feet when the women entered. A few moments later Pendlebury came in, closely followed by Natty Scroat and Trooper Stone. Everyone was dressed in shooting clothes.

Latimer sat at a reading desk and spread the contents of his slim briefcase before him.

There was silence, and then Nightingale said: 'Come on, man, can't we get on with it?'

But Latimer still waited until a clock began to chime the hour, then he opened a large stiff envelope.

Sarah had no trouble following the legal jargon. The will seemed quite simple. It was all as Latimer had described it to her in his office. After provisions for various servants, which included large pensions for Natty Scroat and Trooper Stone, there was a generous bequest to Doctor Pendlebury. The main revenues of the estate were then to be equally divided between Professor Perceval, Jane Crow and Tobias Nightingale. If all were to die, and Sir Toby without issue, then the estate would be administered by Doctor Pendlebury for the benefit of the existing tenants.

Towards the end, Latimer looked up and said, 'There is one addition from Sir Silas, which is more in the nature of a request. It reads as follows: "Although I have made separate provisions for my natural granddaughter, Jane Crow and my legal heir and nephew, Tobias Arthur Horace Nightingale, it is my dearest wish that they should marry and thus preserve the bloodlines of the Nightingales, as well as much of the fortune, so that it will benefit future generations of our ancient and honourable family."'

Sarah glanced towards Jane, who sat looking towards Latimer without any discernible expression. Then she turned to Nightingale, who was suddenly beaming with pleasure. 'Is that it, then?' he asked rising from his chair.

'That's it,' Latimer answered, folding away his papers.

'And what about this man, Perceval? Does he get anything for not turning up?'

Latimer replied: 'Legally he still has a claim to his portion of the estate, although his absence complicates matters. I would advise settling on the terms of the will to avoid a protracted wrangle.'

Nightingale shook his head. 'If he can't be bothered to be here, he can whistle for it. I want you to fight him, Latimer.'

'As you wish.'

Nightingale now turned to Jane. 'Well, my dear, what a pleasant surprise. And how do you feel about Uncle Silas's plans for our future?'

Jane looked at him for a moment, as the implication of his remark became clear to her. 'It was only a suggestion, you know,' she said after a further pause.

Nightingale waved airily. 'Who cares about all that legal nonsense? It was Uncle Silas's intention that we should marry. That's enough for me.'

Jane was about to say more when she saw Latimer's expression and noticed that he almost imperceptibly shook his head. 'Let's discuss it later,' she said with sudden sweetness. 'I'm sure all your guests are eager for the shoot to begin.'

'You're right,' Nightingale answered and he called out: 'We're off in five minutes.' He turned back to Jane. 'We can make all the necessary arrangements later.' He smiled and turned to Scroat. 'I want her next to me during the shoot. We'll be able to get to know each other better between drives.' He slapped his hands together in sudden elation. 'This really is a celebration day for the Nightingales. I want it to be a family matter. Inform all the guests that the revels end at lunchtime,' he instructed Scroat. 'They can all clear off and we can have the place to ourselves.' He took Jane's hand. 'What do you say to that, my dear?'

She looked about her in sudden confusion and said, 'I'd like Sarah to stay.'

'That's fine,' he said. 'Select whoever you wish.' Then he gestured to Pendlebury, Stone and Natty Scroat. 'Come along, we'll inform the others that there's been a change in the revels – a historic day.'

He led them out and Latimer gestured for Sarah and Jane to hang back. He told them he had arranged to meet Greaves in the library, and that they should come as well.

When they had assembled, Latimer checked that they could not be overheard, then said urgently, 'I invented that part in the will – the clause saying Sir Silas wanted Nightingale to marry Jane.'

'Why?' Sarah asked.

Latimer looked from the window: outside he could see Natty Scroat talking to a group of guests in the drive. He turned back to the others in the room and said, 'Because Toby worshipped Sir Silas and he grew up believing that every order the old man issued was to be obeyed. It won't occur to him that Jane may not want to comply with Sir Silas's request. As far as he's concerned, it's all settled. If he was going to kill her, there's no need now. Don't you see – she's protected if Nightingale thinks she's to be his wife.'

The door suddenly opened and Natty Scroat looked in. He seemed surprised at the gathering, but he directed his remark at Jane: 'Sir Toby is waiting for you, Miss.'

Jane hesitated but Latimer nodded for her to go. 'I've got to get my gun,' she said.

'I've got it here, Miss. I collected it from your room,' Scroat said.

Jane left and the others paused until Scroat was out of earshot.

'I suggest you get out of Gaudy when the shoot stops for lunch,' Latimer said. 'Now we'd better join the others.' He paused again, 'Oh, Greaves, I just want a further word with you. I have an idea how we can actually get all of you to the little chapel without creating much fuss. Perhaps Sarah could fetch the guns while I explain?'

'Sure,' Sarah said. 'I'll see you in the main hall.'

She made her way to her room and when she finally reached the entrance the shooting party were just departing. After a few minutes she decided to hurry the men along. When she walked back to the library and glanced in from the doorway it appeared to be deserted, but then she heard a shuffling sound and saw

Latimer rising unsteadily from behind a table. She hurried over and saw that Greaves was crumpled on the floor beside him, lying very still.

She knelt beside him and found his pulse: he was alive and breathing, but deeply unconscious.

'I think it was Stone,' Latimer said in a dazed voice.

'Are you fit enough to come with me?' Sarah asked.

'I think so,' Latimer answered, shaking his head. 'But aren't you worried about Greaves?'

'He'll live,' Sarah said. 'But somebody else is in danger of their life.'

They hurried out into the stableyard and Sarah found Greaves's Riley, hood down, parked among the other cars. To her relief the keys were in the ignition. 'Get in,' she ordered Latimer and she gunned the engine and roared away.

Swerving past the front of the house and ignoring the gravelled drive, she set off across the lawns in the direction of the woods where the shoot was to take place. As they accelerated past the lake, Sarah called out to Latimer: 'Do you notice anything?'

'What?'

'The surface of the lake is falling.'

'Can you go any faster?' Latimer shouted.

The car reached the top of a low hill and before them Latimer and Sarah could see a curious tableau being enacted. Nightingale, Trooper Stone and Jane stood at the edge of the Whirling Pool, while Trooper Stone was pointing towards the lake and shouting something to them. Then Stone began to advance on Jane, still shouting.

Jane swung her shotgun round to point at the menacing figure. Now Nightingale dropped his own weapon and reached out to grab Jane's shotgun. It looked as if he was trying to pull her towards the water-filled pit.

As Sarah and Latimer clambered from the Riley, the struggle

continued; then there was a sudden report from Jane's gun and Trooper Stone was thrown back as the full force of the charge hit him in the chest.

'He's trying to kill Jane!' Latimer shouted.

Sarah had almost reached the struggling couple. Nightingale and Jane Crow were still fighting for possession of the shotgun. It seemed as if Nightingale might be gaining the advantage, but suddenly Jane managed to swing the butt so that it struck the side of his head. He stumbled but did not release his grip. Jane fought on, then, as if in desperation, threw herself on to her back at the edge of the pool so that Nightingale, still holding on to the weapon, toppled forward on top of her. Jane raised her right leg as she fell, planted her foot firmly in Nightingale's stomach and gave a final heave. Letting go of the gun, Nightingale turned a somersault through the air and was swallowed into the black hole at the centre of the pool.

Sarah ran towards Jane, who was attempting to rise from the ground. Ignoring her, Sarah did not hesitate – without altering her pace, she put both hands above her head and dived into the whirling water.

She was ready for the icy shock, but there was little light in the murky depths of the pool. Sarah could feel her body bumping against floating objects as she was tumbled by the surging water. *Rats*! she remembered, but forced the thought from her mind. She had something else to worry about. A powerful current was sucking at her body, stronger than anything she had ever experienced before. Sarah could feel herself being pulled helplessly towards the centre of the pool and her body banged against the wheels and cogs of the machinery. She began to feel her lungs burning – but she still had not found Nightingale.

Then she felt his dim form, thrashing in the water. The game bag slung across his shoulder was jammed between two massive cogs. Sarah seized hold and fought to tear it free. Nightingale seemed unable to help her: his body was limp as it banged against her, drawn by the powerful current that sucked at them both.

Finally, Sarah managed to release the game bag and immediately they were pulled with increasing force towards one of the massive outlet pipes.

Drawn into the vortex of a whirling current, Sarah and Nightingale were sucked into one of the cast-iron outlets and drawn along its length, their bodies bumping and scraping along the rough sides of the pipe. It seemed to Sarah that their strange journey would have no ending, and she did not think she could hang on to consciousness much longer. A roaring sound filled her head and the dark of the narrow tunnel gave way to a more profound blackness. The pain in her lungs was now like heated pokers burning through the walls of her chest.

Then, quite suddenly, her limbs were free again and the driving force of the current diminished to a gentle drift. Still holding on to the game bag slung about Nightingale, Sarah kicked out for the surface of the river.

She broke into the daylight with a gasping sigh and gulped in great healing lungfuls of air. Gaining her bearings, she struck out to tow Nightingale's inert body to the riverbank. She summoned what felt like her last reserves of strength, crawled on to the embankment, and heaved Nightingale up beside her.

He still had a pulse but she could detect no sign of breathing so she thrust him on to his back and began to give mouth-to-mouth resuscitation. At last he gave a rattling gasp of breath; and Sarah turned him on his side to start forcing the water from him. Then a thought came to her.

'That's how he did it!' she exclaimed in sudden realisation. Nightingale blinked awake and his eyes flickered over to Sarah. Then he slowly sat up. 'Did we come through the Whirling Pool?' he asked.

Sarah nodded.

'No one has tried that and lived before now,' he said with a note of pride. Then his brow wrinkled into a puzzled frown. 'She tried to kill me. Why? And I was going to marry her.'

'I think I know why,' Sarah answered, then she looked along the wall of the estate.

'Are you ready to get us back inside?' Sarah asked. Nightingale rose unsteadily to his feet. 'I think so,' he replied.

They made their way back upstream to the little bathing jetty and, without pausing to search, Nightingale pressed two bricks and a large section of the wall swung open. The gap was wide enough for a large man to enter. Sarah followed him down the flight of steps that was now revealed. The doorway swung shut and they were in total darkness. She realised that they were still on the far side of the iron cage but she could see nothing.

Suddenly a light flared from the other end of the tunnel and she saw that it was Greaves, who had lit the gas lamp. He walked purposefully towards the dog cage, carrying a shotgun at the ready, then stopped in astonishment when he saw Sarah and Nightingale beyond the cage.

'Good God, you're alive,' he called out. 'I was coming to look for your bodies in the river after I'd killed the dogs.'

'Of course we're alive,' Nightingale replied. 'And I'll thank you to leave my dogs alone.' Without hesitation, he unlatched the cage and walked in among the giant prowling creatures. Instead of turning on him as Sarah expected, they stood meekly by his side. 'Come on,' he said to her. 'They won't hurt you while I'm here.'

Shrugging wearily, Sarah followed him into the cage.

'Better not let them out,' Greaves said carefully, as Nightingale reached for the next latch.

'Rex, Nero, over there,' Nightingale ordered; and the dogs obeyed.

Despite her exhaustion, Sarah was overcome with curiosity. 'Why do you keep them down here?' she asked.

Nightingale reached out and fondled the massive creatures before he answered. 'That was Uncle Silas's idea,' he replied. 'They killed my tutor, Mr Hostler, a while ago. No one can control them except me and Natty Scroat, so I have to keep them caged.' He leaned down and buried his head in one of the dogs' coats. 'Poor boys, nobody loves them but me. You're quite safe while I'm here,' he reassured them again, but Greaves kept the gun trained until the door was closed.

'Where are Jane and Latimer?' Sarah asked as they made their way along the tunnel.

'Back at the house by now,' Greaves answered, and he gestured towards Nightingale. 'Did you know he tried to kill Jane?'

'I don't think it was quite like that,' Sarah said. Then they heard another sound and saw Natty Scroat standing at the entrance to the tunnel. He was overcome to see Nightingale. 'I knew they couldn't kill you, Sir Toby,' he kept repeating.

'How's Trooper?' Nightingale asked.

'Dead as a doornail, sir,' Scroat answered. 'I found the ghost he saw as well. Come and look.'

He took them out of the wood and past the Whirling Pool, which had now been turned off. The level of the lake was still low and when he led them to the muddy embankment they looked down on a terrible sight.

Just below the surface the body of a young woman clad in a white dress floated in the cloudy water, her sightless eyes looking up through the depths as if in yearning for the cloudless sky. Her long blonde hair billowed about her. The body had been weighted to prevent it from rising to the surface.

'Do you know her?' Sarah asked.

Nightingale shook his head. 'This must have been what Trooper was trying to tell me about,' he said. 'I wonder who she is? Trooper thought it was the ghost of my mother. He must have seen her when the level of the lake fell the other night. I wish I'd listened to him then. Poor old Trooper.'

He turned to Scroat. 'Feed the dogs and bring them up to the stables,' he said. 'They've been down in that damned tunnel long enough.'

'Let's get back to the house,' Sarah said determinedly. They climbed into the Riley, which was still parked nearby.

Gaudy seemed deserted when they reached the drive. The rest of the weekend guests had departed, but they found Latimer and Jane in the library drinking champagne. When Nightingale entered the room, Latimer lowered his glass and attempted to place it on a table. He misjudged the distance and the crystal goblet shattered on the parquet floor, but Latimer did not notice.

'Thank God you're alive,' he began, but his relief seemed half-hearted.

Sarah crossed the room quickly to where Jane leaned against a bookcase. She collected the shotgun that rested close to her and passed it to Greaves.

'It's all over,' Sarah said. 'I know who the woman in the lake is.' Jane and Latimer exchanged glances then she nodded towards the shotgun Greaves held.

'It wasn't loaded,' she said and now there was no trace of an American accent. 'But that one is.' She nodded to Latimer, who now stood holding an automatic pistol at Nightingale's head. 'Put down the shotgun, Greaves,' Latimer called out. 'Darling, come over here.' Jane walked over and stood next to him. Nightingale seemed strangely detached from the events taking place around him. He reached out and picked up an elegant box from the table next to him. 'What's this?' he asked in almost a dreamy voice.

'Cocaine,' Latimer replied. 'Hand it to me, please, it's quite a valuable amount, I'm glad to say.' Then he turned to Jane.

'Sorry, darling, it looks as if that's all we're going to take out of Gaudy now.' And to Nightingale: 'You have no idea how much of this it took to hook those dogs of yours.'

Nightingale looked up from the box with a flash of sudden anger and his body stiffened with rage. 'You gave this to my *dogs*,' he said in a furious voice.

'How do you think I got them to eat Professor Perceval?' Latimer replied.

'You unspeakable cad!' Nightingale shouted. 'To corrupt creatures as noble and innocent as dogs with your filthy habits.'

Latimer held his hand out for the box, but instead of passing it over, Nightingale threw the contents over Latimer and Jane in a sudden angry motion. The cloud of white powder clung to their clothing but Latimer did not bother to brush it away. Instead he raised the automatic and for a moment Sarah was sure he was going to shoot Nightingale. But then Latimer just shook his head and half lowered the gun. 'What's the point in killing you now?' he said with a mirthless laugh. He turned to Jane and said, 'Collect all the weapons in here. We're getting out,' then, to Greaves, 'I'm afraid we'll have to take your Riley. Fortunes of war.'

'Do you think you'll get far?' Sarah asked.

'Who knows?' he said with a smile. 'But one must make the effort. At least the gates of Gaudy are now open.'

They backed out of the room with Jane holding the two shotguns she had picked up; then came the sound of the key being turned. Sarah and Greaves hurried to the small medieval windows – but they were locked.

'Even if we break one, it's too small for any of us to climb through,' Sarah said.

Nightingale was sitting in a chair studying the empty box that had contained the cocaine. Suddenly he got up. 'I must go and see how my dogs are,' he said in a matter-of-fact voice. He walked to one of the bookcases and pushed open a concealed door. Sarah and Greaves exchanged astonished glances and then followed him.

By the time they reached the front of the house Latimer and Jane had reached the Riley. A moment later Latimer had started her and was heading for the main gate.

Nightingale watched for a few seconds and then called out: 'Scroat, get the dogs.'

Moments later, the two monstrous creatures bounded from the stables and gambolled around Nightingale. 'Rex, Nero, *there*!' he called out, pointing towards the Riley. 'Seek.'

The dogs turned away on his instruction and hurtled towards the open car that was now following the path of the curving drive, at right angles to them. Because of the heavy gravel, Latimer was unable to drive at top speed; but the ground did not inhibit the dogs. They streaked towards the Riley on a line of interception that reminded Greaves momentarily of the flight of arrows.

Out on the far roadway the dogs could not have caught them, but Latimer still had a few yards to go when they finally closed the gap. Leaping like stags, they sailed through the air and landed inside the moving car, which wobbled wildly out of control for a few yards until it smashed into one of the horse chestnut trees that lined the drive.

'Oh, my God, the cocaine on them!' Sarah cried out. She started running towards the Riley, shouting: 'Call off the dogs, Nightingale.'

But the terrible screams coming from the wrecked car drowned out the sound of his whistle.

· Epilogue ·

It took some time for Doctor Pendlebury to return with the police. He had telephoned from the village and a chief inspector, accompanied by a detective-sergeant, had come from Oxford in response to his summons. When they arrived at Gaudy, Sarah and Greaves were in the library with Nightingale and Natty Scroat.

'What on earth has happened?' Pendlebury said in a bewildered voice, when he entered the room with the policemen. 'Where is Latimer? I understood you were drowned when he sent me to the village,' he said to Nightingale.

'Latimer and his companion are under the tarpaulin you may have noticed in the drive,' Greaves said. 'I'm afraid things have changed a bit since he sent you to the village.'

Chief Inspector Lonsdale was a methodical man. He could tell he was in for a complicated time, but was pleased that a Scotland Yard Superintendent was actually at the scene of the crime – whatever it turned out to be. In his experience the rich and powerful did not make his job easy; they tended to regard searching questions as an impertinence. A bit of brass would make the going softer and it would mean there was someone for him to pass the buck to if matters proved to be difficult.

'Have you got that tape recorder working, Sergeant Wilkes?' he asked.

'All right now, sir,' the sergeant replied.

Lonsdale sat back in an easy chair and pointed at Nightingale with a plastic lighter. He was beginning to enjoy the role of interlocutor. 'I've already heard some of what's been going on here from Doctor Pendlebury. Perhaps we could begin with your version of events, Sir Toby.'

Nightingale shook his head, still dazed. 'I haven't the faintest idea of what's been going on,' he answered.

Lonsdale sighed and lit a cigarette. 'Can *anyone* tell me what's been happening here?' he asked, blowing a stream of smoke in the direction of Pendlebury. 'How about you, sir?' he appealed to Greaves.

'It began with the death of Mr Hostler,' Greaves began.

'Then Professor Perceval was murdered,' Sarah volunteered.

'Where's his body?' Lonsdale asked.

'I'm afraid it's been eaten, as was Mr Hostler's.'

'*Eaten?*' Lonsdale repeated with a little less certainty.

'I still have a finger,' Greaves said drily.

Lonsdale inhaled some smoke and tried to look unconcerned. 'Who was Hostler and why was he killed?' he asked eventually.

'Mr Hostler was Toby's tutor, his death was an accident,' Sarah said. 'Something that started as a bit of horseplay. Hostler was afraid of the dogs, the others were taunting him; they only intended to scare him. Latimer knew that they had been conditioned to kill, but he was in town. Sir Toby set the dogs on his tutor for fun – he didn't know they would tear him to pieces.'

'I knew nothing of this,' Pendlebury chimed in. 'I was away from Gaudy the night it happened – I have witnesses and will call them if you wish.'

The Inspector held up his hand to silence the doctor and looked at Nightingale, who sat in his chair and nodded his agreement.

Sarah continued: 'Latimer learned what had happened when Silas Nightingale contacted him so that he could cover the business up. Latimer took care of it – as he did with all the family's dirty linen. He was visiting Hostler's brother to explain that Mr Hostler had died unexpectedly when he first met me. I was just the sort of person he was looking for to develop the plan he had made to get his hands on the Nightingale money.'

'And where is John Latimer now?'

'His is one of the bodies beneath the tarpaulin. He planned the whole business,' Greaves said. 'The first murder he intended to happen was that of Professor Perceval, who was to share in an inheritance. Latimer was plotting to get his hands on it all.'

'How did he do it?'

Greaves rubbed a bruise on his chest before he answered. 'Professor Perceval's hobby was finding ancient rights of way. Latimer arranged for a fake map to come into the Professor's possession, supposedly showing a lost pathway on the embankment outside Gaudy's walls. When Perceval turned up to track it down, Latimer drowned him in the river. Later he fed his body to Nightingale's dogs.'

'Who was murdered next?'

'Sir Silas Nightingale,' Sarah said. 'That's when I come into the picture.'

Pendlebury interrupted. 'How could he possibly have been murdered?' he asked, turning to Sarah. 'Remember how it happened. *You* were there as well.'

Sarah nodded. 'Nonetheless, Latimer killed him. He wanted me there as a witness, so that I would confirm it was an accident. I think it may have been vanity as well. Proving he could get away with anything.'

Pendlebury still wasn't satisfied. 'But we all saw Sir Silas die. It was a classic case of heart attack.'

'No,' Sarah said. 'When Latimer was supposed to be stopping Sir Silas from drinking from his tankard in the Turkish bath, he slipped a drug into the mixture. Then, when he was supposedly giving him the kiss of life, he passed an even stronger dose into his mouth, just to make sure. I realised that a little while ago, when I was breathing air into Nightingale on the riverbank.'

'How could he have done that without killing himself?' Pendlebury said in disbelief.

'Latimer took a big gamble,' Sarah said looking hard at the doctor. 'He had the lethal dose of the drug in a gelatin capsule in his mouth. It was half melted when he spat it into Sir Silas's mouth. That was what finished him off.'

Pendlebury seemed to shrink back at this.

Lonsdale sat forward in the chair. 'And who was murdered next?' he asked.

'The real Jane Crow,' Sarah said.

'And where is her body?'

'In the lake.'

'Isn't that Jane Crow in the car with Latimer.' Scroat asked.

Sarah shook her head. 'The woman in the car was John Latimer's accomplice. They collected the real Jane Crow from the airport and brought her here, then they killed her and hid the body in the lake. They obviously didn't have time to feed her to the dogs. I imagine they intended to do that at a later occasion. That was why the phoney Jane Crow fainted the first night at Gaudy; when Sir Toby demonstrated the whirling pool. Latimer was against the demonstration, he tried to stop the expedition. They both knew if the level of the lake was lowered the real Jane Crow's body would be exposed. She fainted to draw attention away from the lake – and it worked. But Trooper Stone saw the body and thought it was the ghost of Toby's mother, that's what terrified him.'

'Poor old Trooper,' Scroat said. 'So who was the woman we thought was Jane Crow?'

'I don't know,' Sarah answered. 'But she certainly wasn't from Arizona.'

'Why do you say that?' Lonsdale asked.

'I've had my suspicions for a long time,' Sarah replied. 'I suppose I just didn't have the confidence to say anything until now.'

259

'And what were these suspicions?'

'Well,' Sarah began, 'on the first night we met, she told me she'd grown up on an Indian reservation near Tucson among the Apaches.'

'So?'

'There aren't any Apaches around Tucson any more. They were Geronimo's tribe, the Chiricahuas, they were all shipped away in 1886 after the surrender.'

'How do you know all this?' Lonsdale asked.

Sarah folded her arms. 'I visited that area years ago. It was a free trip for the holiday section of the paper. It's all in my cuttings book.'

'Is that all?'

'There were other things. I told her I'd seen the Papagos Indians mountain-climbing in Canada. The Papagos *are* from Arizona. The whole tribe are farmers and mostly very fat; they don't go in for mountain-climbing. She should have known that.'

'And?'

'She also said it never rains in the desert in Arizona. That's not true – they have flash floods there. In fact at some times of the year the rain is quite dangerous.'

'Anything else?'

'I think it was her who set fire to the Bryant Hotel in order to gain my confidence. You don't usually suspect someone who is supposed to have saved your life, and it gave her the opportunity to claim that she had lost all of her documents in the fire – all except her birth certificate, that is.'

'What then?'

'We were in Latimer's chambers the first time she was supposed to have met him. I pulled over his coat-stand and Jane knew which umbrella belonged to Latimer without asking. It was quite distinctive – ivory-handled with bands of gold.'

'Go on,' Lonsdale instructed.

'It was Jane who put the cocaine on the dress she was going to wear to the ball. She must have done it when she pretended to be drunk and left the lunch early. She knew that would prevent us from escaping past the dogs.'

'Why did she kill Trooper Stone?' Lonsdale asked.

Sarah shrugged. 'I suppose he was showing Sir Toby the body in the lake. Latimer intended to feed it to the dogs at some later time and get rid of the evidence. If she'd managed to drown Sir Toby in the Whirling Pool, all of the suspicion would have rested on him. And she would have inherited the entire estate.'

'And shared it with John Latimer,' Pendlebury added.

Sarah stood up and walked over to him. 'And with you, Doctor,' she said softly.

'With me!' Pendlebury said in outrage. 'Don't be so ridiculous.'

'Oh yes,' Sarah insisted. 'You cooked up the entire scheme with Latimer. Only you could get the drugs that killed Sir Silas; you made up the gelatin capsule for Latimer and you signed the death certificates for Dr Hostler and Sir Silas. Also you had the knowledge of anatomy that enabled you to dismember Professor Perceval's body so that it could be fed to the dogs.'

'This is all pure speculation,' Pendlebury blustered. 'You don't have an atom of proof.'

'Oh, but I do,' Sarah said in the same soft voice. 'Perhaps Chief Inspector Lonsdale will have a word with me in private and then allow me to conduct a demonstration.'

A short while later they assembled in the stableyard. Sarah spaced everyone in a row before turning to Nightingale. 'You say Rex and Nero will only obey you and Natty Scroat?' she asked.

'They'll tear the throat out of anyone else,' Nightingale said lightly.

'But you can control them?'

'Certainly.'

'Go into the stable and bring them out,' Sarah instructed. 'Then let them inspect each of us in turn.'

Nightingale followed her orders and the dogs padded down the line. At each person, they gave a low menacing growl. But when they reached Pendlebury, who was last in the line, they wagged their tails and pulled forward in a fawning fashion to lick his hands. The doctor was defeated: he looked towards the sky helplessly. After Lonsdale had instructed the sergeant to take him to the waiting car he turned again to Sarah.

'Why were the dogs so friendly to the doctor?' he asked as they returned to the house.

'The cocaine,' Sarah explained. 'Pendlebury was the one who hooked the dogs: he did it when he was going for his swims with Sir Silas.'

'Beastly man,' Nightingale said with conviction. 'I shall see his name is removed from the list of Corinthians.'

Lonsdale checked that he had all the answers he required, then gave Sarah and Greaves permission to leave. Scroat entered the room to announce that their luggage was stowed in the pony-trap and there was forty-five minutes before the next train to town. Nightingale walked with them to the front of the house and stood in the drive as they climbed aboard.

'Pity about that girl,' he said when they were seated behind Scroat. 'Who do you think she really was?' he asked Sarah.

She thought for a moment. 'Someone who'd been in London some time, at least judging from the way she knew how to shop.'

Nightingale glanced towards the lake. 'Still, it's a damned shame. She could ride and shoot, I would have thought she'd have made me a splendid wife. I'm sorry things didn't work out better.'

He nodded curtly to his servant. Scroat gave a flick of the whip and the pony pulled away. 'If we ever find another like her we'll give you a call,' Greaves called out. As they headed for the gates of Gaudy they looked back to watch his figure receding into the past.

Sarah stopped at a telephone booth in the station and called George Conway. He was sitting in his office waiting for a meeting to start.

'How are you, George?' Sarah began.

'Top of the world,' he answered testily. 'I'm about to go into an ideas conference and tell them I haven't got a bloody thing for them to put into the television adverts.'

'Oh but you have, George,' Sarah said, and she began to outline the story.

He was still making notes some time later when Alan Stiles put his head round the door of his little office and said, 'The editor's called. They want you in there – now.'

George waved him away, 'Tell them I'll be along soon. Start without me.' Stiles looked at him for a moment and then slowly shook his head as if to signify madness. He walked back to the news desk smiling happily to deliver George's message.

When he finally hung up, George looked down at the sheaf of notes with elation. After arranging them in order he sauntered towards the editor's office. He knocked lightly and entered, to find Fanny Hunter in full flow.

George looked towards Brian Meadows, to apologise for his lateness, but the editor frowned and nodded for him to sit down in silence.

'. . . so that's it,' Fanny said finally, with a glance of triumph towards George. 'The whole of dog week is sewn up. Nothing will stop this being a memorable week for all dog-lovers who read the *Gazette*.'

'Brilliant, Fanny,' Mantle said with admiration. 'The readers are going to love it.'

The editor looked towards George. 'So what have you got for us?' he asked.

Conway paused to savour the moment. 'One of the best stories I've ever handled,' he answered mildly. 'But I think it's going to create one or two little problems with Fanny's dog week...'